Reunited

Reunited

L B Cotton

Mini Matti Books

Reunited

By LB Cotton

First published in 2022 by Mini Matti Books.
info@minimatti.com

Front cover by Nora Bek-Pedersen

Edit by Joanna S Hawkins and Keith Anderson

American English is the editing language

ISBN 978-1-7398665-2-5 Paperback
ISBN 987-1-7398665-3-2 eBook

Follow LB Cotton on social media:
Facebook: LB Cotton
Instagram: @lbcottonauthor
Twitter: @LBCottonAuthor

www.lbcotton.com

Never too late to say sorry.

Acknowledgment

They say writing the second book is almost harder than writing the first. I don't know whether that is correct or not. Writing this one wasn't difficult but making sure that it was good enough was hard. I wasn't ready to write the follow-on to My Montana Ride. My intention with this book was that it would do something completely unrelated to My Montana Ride. And yes, to a certain extent it is but somehow it has ended up with a connection to My Montana Ride.

It has been a journey I have enjoyed, and I hope you will enjoy reading it.

I want to give a special thanks to the very talented young artist Nora Bek-Pedersen for the lovely cover design. This is her first cover and I'm pretty sure it won't be the last. Also, a big thank you to Joanna Hawkins and Keith Anderson for the editing. Sorry, it was short notice. I would also like to thank my Inspired group who have been there for me ever since I started this journey. You have put up with my strange WhatsApp messages and pushed me on when I needed it.

And a big thank you to all my friends who have patiently listened to me and given me support.

Last but not least I want to thank my family for their love and support.

{ 1 }

It had been a bit of a crazy start to the week. Everything seemed to have been against him, and it was only Tuesday. Jason wanted to finish work early, one last email to do and he would be ready to leave. Despite feeling quite shattered and frustrated after two very busy days, he wanted to head to the gym. One thing he had learned over the years was that exercise helped him to clear his head. So, a good session in the gym was what he needed. Helen had called him earlier to see if they could meet at their favorite restaurant for dinner. She had vacation plans she wanted to discuss with him and, despite not really being in the mood for that kind of discussion, he had said yes. Sometimes it's just easier to run with it and hopefully, after a good session in the gym, he would be in a better mood. They had arranged that Helen would meet him there.

Jason was trying to think how long he had known Helen. He worked out that it had to be about five months now, which was a bit of a record for him. His life was work and gym and not a lot else, which was the reason previous girlfriends had lost interest in him. Helen was different from the others he had dated in the past, as she was a bit of a fitness fanatic. She spent most of her free time in the gym or out socializing. Staying at home was not her thing. *Being seen*, as she called it, was something she found very important. They first met at the gym when she was on the running machine next to him. Jason had found it difficult to take his eyes off her and they soon got talking. By the end of the session, Jason had invited her out for dinner. Soon they were regularly dining out together, well almost every evening if he wasn't away with work.

He hadn't told Helen yet that he had put his name forward for the Head of Investment. This was a position for which he had aimed for almost from the day he had started in the company. If he got it, it would mean he would have less free time, which would mean less time to spend with her. He wasn't sure if she would be okay with that. Come to think of it, he was pretty sure she wouldn't be okay.

For a minute, Jason wondered who else could be interested in the new position. No names had been mentioned in the conversations he had had with various people. John Jackson, one of his best friends, had also put his name forward. However, due to family circumstances, he had now withdrawn his application. Jason hadn't heard the details but could only assume it must have been very serious for John to pull out. Head of Investment was an attractive position that would mean a better income. It could also open up doors for bigger things in the future. The interview was taking place next Monday and for the last few weeks, he had worked hard to prove he was the right person for the job.

Right last email was done. He took a quick glance at

the list of things that Mrs. Anderson, his PA, had given him that morning. It looked like he had cleared the list, well, apart from one thing. She had even highlighted it, so he couldn't miss it, as she knew he would try to avoid it. His dad had called again yesterday as Jason hadn't got back to him, despite having called three times the week before. Mrs. Anderson had promised Jason's father that he would call him back today. For a second, Jason was debating with himself if he should call him. A quick look at his watch told him it was already later than he had hoped. As he wasn't in a good mood, he decided it could wait until tomorrow.

Jason was trying to think about when he last spoke to his dad. It didn't seem that long ago, and he remembered he had promised him he would try to make it home soon. Well, he hadn't got around to it yet. Work had been very busy and what little free time he did have, he had spent with Helen. It annoyed him that his dad didn't seem to understand how important his job was to him, and he knew exactly what his dad would say.

"We would love to see you, son," as if his mom was still there. She had died a couple of years ago and Jason found it irritating how his dad kept talking like she was still there. In the beginning, he had tried to correct him, but his dad wouldn't have it. Growing up, he and his dad had been very close. They had done a lot of things together and Jason had spent hours watching his dad, either repairing or building things. But since the funeral, their relationship hadn't been the best. That day had ended with a big argument between them, and Jason had left as soon as the funeral was over. He

had only been home a few times since and hadn't stayed for long. Deep down, he knew he ought to visit more often. At some point, he would have to sit down with his dad and talk things through but now was not the right time. His career was at an important stage right now and required all of his attention.

A quick look at the diary told him it was coming up to the second anniversary of his mother's death and it would have been her birthday too. Those were two dates Jason knew he would never forget. Two years ago, he made a last-minute decision to go home and surprise his mother on her birthday. Little did he know that would be the last time he saw her. She died suddenly, a week later. Hard to believe that it was that long ago. It didn't feel like that.

On his desk was a picture of his parents from one of their anniversaries. Which one of them he couldn't remember. It didn't matter because the date would be on the back. His mother had always put dates on the back of their photos. Jason picked it up and looked at it. Her sudden death had come as an enormous shock for him and, to begin with, he had found it hard to speak to anyone about it. Instead, he had buried himself in work. His mother had always been there when he needed to talk to someone. She never pushed him to tell her anything. Nor did she ever tell him what he should do. She had said nothing bad about any of his girlfriends, as she claimed she couldn't judge them when she hadn't met them. In fact, she had only ever met one of them, the first one whom she loved, but sadly, that hadn't worked out. Her favorite saying when he had ended a relationship was: *"Their loss your gain, my dear"* or *"one day you will find the right one."* He could hear her saying it in his head now, and it made him smile.

His phone was buzzing with a new message from Helen. She wanted to let him know she was at the gym waiting for him. *I wonder what you would have thought of Helen.* He looked at the photo. Would she be the one? Somehow, he had his doubts.

Jason grabbed a pen and made a note on his desk to call his dad in the morning. Maybe it was time for him to mend his relationship with his dad. After all, he was the only family he had left. A brother of Jason's mother lived somewhere over on the west coast. When he was young, his mother had told him about Uncle Tim. He had left his parents very young after a fallout over something and had not returned home until Jason's grandfather had died. Jason vaguely remembered that day, seeing his uncle for the first and only time. When Jason's mother died, they tried to contact Uncle Tim to tell him what had happened but were told it had nothing to do with him. Jason had found Uncle Tim's reply strange and remembered at the time thinking he could never do that to his dad. Suddenly, he realized he was fast becoming a copy of Uncle Tim. A harsh reality, but the truth, and he made the decision that he needed to change. After a quick glance at his watch again, he promised himself that his dad would be the first call tomorrow morning.

Mrs. Anderson came into his office looking very serious. She even closed the door behind her, which concerned Jason.

"Sorry Mr. Wild, but there is a Mr. Henderson on the

line who insists he needs to talk to you now. I tried to ask if it could wait until tomorrow, but he says it is a matter of urgency."

Jason wasn't aware of a client called Henderson and wondered who it could be.

"Sorry, I know you wanted to get going, but he insists it is urgent that he speaks to you now. Shall I put him through?" Although she knew Jason was ready to leave, there was something in the tone of Mr. Henderson's voice that made her feel it was important that Jason took the time to hear what he had to say now.

"Okay, but it better be important." Jason reached out for the phone on his desk. This just about summed up the first two days of his week. Little did he know that the call would change his plans. Not just for the evening, but for the weeks ahead.

"Jason Wild speaking," and he glanced at his watch. He hoped he could sort out whatever it was that was so important that it couldn't wait quickly and be on his way. If there was one thing Helen didn't like, it was him being late.

"Hello, Jason. It's Alan Henderson, your father's neighbor."

"Hello Mr. Henderson, is everything okay?" Jason almost froze when he realized who he was speaking to. Suddenly he knew things were about to get a lot worse. Jason clearly remembered the last time Mr. Henderson had phoned him at work. It was when his mom had a heart attack.

"I am afraid I have some bad news. Your father is in the hospital, and they think it is quite serious. I know you two haven't seen a lot of each other the last couple of years, but I thought you ought to know."

Jason's legs gave away and he collapsed into his chair. A thousand questions were running through his head. In the end, he took a deep breath.

"What happened? How serious is it?" At the same time, he was trying to work out how quickly he could reach the hospital.

Mr. Henderson explained that he had gone across in the morning to see what was going on as Duke, Jason's dad's dog, was barking a lot.

"I found him on the floor between the bathroom and bedroom. He was unconscious so I called for an ambulance. The police turned up as well. They thought he might have been a victim of a robbery, but couldn't find any signs of a break-in. The paramedics think he tripped and hit his head in the fall and knocked himself out."

"How long has he been lying there?" Jason was still feeling sick now. The thought of losing his dad made his stomach turn. At the same time, he was getting angry with himself. If only he had taken the time to call his dad.

"I saw him last night when he was walking Duke. He looked fine and told me he was hoping you would have time to come home soon."

"And how serious do they think it is?" This was terrible timing for him. He hoped to get a promotion after the interview on Monday. However, he knew it wasn't by any means a forgone conclusion. He needed to prove he was the right person for the job. On the other hand, this was his dad, the only actual family he had.

"They said that he has a broken hip. He was unconscious, and he felt rather cold. He hit his head in the fall. How badly I don't know, but it was a lot of blood. Don't worry, we have cleaned it all up now."

Hearing that the police had been involved sent a shiver down his spine. Jason took another deep breath. There was really only one thing to do. The question was how quickly he could get to the hospital. Suddenly, it felt like he couldn't get going fast enough.

"Thank you, Mr. Henderson. I will head home and pack a few things and start driving. I hope to be there before midnight. Do you have the number for the hospital?" As he was talking, he wrote: "not good news" on a piece of paper, which he passed to Mrs. Anderson. She had entered his office, as the call lasted longer than she had expected. His phone was going mad with messages. They were all from Helen.

"Sorry, I don't know it off the top of my head. I will get my wife to find it, just one moment." Jason could hear Mr. Henderson asking his wife to find the number.

"Don't worry, Mr. Henderson. My PA will find it and I will see you tomorrow."

"Okay. Will leave the outside light on and we will keep Duke here for the night. Drive safe and we will see you in the morning."

"Thank you, Mr. Henderson." Jason hung up and just sat there, staring at his desk. What had just happened?

"Everything okay, Jason?" Mrs. Anderson was standing in

front of him and had watched his face turn white. This could not be good news. She had seen this happen once before when he had received the call about his mother's heart attack. The look on his face and the notes on the paper made her fear the worst. She walked across to close the door to his office so no one else could hear their conversation. This was clearly a private matter. There was no need for anyone else to hear about it. Jason was holding the photo of his parents but still not saying anything.

"Is it about your father, Jason?" She went round the desk and was now standing next to him. When he didn't reply, she carried on: "What has happened to him, Jason?" She knew from the last time she had to get him to speak. The office phone was ringing but instead of answering it, she diverted it to voice mail. It was most likely Helen, and she could wait. Jason turned to face her and explained who Mr. Henderson was and what he had told him.

"I need to go and see my dad." Jason glanced at the diary to see what he had coming up. He had so much he needed to do before Monday. It couldn't have happened at a worse time.

"Don't you worry about the appointments. I'll take care of that. Right now, you need to go and get your car and start driving." Mrs. Anderson had spotted him looking at the calendar. "You need to do one thing before you leave. Your so-called girlfriend has been ringing me as you didn't answer your phone. All I can say is that she doesn't sound too happy. I will give you one piece of advice. If your friend can't understand your need to go and see your father, she is not worth holding on to." She headed back to her desk to find the hospital number.

That's exactly what mom would have said. He looked at the picture again. He knew that Mrs. Anderson had never thought highly of any of his girlfriends. Well, time to break the news to Helen. He knew his change of plans wouldn't impress her. There were lots of messages and several missed calls from her on his phone. He didn't bother to listen to any of them. Instead, he took a deep breath before dialing her number.

"Where are you?" She was so loud that Jason felt sorry for anyone standing near her. Judging by the tone of her voice she was definitely not in a good mood. Before he had a chance to say anything, she carried on: "Why are you not answering my calls?"

Helen was one of these people who didn't tolerate a sudden change of plan. They, or more precisely, she, wanted to talk about vacation plans tonight. Jason had a feeling she had already planned where they were going. All she needed was the confirmation he could go and his credit card so she could book it.

"Sorry, but something came up and I have to change my plans. Going to cancel this evening." He tried to explain what had happened to his dad and that he needed to get to the hospital asap.

"Why? Can't that wait until tomorrow? You promised we would discuss our vacation plans'?"

"Well, as I have just told you, my dad is seriously unwell in the hospital. Therefore, I need to get there asap." He couldn't help but feel disappointed at the lack of understanding from her side. It didn't really surprise him, and his thoughts turned to his mother. He could hear her saying,

"When will you be back? Before the weekend? Don't forget we've got a party after the show on Saturday. We just have to be there." Helen was a former model and was now working with one of the big fashion houses in New York. Her job was to help them promote their products, which involved going to a lot of fashion shows. He wasn't sure why she needed him to tag along.

"Right now, I have no idea when I will return. Can I just remind you we are talking about my dad here. He is all I have in terms of family. I'll keep you updated when I know more. Got to go now." Jason had had enough and hung up. She wasn't going to change her attitude so there was no point in carrying on. Besides that, he needed to get going. First, he had to get back to his apartment to pack a few things and get his car. Then there were at least four hours of driving ahead of him to reach his father's house. As he was leaving Mrs. Anderson handed him a piece of paper with the number for the hospital.

"Now drive carefully and don't worry about things here. I will take care of it. Promise you'll call me if you feel you need to talk at any point this evening or night. Okay?" She gave him a very firm look, so he knew she meant it.

"Thank you. Hopefully, everything will be okay. I'll call you tomorrow when I have spoken to the doctors."

"Yes, let's talk in the morning. I hope it isn't as bad as it sounds right now. You'll both be in my prayers tonight."

"Thank you, Mary. I don't know what I would do without you," and he gave her a hug. Jason only used her first name when things became very personal, like when his mother died. Since her sudden death, Mrs. Anderson had not only been his PA but also like a mother to him. The way she reacted and spoke to him was so much like his mother. She had been the one who had helped him get through it. In fact, she was the only one he would speak to about personal matters. They had spent many evenings in the office talking about his mom.

He left the building and flagged a taxi to take him home. It wouldn't be quicker, but the thoughts of the subway full of people didn't appeal to him right now. He needed to gather his thoughts and make a couple of calls. Once he had given the driver instructions, he got the note with the phone number for the hospital and dialed it.

"Miss. Andrews here. How can I help?" And again, he explained who he was and why he was ringing.

"Hello, Mr. Wild. Thank you for getting in touch with us."

"How is my father?" Jason was anxious to hear any news.

"He is stable and comfortable. Would you like me to arrange for you to speak to a doctor?"

"I'm just heading back to my apartment now. Need to pack a few things and get my car. I hope to be at the hospital before midnight."

"Okay. I can get a doctor to call you shortly. Or you can speak to them in the morning. Where will you be staying Mr. Wild?"

"At my father's house. Why?"

"You don't need to come here first. Your father is stable and sleeping. Think it would be better if you got some sleep after your long drive. Dr. Peterson, who is in charge of your father's care, will be here in the morning. I'll make sure that Dr. Peterson knows you are coming. He and nurse Taylor can then explain everything to you."

Taylor? The name sounded familiar to him but thought no more of it.

"No need for the doctor to phone me. I will come in first thing in the morning. Please call me if there are any changes. You can reach me on this number. Oh, and please don't tell dad I'm coming."

"No problem, Mr. Wild. I got your number, and we will call you if anything changes in his condition. And don't worry, we won't tell him." Miss Andrews made a note of his number.

Next on the list was his boss. Mrs. Anderson had said she would take care of all his appointments in his calendar, but he had told her he would call Mr. Patterson and explain what had happened.

"Take all the time you need Jason, family is important. Don't worry about the interview. We will work something out. Keep me posted on the situation and I hope your father will be okay."

"Thank you, I will update you on how it's going, and I will try my absolute best to make the interview next Monday."

"Jason, if you can't make it, we will just reschedule it, okay? Your father is more important." Mr. Patterson had sounded very serious, and Jason decided it was probably best not to argue with him.

"Okay, thank you. I'll do my best to keep you posted."

The taxi had pulled up outside his apartment building. Jason quickly paid, grabbed his bag, and jumped out. It felt like forever for the elevator to come down, even though there wasn't anyone around. He began to wonder if it would be quicker to take the stairs when the doors finally opened. To his relief, there was no one in it and Jason jumped in and pressed floor 3. Once inside his apartment, he collapsed into a chair and sat there for a couple of minutes. He went over what Mr. Henderson had told him again, trying to understand what had happened. Finally, he got up, quickly packed a bag, and glanced at the fridge to see if there was anything he could eat. There wasn't a lot in the fridge; there never was. He decided he would find something when he stopped for fuel.

{ 2 }

Jason managed to leave New York without too many hold-ups and was now making good progress. Only another three hours or so to go, he thought. It was cloudy but dry which made it easier for driving, and, with a bit of luck, he would reach his dad's house around ten. Before leaving he had looked up a hotel near the hospital but then realized how silly that would be. He had a key to the house and there was a bed for him. Not only that, the house was less than ten minutes from the hospital which was closer than the hotel he had found. Besides that, Mr. Henderson had said they would turn the light on. If he knew them right, they would stay up and check that he made it back. So why did he even think of checking into a hotel? The fuel gauge light came on and he pulled into the next gas station.

While drinking his coffee Jason had searched the radio in the hope that there would be something he could listen to, but nothing took his fancy. Back on the road, he started to think about what state the house would be in. There had to be a reason for his dad to fall over like that. Was the house that untidy? He didn't remember finding it untidy the last time he was home but that was over three months ago, if not more. Judging from what the nurse had said earlier, it looked like this could turn into a longer stay in the hospital, that was if his dad pulled through. What would he do if he didn't? That last thought sent a shiver down his spine. Jason took a deep breath and decided he couldn't and wouldn't allow himself to think that his dad was going to die. So instead, he turned his thoughts to his old school friends. Would any of them still be around? Knowing his luck, they had probably left town like him. Besides that, Jason had never really done anything to keep in touch with any of them. Through his mother, he knew that a couple had gotten married and had children. She had also told him about Julia getting engaged to someone he didn't know, but he hadn't heard if they had got married. Jason wondered what would have happened if he had stayed all those years ago or if Julia had come with him. Would they still be together now? Anyway, it didn't happen, and she was most likely married by now.

He and Julia had been friends since their early school days and by the time they were in their mid-teens, they were dating. When Jason decided to move to New York, he suggested to her she should come with him. At the time Julia didn't feel she could leave her family, and they broke up. Jason had never forgotten that day. This was the first and only time he had really cried. It wasn't even a breakup but more putting their relationship on hold. Jason had promised Julia that as soon as he was settled in New York, he would come back and get her. Well, that never happened. He could see her face and her shoulder-length brown hair with the natural waves in it and began to wonder what she is doing now.

The further west he got, the lighter the traffic was, which made driving easier. Unless something happened, he would definitely be at the house by ten. The GPS said an hour and a half to go, not that he really needed it for guidance, but it would tell him if there was an issue ahead. There was nothing worse than being stuck in a traffic jam near the end after a long drive. Jason decided to call the hospital to hear if there had been any change in his dad's condition. A very kind lady put him on hold and went to find a nurse.

"Hello, Jason." Her voice shocked him, and he nearly lost control of his car. It couldn't be, could it? He was pretty sure he recognized the voice at the other end of the line. But what was she doing there? It took him a few seconds to reply.

"Julia, is that you?" Hearing her voice had caught him completely off guard and he decided it was best to pull over and stop the car.

"Yes, it's me. I understand you are on your way home to see your father?" It had been a long, stressful day for her, and her shift had ended over an hour ago. The nurse that was due to take over had called in sick at the last minute and stupidly enough, Julia had offered to stay until the replacement arrived. She still had some paperwork to do. The last thing she really needed right now was to speak to her ex-boyfriend. Since Frank Wild had been admitted to her ward earlier in the day, she knew it was highly likely that she would see or speak to Jason at some point. However, she had hoped it could wait until the morning.

Jason didn't know what to say to her, so went straight on to ask about his dad.

"Mr. Henderson called me earlier and told me what had happened. How is dad?" He was finding it difficult to think. Suddenly, there were even more questions running around in his head.

"Well, he is still critical, but stable. They have fixed his hip, but he hit his head badly in the fall, so we are keeping him sedated for now. That will give his brain a rest and a chance to recover." There was a little part of her that couldn't help but feel sorry for Jason. Julia remembered the day of his mother's funeral and how he had left. Everyone had heard how Jason and his father had argued. She hadn't seen him in town since but had met Frank a couple of times. He had informed her that Jason had a very demanding job with very little time off. So, he didn't come home very often.

"What do you mean by *fixed his hip*?" Jason was trying to concentrate on what Julia was saying rather than on the fact that he was talking to her. What was the chance that it would be her looking after his dad? He then realized why nurse Taylor had sounded familiar to him earlier. But if she was called Taylor, would that mean that she hadn't got married yet?

"He broke his right hip in the fall," Julia explained it was a very common injury, especially among older people that had a fall.

"Is he going to be okay?" Jason didn't know what else to ask.

"We won't know until he wakes up, Jason. The best thing you can do right now is to get here safely. I presume you are staying at the house?" She had spotted the replacement nurse coming in, which meant she could go home as soon as she had finished talking to Jason.

"Yeah, that's the plan. I am about an hour away now. What time can I visit him in the morning?"

"It would be good if you could be here at 10 am. The morning rush is normally over by then and there should be a doctor here. There is a note here that says you would like to speak to the doctor in the morning?"

"Yes, I arranged that earlier with one of your colleagues."

"That's fine. I will make a note to Dr. Peterson. I know for a fact he would like to explain to you what they have found and done so far." She knew it meant she would have to face Jason in the morning, but there was nothing she could do about that. It was her job to speak to the relatives of the patients she was looking after. Right now, she was just longing to get home.

"Yeah, I can make it for 10. Will you be there?" What a stupid question, he thought. Of course, she would. She worked there. It suddenly dawned on him that he would be seeing a lot of Julia over the next couple of days. And from what she had said it sounded like it could be a while before, or even if, his dad made it out of the hospital. How was he going to tell Helen that he was unlikely to be back by the weekend? She is definitely not going to be happy, he thought.

"Drive safe Jason and yes, I will see you in the morning." Julia could feel she was blushing. Luckily no one was near her to see it. It surprised her a bit to find that part of her was actually looking forward to seeing him again. Why? He had left her ten years ago and hadn't come back as promised or even tried to stay in touch. So why would she look forward to seeing him again?

"Thanks, Julia." Jason didn't know what else to say. She sounded a little short with him, and he couldn't really blame her after what had happened all those years ago.

"No problem, that's my job. Right, I better go. My shift ended a while ago and as I'm back on again in the morning I want to get home and have a rest. I will see you when you get here tomorrow. Bye for now." She quickly hung up before he had a chance to reply. What a day it had been. She gave the new nurse a few notes and finally made her way home.

Jason needed some fresh air and got out of the car. This was turning into an even bigger nightmare. Firstly, his dad was in the hospital with a head wound, and his ex-girlfriend was looking after him. Secondly, his current girlfriend was back in New York, not happy because of him changing his plans for the evening. What did a head wound even *mean*? Would he ever be able to speak to his dad again? He was trying to think when he had last spoken to him. It must have been about six weeks ago when he had phoned and asked if Jason would like to visit him for his birthday. Jason had given him some excuse about an important meeting he had to go to. He remembered at the time that he had felt a bit guilty. Now he was standing here on the side of the road, not knowing if he would ever speak to his dad again. If only I had gone to see him, he thought, and he could no longer hold back the tears.

"This has got to stop." He had said it out loud in an angry tone and almost frightened himself. He really only had himself to blame for this mess. Why had he let it get so out of control?

"It's time to grow up Jason," and he promised himself that from now on he would try to visit his dad every month. It wouldn't be easy, but it was something he had to do. Well, that was if his dad survived. And then there was Julia, the girl he had promised to come back to but never did. There was no way of him avoiding seeing her. How would he react when he saw her? Would she still be that lovely girl he had known ten years ago? He imagined her still to be, just now a beautiful lady instead. He could picture her with her long, light brown hair with the waves and her brown eyes. Why hadn't he kept his promise to her? He took a deep breath and jumped in the car to continue the drive.

It had just gone ten pm when he pulled up outside his dad's house. He turned the engine off and just sat there for a while looking at everything. It was difficult to see in the dark, but the bit of the place he could see looked slightly overgrown, and the house looked like it could do with a coat of paint. Right, he took a deep breath and got out of the car. Mr. Henderson had, as promised, been over and put some lights on for him so he could see where he was going. He grabbed his bag and headed for the door. He felt nervous about what he would find once inside. Mr. Henderson had said that he and his wife had been in and cleaned up the blood, so he didn't have to face that. Seeing blood wasn't one of Jason's strong points. Back when he was a child, he remembered passing out twice because of blood and didn't fancy that experience again. Jason was now standing in front of the door and for a second waiting for someone to open it. Finally, he got the key out and put it in the keyhole. Now would it work? There shouldn't really be any reason why not. He turned it and the click sound told him it was now open... Jason carefully pushed the handle down and the door opened. He took another deep breath and slowly entered the house.

Jason wasn't sure what he had expected to find in the house. Nothing had really changed. He put his bags down and slowly began to make his way around the house, starting with the kitchen. There was a small pile of what looked like the local newspaper on the kitchen table. He spotted a small pile of mail and picked it up. He did a quick flick through it. They were all addressed to his mother, and none of them had been opened. Now it was almost two years since she died, so why had his dad not opened them or gotten rid of them? He put the letters down and slowly made his way through the rest of the house, checking every room on the way. It didn't look like his dad had changed anything since his mother died. All her clothes were still there, even her slippers were parked by her side of the bed in the bedroom. Finally, he reached his old bedroom and found that the bed was ready for him like it always was. It had the same old quilt on that she had made for him when he was ten or eleven. And there were a couple of decorative cushions on top that she had made. His mother would put cut-outs from the local paper on his desk of things he would have found interesting, yet there was nothing but dust, indicating that no one had been in there since. Jason suddenly realized that one of the last things his mom would have done before she died would have been to tidy his room after his last visit the weekend before.

Jason remembered that weekend well. He had made a last-minute decision to go home and wish his mother a happy birthday. It had been a lovely weekend. He had taken them out for a nice dinner in the evening as a birthday treat, even though his mother claimed it was far too much to spend on her. They had talked about his life in New York and what there was to see. He had even suggested that they should come up and stay in his apartment so he could take them on a sightseeing tour. Nothing had indicated to him that there was something wrong with his mother. A week later, she had a heart attack and died. Jason's dad had woken up in the morning and found her dead in her favorite chair. No one knew why she had gotten up or why she had chosen to sit in the chair instead of going back to bed. The autopsy had found nothing, and the doctor had concluded that she simply just *"slipped away in her sleep,"* as they said. It had all been an enormous shock and difficult to understand for not only Jason and his dad, but for all the neighbors and friends, too.

Jason went back to the kitchen to get a drink. In his search for a beer, he discovered that there wasn't a lot of food in the fridge or any of the cupboards. What was his dad living on? Finally, he found a beer in the back of a cupboard, and before opening it he checked to see how old it was. As he was sipping it, he looked at all the family photos that were hung up or standing on shelves. There were some in every room of the house. Both his parents had been keen on photography. There was one in the kitchen that caught his eye. It was him as a ten-year-old standing together with his mom. He was holding a small trophy and she looked so happy. Jason remembered that day very well. He had won a math competition at school, beating some of the older students. The clock on the wall struck and Jason looked at it. Was it really midnight? He finished his beer and headed for bed. It had been a long day.

*

All he could hear was women shouting, but none of them were saying the same thing. It felt like he was being pulled in different directions by them. They all wanted him. He couldn't see their faces, their voices sounded kind of familiar, but he wasn't sure. Why won't they just leave me alone? He was trying to figure out how he could escape from them. First, he tried to hold his breath so they couldn't hear him, and for a second he thought he had escaped them. Just as he started to relax again, the banging was back. This time, he pulled the pillow over his head to keep the noise out and after a little while, it seemed like it had worked. He waited a bit longer; yeah, it definitely sounded like they had given up. He could finally relax and get some sleep.

"Bang, bang, bang." He sat up in bed. What a nightmare that had been. He was trying to work out what it all meant when he heard the banging again. Then he realized it wasn't a bad dream. Something was banging, but what? Jason turned over to grab his watch so he could see what time it was. He took another look. Did it really say nine am?

"Bang, bang." There it was again. It sounded like someone was knocking on a door, but why? Why would they knock on his door? Suddenly he was wide awake and remembered where he was. There it was again, the knocking. Who could that be this early in the day? He quickly jumped out of bed, grabbed a shirt, and went to see who it was.

"Morning Jason. Sorry if I woke you up, but my wife has sent me over with some breakfast for you as she was concerned that you wouldn't have anything to eat." Mr. Henderson handed him a little basket with a few bits in it.

"Morning Mr. Henderson. Don't worry about it, good job you woke me up. I have a meeting with the doctor at the hospital at ten am. I must have forgotten to set the alarm when I went to bed. " Jason took a quick look in the basket. "This looks very nice and it's very kind of her to think of me. Please thank Mrs. H from me." He used Mrs. H as an old habit, one he had started when he was a young boy. He and Andrew, their son, had made up a game where Mrs. H. was a code for snack time. Unlike Jason's mother, Mrs. Henderson always had snacks available for them.

"No problem. Please let us know if there is anything we can do to help. I think it will be best if we keep hold of Duke for now while you go to the hospital."

"Will do and yes, that would be very good if you could." Jason had almost forgotten about the dog. Poor old Duke. It wouldn't be fair to leave him alone while he was visiting his dad. For a start, he did not know how long he would be there, but it was likely to take care of most of the morning.

"Well, once again, thank you for this. I better get ready and get going." Breakfast wasn't normally something he had nowadays, but he thought it would be rude not to take it. Besides that, as he discovered last night, there wasn't a lot of food in the house.

"Before I forget, you are coming over for supper tonight." Mr. Henderson had been given strict instructions by his wife to invite Jason over for supper. "She said she didn't want you to worry about food today and you can then give us an update on your father's condition."

"Thank you. I would love to come." Jason hadn't thought of anything beyond his trip to the hospital, let alone what he was going to eat.

"Would seven o'clock work for you?"

"Seven will be fine by me and tell her I will look forward to it." Jason couldn't help but smile. He had always got on very well with the Hendersons.

He put the basket on the kitchen table and took a closer look at what Mrs. Henderson had sent him. It looked like she hadn't forgotten what he used to like for breakfast. Jason had spent many hours and sleepovers at their house. Their son Andrew was the same age as him and they had been practically inseparable back then. Wonder what he's doing now, he thought. Jason remembered how Andrew had always talked about engines and he was always taking things apart to see how they worked. The pair would borrow books about engines at the library but as Andrew didn't enjoy reading, it became Jason's job. Despite reading a lot of books about various mechanical things, it had never really been of interest to him. Numbers were Jason's thing and that was why he had moved to New York. Andrew had stayed local and trained as a mechanic. Jason remembered his mom telling him a few years ago that Andrew had married his girlfriend and something about his wife expecting their first child. He couldn't remember hearing about the child being born but was pretty sure he would hear about it later. For as long as he could remember, the Hendersons had lived next door to his parents, and they were all of a similar age. Andrew had an older sister as well, and Jason knew she was married and had two kids. Her husband was an engineer of some sort, and the last he had heard was that they lived in Atlanta, Georgia.

Right, he had better hurry and get dressed and then head to the hospital. The last thing he wanted to be was late, as that would just make it all even more awkward than it already was. He took a quick look at the messages on his phone. None of them were from the hospital, which could only be a good sign. There were a few messages from some clients who had accepted the changes to their meetings with him. It looked like Mrs. Anderson had already rescheduled most of them. She had attached a list of them with the time and place to be confirmed once she had spoken to him later in the day. She had also copied him in on all the other emails to keep him updated with what was going on. Finally, there were several messages from Helen. She wanted to know when he would be back and also pointed out how important it was that he came back for the weekend.

He quickly sent Mrs. Anderson a note to say he had arrived safely last night and was now heading to the hospital. He didn't read and reply to all of Helen's messages. Instead, he just sent one stating that he had arrived and would speak to her later.

There was just enough time for a quick shower and a shave while the coffee was running through the machine. Then a quick look in the basket to see if there was any he could take with him. Jason wasn't hungry now, but he didn't know how long he would be gone, so he grabbed a roll. Finally, he made his way out of the door, he was feeling nervous about what the day would bring. How bad was it with his dad? He feared the worst and it wasn't helped by knowing that Julia was going to be there. How awkward was that going to be? What would he say to her? There was no way around it. He had to face up to the fact that this wasn't going to be an easy day, he was pretty sure of that.

{ **3** }

There was hardly any traffic, and Jason reached the hospital quicker than he had expected. It all looked a bit different from what he remembered, and the hospital looked like it had expanded. There were some new buildings he didn't remember being there before. Not that he had been there a lot and the last time was back when he was at school. There was one that he particularly remembered. He and Andrew had been playing a game to see who dared to climb the furthest out on a thin branch in the big tree at the bottom of the backyard. He had won, but the price had been a broken arm. Jason could still remember the look on his mom's face when they told her how it had happened, and they had both been told off for playing such a dangerous game. At the time they had found it difficult to understand why it was dangerous as the branch hadn't been that high off the ground.

Jason had parked the car near the entrance and turned the engine off. He sat for a while trying to work out what he would say to Julia when he met her. Finally, he took a deep breath, open the door, and got out of the car. Right here we go he thought and headed for the entrance. Once inside he looked for the signs to ICU. Julia had briefly explained to him last night how to get to the ward and had promised him it was straightforward as long as he followed the signs. It was fairly busy with people coming and going in all directions. There was a shop and small cafe just inside the door to the left. On the right was an information desk and then there were several elevators. Finally, he spotted the sign for ICU and headed straight across the hall toward the door. He pressed the button and went through. There was a big sign with different departments on it. One of them was ICU and it had a blue arrow on it. After passing through a couple more doors he suddenly found himself standing out-side a door saying "ICU" and underneath the handle was a sign. "Visitors, please report to reception." That had to be it, and he went to press the button for the door to open. As he entered, a couple of people dressed in blue clothes came out. They both nodded towards him and said morning, and he politely nodded back. A nice lady at the reception desk asked if she could help him and he explained who he was and why he was there.

"Just one moment Mr. Wild. I will see if I can find Dr. Peterson. He is the one that is overseeing your father's treat-ment and care. Won't be a moment," and she disappeared around a corner.

While he was waiting, he looked to see if he could see Julia anywhere. There wasn't a lot to see. Everything seemed to be behind yet another set of doors. There were a couple of double doors with windows leading into what looked like rooms with beds from what he could see. Behind him were a couple of other doors with signs: "Meeting room" and "Relative room". Every time the doors to the bed areas opened, he could hear lots of beeping noises, but there was no sign of Julia. Maybe she had changed her shift now that she knew he was coming in. He couldn't blame her for doing that and fully understood if she didn't want to see or speak to him.

"Mr. Wild?" A man in a blue outfit came walking across toward him. He had put his hand out to shake Jason's hand. "I'm Dr. Peterson and the one overseeing your father's treatment." He turned to the reception lady and told her he would be in the meeting room if anyone needed him.

"Let's go in here," he opened the door and Jason walked in. There was a table and a few chairs and not a lot else in there.

"Please take a seat. The nurse who is overseeing your father's care will join us in a minute." Jason did as he was told and sat down on the other side of the table across from Dr. Peterson. He was trying to work out from the look on Dr. Peterson's face if there was good or bad news to come. Meanwhile, Dr. Peterson had put a folder on the table which he had opened, and was now looking through the papers.

Jason was so busy looking at Dr. Peterson and his papers that he didn't notice Julia entering the room.

"Sorry about that. I just had to finish some paperwork." She quickly closed the door behind her. Jason felt like something hard had hit him. There she was, right in front of him. She had her hair tied back but still looked as beautiful as he remembered. Her face looked very serious and, for a second, he didn't know what to do or say.

"This is Julia Taylor, the nurse that is in charge of your father's care." Dr. Peterson turned to Julia and was just about to introduce Jason, but Julia beat him to it.

"Thank you, doctor. Mr. Wild and I know each other back from our school days." She looked at Jason, smiled, and went to sit down next to Dr. Peterson. On the way to work this morning, she had caught herself thinking about Jason and what he would look like now. It had been ten years since she last had spoken to him. She had only seen him once since, at his mother's funeral two years ago, but hadn't been up close to him. Now he was sitting straight across from her, and she noticed that he hadn't really changed a lot, still as handsome as she remembered. Just looking at him made her heart rate go up and she knew instantly that she would have to be very careful and stay strong. The last thing she needed right now was another heartache.

"Hi." That was all Jason could say.

Dr. Peterson had found the papers he needed.

"That's great. Then we can get on to talk about your father, Mr. Wild." Dr. Peterson shuffled the rest of the papers in the folder and then went straight on to explain what they had found so far.

"We are still not sure what caused the fall. The scans we have done so far haven't given us anything to be concerned about apart from a small hairline fracture on the side of his head which has caused a small bleed to the brain. We are very confident that it's a result of the fall and not something that happened before. I think we can rule out a stroke. One thing we did find was that your father was slightly dehydrated when he came in which could have been a contributor to his fall. Once we wake him up, we will do some more tests and hopefully, that will give us some clues, but I have to warn you we might never know the full answer. Your father broke his right hip in the fall. We have fixed that. He will be kept sedated for now to give his brain a chance to recover. Now, are you aware of your father suffering from anything? Does he take any medication?" Dr. Peterson was looking straight at Jason over his reading glasses, which, for some strange reason, reminded Jason of his science teacher back in his school days.

"No, not that I know of. To be fair I haven't seen a lot of him since..." Jason was trying to think what to say, "well since my mother passed about two years ago. We had a bit of a fallout back then and have mainly spoken on the phone since. Sorry I can't help you more with that." He was staring at the floor now trying to avoid looking at either of them. This is so embarrassing, he thought as he realized he had a complete lack of knowledge of his father's daily life or well-being.

"That's okay. We can contact his doctor to find out." Dr. Peterson turned briefly to Julia and asked her if she could organize that with the reception. He then looked at Jason.

"The important bit is that you are here now. We will do our best to try and understand what made your father fall. Any questions?" Dr. Peterson had picked up the folder with all the notes and looked like he was ready to leave. Jason could only think of one question right now.

"How long do you plan to keep him sedated? Oh, and do

you think he will be able to come home again?" He knew the last question was impossible to answer right now, but he couldn't help it. He needed to know.

"That is difficult to say. Regarding the sedation, that will depend on the swelling going down. Now that might take a couple of days or a week, or maybe even longer. We just don't know. In terms of him being able to get home. Well, that will depend on whether the brain has suffered any damage and if so, how badly it is. He might have some brain damage; he might not. We just won't know until he is awake. Sorry, I can't give you more than that for now. I know you are a busy man, but there are things in life that even we doctors can't control. Do you have any work commitments or travel that you have to do in the next couple of weeks?" Dr. Peterson was now standing up and ready to go.

"Well, for now, I plan to stay until Sunday. However, I was hoping I could get to New York for an important meeting on Monday which I can't postpone that easily. Of course, I would return to here straight after it." He used "meeting" rather than "interview" as he thought it sounded better.

Julia could feel herself getting angry after what Jason had just said and decided it was time to let him see his father. Maybe it would make him realize how serious this was. Was his work really that important to him? It would explain why he never came back or even contacted her after he moved to New York.

"Let's take you to see your father." She pushed her chair out and stood up.

"Well, hopefully, we will have some answers for you by

the weekend. I appreciate you have a lot to think about right now. Should you have any questions, just let the nurses know." Dr. Peterson reached out to shake Jason's hand.

"Thank you, Doctor, for taking the time to speak to me. It's still all a bit of a shock for me."

"Nice to have met you, and I wish you and your father all the best." Dr. Peterson left the room leaving him alone with Julia.

Jason, who was normally a very confident type found himself in unfamiliar territory. His life had been turned upside down overnight. Yesterday morning he got up and headed to work feeling happy with life and now a day later he was about to see his father in a hospital bed relying on others to help him. Jason belonged to the type of people who had their week ahead planned by Sunday evening. So not knowing what the rest of the week would look like, let alone the next day was not something he found easy to handle. He looked at Julia, in the hope that she might be able to help him out, but she didn't exactly look like she was going to rescue him. Could he blame her for that? After all, he was the one that had left and not returned or stayed in contact.

"Ready to see him?" Julia was standing by the door, looking impatient and Jason didn't have any other option than to follow her. After they had spoken last night, she had found it difficult to get him out of her head. There was something there that she couldn't quite put into words. Did she really still have feelings for him? She had thought long and hard about it and had promised herself on the way to work this morning that she would stay professional and not let her feelings take over. She realized it wouldn't be easy for either of them, but she had to leave her personal feelings out of it.

Well, too late to pull out, and Jason walked towards the door.

"Yeah, I'm ready." He avoided eye contact with her and tried to sound like he was in full control, which was far from the truth.

On the way in Julia had explained to Jason that his father was wired up to various machines, and they would beep at times. They reached the bed and Jason was standing at the end like he was frozen to the floor. His dad looked so helpless lying there with lots of wires and tubes. Julia had found a chair and suggested to Jason that he should sit down. He was looking rather pale, and she was concerned that the shock might make him pass out. As he sat down Jason could feel himself losing control, and he was doing everything he could to not show the tears, not here in front of everyone. Julia had spotted it and pulled the curtains around the bed to give him some privacy. She put her hand on his shoulder to try and comfort him and at the same time, trying hard not to get too personal. Deep down she felt sorry for him, and she knew what he really needed but she couldn't give it to him. That would be a step too far for her.

Now stay professional she told herself. She took a deep breath.

"It's okay Jason. You're not the first person to find all this overwhelming and frightening." She then explained what the various machines were doing and why they were beeping.

Jason couldn't stop staring at his dad. He looked so thin,

and frail surrounded by machines that would suddenly start beeping. He had a massive bruise on one side of his head, starting above his eye. Jason couldn't help but think, would he ever be able to speak to his dad again? Would he survive this? So many things were going through Jason's head as he sat there staring at his dad. He turned to look at Julia, hoping she would have some answers for him. Deep down, he knew she couldn't tell him what the outcome would be, but right now, he had no one else to speak to. Julia could see Jason was struggling, and to her surprise, she had to fight very hard not to show her feelings. It would be so easy to just give him a big hug, but she couldn't risk it. One hug could easily lead to more and that was not a road she was prepared to go down again. No, she had to stay professional.

"Jason, I know this looks scary in your eyes, but he is in the best place right now. I can't promise you anything apart from the fact that we will do our very best to help him. At the moment, he is stable and resting, and should anything change, I promise you we will contact you straight away, even if it is in the middle of the night. Now you have to stay strong and think positively. Remember that Dr. Peterson said that they have found nothing on the scan apart from the small bleed. Take that as a good sign. Now you are welcome to stay as long as you like and if you have any questions, just ask one of us."

"Thank you." He didn't know what else to say. He desperately wanted to put his arms around her and bury his head in her shoulders, but he knew he couldn't.

"Now I have to get on with my work but take a seat and

spend a little time here. Hold his hand and talk to him; some experts believe that's some of the best medicine for these kinds of patients. Any problems, just press the button here and one of us will come." She pulled the curtains back again.

Was she going to leave him alone here? He muttered another "thank you" and sat down in the chair again. As Julia was heading towards the door, he couldn't help but ask:

"Could we talk at some point? I mean, away from here?" What had he just done? He looked around to see if anyone had heard him and, to his relief, there were no other nurses or doctors in the room. Julia stopped for a second, turned, and looked at him.

"I'll think about it," she said and left.

Why did I ask? He nearly said it out loud, but then it suddenly dawned on him that she hadn't actually said no.

Jason spent the next hour just sitting there holding his dad's hand and thinking of all the things he wanted to say to him. If only he had taken the time to return his dad's calls or tried to visit more often. Now it could be too late and all because of the argument at the funeral. However hard he tried; he couldn't remember what they had argued over. In fact, he couldn't remember much at all from that day. After Mr. Henderson had told him about his mother's heart attack, he rushed straight home to be with his dad. Together they had arranged everything surrounding the funeral. They had both been overwhelmed by the number of things that had to be done before the day of the funeral, but somehow, they had managed it together. So why it had ended in an argument was still a mystery to Jason.

Two of the machines started beeping and brought Jason back to the present. Before he could press the button, a nurse appeared, looked at one of the machines, and pressed a button.

"Everything okay?" Jason felt nervous and gave his dad's hand an extra squeeze.

"Yeah, everything is fine. Just need to change this bag as it is empty." She had brought one with her and it didn't take her long. She then checked that it was running before walking off again.

Jason had no idea how long he had been sitting there by his dad's bed. He had been thinking of going home a couple of times but couldn't seem to get up and go. In the end, he decided that it probably would be a good idea to get some work done. One last look at his dad and he headed for the exit. On the way out, he had a quick glance around to see if he could see Julia, but she seemed to have vanished. Before leaving he checked with the reception that they had both his number and the one for the house. And he made her promise that if anything changed, they would phone him straight away, even if it was in the middle of the night. Once outside in the fresh air, he took a couple of deep breaths and reached into his pocket for his phone. It had been on silent since he entered the hospital earlier, mainly so he wouldn't get distracted by any calls or emails. There were a few missed calls, several text messages, and emails for him to deal with, so it looked like he would have plenty to do for the rest of the day. For a second, he debated with himself whether to reply to some of the messages straight away but decided it could wait until he was back at the house. He quickly put the phone back in his pocket before he would change his mind and headed for the car.

As he passed the grocery store, he remembered the nearly empty fridge and stopped to do a bit of shopping. This wasn't something he did often, so it took him a little while to work out where to go and what to get. As he walked around the store he wondered if his dad was struggling financially and if that was the reason for the lack of food in the house. Jason was well aware of his dad's financial situation as he had helped him set it all up after he retired. He knew all about both his parents' savings, so unless his dad had done something really dramatic, there shouldn't be a problem. He made a mental note to himself that he needed to check out what the situation was. Luckily when they had set it all up his dad had said that Jason had to be one of the administrators for it in case something happened. And that meant it should be fairly straightforward for him to check things out later.

As he parked the car in the driveway, he glanced across to the Hendersons and thought about whether he should collect Duke. In the end, he decided it would make sense if Duke stayed with them until the evening and that way, he could get on with some work. But first, he had to have something to eat, as his stomach had become very loud. He looked at the clock on the wall. No wonder he was getting hungry; it was close to two pm already.

It didn't take him long to make a couple of sandwiches using some of Mrs. Henderson's bread and some ham he had just bought. While he was eating them, he looked through the long list of emails on his screen and made a couple of notes on things he needed to speak to Mrs. Anderson about. As soon as he had finished his sandwiches, she was the first call on his list as he knew she would be waiting to hear from him.

"Mr. Wild's office here. How can I help?" Jason couldn't help but laugh a little. Mrs. Anderson always sounded so cheerful when she answered the phone and he decided to have a little fun with her.

"Hi, Jason Wild speaking. Can I speak to Mrs. Anderson?"

"Jason, it's you. I haven't stopped thinking about you all morning. How is your father? How bad is it? Is he going to be okay? Sorry for all the questions. How are you doing?" She had said it all so fast that Jason didn't get it all, but he knew what he wanted to tell her.

"I am fine and hopefully dad will be as well, but it is going to take time." He told her what the doctor had told him that morning and that he most likely would be stuck there for a while. He thought for a moment about whether to tell her about Julia but decided it could wait. Instead, he mentioned the interview and asked her what he should do. Should he go or should he stay? And what about all his clients and the meetings that he had planned?

"Jason, this is your father we are talking about, and you are all he has got. He needs you right now, and everything else is irrelevant. Don't worry about things here, I can handle it and besides, you can work from there. And you know that your interview can be moved if you can't make it on Monday. The most important thing right now is that you spend some time with your father. Think positive and believe that he will be okay, which I am pretty sure he will be. But please do me a favor and sort out your lady friend. Not sure what you have told her, but I could do without her constantly phoning me."

"Sorry about that. I will call her straight away." Jason was rather disappointed that Helen hadn't listened to what he had said to her. He began to wonder if it would ever work out with her.

Mrs. Anderson went through the list of emails she had sorted for him and gave him a list of what he needed to do. She had also postponed most of the appointments on the calendar, but there were a few that couldn't wait too long. They arranged that he would do them via a video link and some of them were already booked that way. It was just a question of re-arranging them at a time that would suit Jason.

"What time of the day would suit you best for them?"

"Let's go for afternoons. That way I can visit dad in the mornings and speak to the doctors if it is needed."

"No problem." Mrs. Anderson made a note to herself that it had to be extra urgent for her to arrange a video call. If she had it her way, he wouldn't be working at all, but she also knew that Jason would never agree to that.

"Thank you so much for all this. Let's keep in touch daily and review on Friday. All being well, I will come back for the interview Sunday night and return here straight after. However, this all depends on how dad is doing by then."

"Sounds like a good plan. Now, look after yourself" She knew she couldn't talk him out of the interview at the moment so there was no point in trying. "Oh, and remember to sort that lady friend of yours out please". She nearly said "if you can call her that" but thought better not. One thing she was very sure of was that Helen wasn't the right girl for him.

"I will be fine. Going over to the neighbors for supper tonight, maybe they can tell me a bit about what dad's been up to. And yes, I will call Helen now."

"Good. I will speak to you tomorrow and I'll email you if there is anything you need to take care of. Have a nice evening Jason and try to relax a bit."

"Thank you, I will try." Jason hung up and turned his attention to the emails, but before he opened the first one, his phone went off. A quick look told him it was Helen, which didn't really surprise him. Despite him telling her he would call her when he knew more, she had tried to get hold of him at least ten times so far today. She had either ignored his message or not understood it. Right. Time for action, he thought and picked up the phone to answer it. Before he could get a word in, Helen had already started.

"Why are you not answering your phone? When are you going to be back? We have a dinner invitation tomorrow evening and I need you there." Firstly, he wasn't aware of the dinner invitation the next day, but that wasn't unusual, as he often would be told at the last minute.

"Look, Helen. I have told you that my dad is in the hospital seriously unwell. He is unconscious and they don't know if he will pull through," he deliberately made it sound a lot worse than it was. Dr. Peterson hadn't said anything about his dad not surviving. "There is no way that I will be back before the weekend. I am sorry if that doesn't fit into your plans, but I need to be here. Now can I ask you not to call the office? You know I'm not there. I will let you know when I plan to return to New York. I hope you understand my need to be here with my dad."

"But......" She tried to break in but before she could say any more, he carried on: "No buts. I am staying here for now. Got to get back to the hospital now, so got to go. Will call you when I know more." He quickly hung up before she could say any more. What planet was she on? What was she thinking? Clearly only about herself and he suddenly realized that she would never change. He needed to end their relationship.

{ 4 }

Jason spent the next couple of hours in full work mode and didn't know the time when his phone went ping. He glanced at the time in the corner of his screen and was surprised to see that it was past five o'clock. Thinking that it was probably Helen again, he reluctantly picked the phone up to see the message. To his surprise, it wasn't from Helen, and it wasn't a number he recognized either. He wondered which of his clients it could be as he opened it.

"Hi Jason, didn't have time to speak to you again before you left earlier today. Hope you are okay. You asked if we could talk. I'm not working on Friday." For a minute, he just sat there staring at the message, reading it again and again. He was confused about what it all meant, well apart from the fact that she was obviously concerned about him, which kind of made him feel good. He thought for a little while about what to reply and in the end, he just wrote that he was okay, possibly still a little shocked. Almost immediately, a reply came back.

"I'm only working in the morning tomorrow. What time are you planning to visit your father?" What did she mean by that?

"I will be there in the morning." He thought for a second before carrying on: "Would be great if we could talk". All he could now hope for was that she would listen to what he had to say. He wanted to apologize in person to her for what he had done all those years ago. And he hoped that they could draw a line under what had happened and somehow move on as friends. It was a big ask, he knew that, but right now he could really do with having a friend to talk to. Mrs. Anderson was the only one he had right now. She was very good, but she worked for him, and she was in New York. He needed someone he could sit and have coffee with and talk things through, such as the letters he had found and the fact that his dad hadn't sorted any of his mother's things.

No instant reply. Was that a bad or good sign? He went to get changed and freshen up a bit before he headed across to The Hendersons'. Just as he was on the way out of the door, a reply came through.

"Yeah, would be good to have a chat. What about lunch at Benny's Café on Friday?" He was not only surprised by the suggestion but also because she had suggested lunch, not just coffee. Benny's Café was where they all used to hang out back in his school days. Was that really still there?

"Does Benny's still exist? Would be good to have a chat. I'm heading over to the Hendersons for supper now. Will see you tomorrow morning at the hospital."

"Okay. See you in the morning. Have a good evening."

Well, that's a small step in the right direction, he thought as he locked the door. He couldn't help but smile.

Jason started to walk out of the driveway and across to

the Hendersons'. He thought for a second about going the back route. Back in the day, he and Andrew used to have a secret path between the two properties through a little gap in the hedge near the bottom of the backyard. It could be fun to try it again, but he decided against it and went the normal way. As he walked up to the front door, he looked around to admire the tidy driveway. Mr. Henderson was a keen gardener who liked everything kept tidy, and that didn't seem to have changed. He knocked on the door and didn't have to wait long before it opened. In front of him was a very happy Mrs. Henderson; she looked as he remembered, but a bit older.

"Hello Jason, so good to see you". And before he could reply, she wrapped her arms around him and gave him a big, welcoming hug.

"Good evening, Mrs. H. Good to see you too. And thank you so much for inviting me over." Once he had extracted himself from her arms, he handed her the basket back.

"This was delicious and much appreciated. And don't worry, I still have a bit left."

"So good to see you, young man. How are you? And how is your dad doing? It was a bit of a shock to see him lying there on the floor helpless." She was still holding his hands as she took a closer look at him. She thought to herself that he hadn't changed a lot.

"I am fine. Dad is stable and I hope he is going to be okay. The doctors are keeping him sedated, for now, to give his brain a rest so we won't know any more until they wake him up."

"Come on in." She had let go of his hands now, took the basket, and told him to take a seat in the living room.

"Duke is in there waiting for you." Meanwhile, she headed into the kitchen. As Jason entered the lounge, Duke looked up and as soon as he realized it was Jason, he got up and went straight to him.

"And hello to you, too." Jason bent down and gave Duke a cuddle and some attention. He noticed that Duke was getting grey now and wondered how old he would be. He had to be ten at least. Jason remembered his parents buying him after he had moved to New York, which was just over ten years ago. Now Jason had, for obvious reasons, never had a lot to do with Duke, but it had never stopped Duke from being very fond of Jason.

"His hearing isn't as good as it used to be, and I think he is missing his master. He doesn't seem as happy as he normally is. Have a seat, dinner will be ready shortly," and Mrs. Henderson disappeared back into the kitchen.

"So, how is life in New York? Your father always talks about how busy you are." Now that his wife had left the room, it gave Mr. Henderson a chance to speak.

"Yeah, work is keeping me very busy, and I love it, but it doesn't give me a lot of free time."

"I take it you are still in the finance business. Whenever I ask your father, he just says that you work with money." Mr. Henderson was a retired banker who had worked his way up in the local bank. He didn't quite get to the branch manager position, but that was only because he ended up retiring before the manager did. Jason remembered once asking him why he didn't move to a different branch to become a manager and Mr. Henderson had replied that he was happy where he was and that was the important bit. Now, as a retired banker, Jason knew he couldn't get away with just saying that he worked in finance.

"Well, kind of, I'm working for an investment company that mainly deals with US-based investments. It's going very well and, in fact, I'm hoping to get a promotion soon." The second he had said it, he regretted mentioning it.

"Oh, that sounds exciting, and I'm sure it will make your father very proud."

"Well, I haven't told him or anyone else about it yet, so please don't mention it." He was trying to figure out what Mr. Henderson meant by that last remark. To avoid any more questions, he decided it would be best to change the subject.

"Speaking of dad. I know I haven't been home a lot lately, so it was a bit of a shock to see him so thin. What does he live on? There is hardly any food in the house. And do you know why he is keeping all of mom's mail? In fact, the entire house looks like she's still around."

Mr. Henderson took a deep breath and looked at Jason with a concerned look.

Jason had never seen his dad cook apart from when they did barbeques. Maybe that could be the problem. But why would his dad wait for him to come home to sort things out? Couldn't he do it himself? He now realized that it wouldn't just be a question of getting his dad back home and settled. He would also have to help him sort out the house. Mrs.

Henderson had overheard the last bit of the conversation as she came in to say that supper was ready.

"Jason, remember that your parents had been together for a long time. It isn't so easy to get on with life afterward, especially when you are older and retired. You are lucky you have your work to do. Your father doesn't have that and therefore doesn't see many people." She had a point there and maybe he had taken the easy option and buried himself in work. He decided it was probably best to stop asking any more questions on that subject. There wasn't a lot he could do right now anyway, not until he knew his dad was going to be okay.

Supper was lovely, but why wouldn't it be? Jason had always loved Mrs. Henderson's cooking as a child, and to his delight, it hadn't changed. He had eaten many suppers at this table as a child, not that he hadn't liked his mother's cooking, but it was always more fun eating here. It was the same with Andrew, just that he preferred to eat at Jason's house. At one point, their parents had joked about how the two boys had swapped their parents.

"This brings back lots of happy memories. How many suppers have I had here in the past?"

"Too many to count," Mrs. Henderson laughed

"Just missing my friend. What's Andrew doing now?" Finally, he found something completely different to talk about.

"He is a mechanic and has his own auto repair shop in Preston, which, as you well know, isn't that far from here. Did you know he is married now, and they have a son called

Colin?" Mrs. Henderson got up and went to find a photo so she could show off her latest little grandson.

"I remember mom telling me he was getting married. Who did he marry in the end?" Jason was trying to think of some of the girlfriends Andrew had when they were growing up. Unlike him, who just had the one, Andrew went through quite a few.

"Her name is Amy, and she is from Preston." Mrs. Henderson returned with a nice photo of Colin and his parents.

"Oh, so no one from here then?" Jason looked at the photo. Andrew hadn't changed at all, he thought and smiled. Mrs. Henderson went on telling him about how they had met, and that Andrew had taken over her father's repair shop as he had retired.

"By the way, Andrew called this morning to hear how your father was. I told him you were back, and he said he would come over this Saturday so you two could have a catch-up if you were still in town. I promised to ask you if that was okay." She had actually called Andrew to tell him what had happened and that Jason was home.

"That would be very nice. Please tell him he is more than welcome. I think I will be here for a few weeks at least."

"Why don't I give him your number, then you can arrange it between yourselves. That would be easier." Mrs. Henderson was a former nurse, and she couldn't help but be concerned about Jason. It must have been an enormous shock for him with his father in the hospital, so she wanted to make sure he had someone he could talk to.

"Great idea. Have you got a pen and paper so I can write

it down for you?" It was now Mr. Henderson's turn to get up, and he returned with pen and paper on which Jason wrote his number.

"Here you are. I'm already looking forward to Saturday now. Sounds like he has a lot to fill me in on." Now having spoken about Andrew, he had to ask about his sister, Felicity, who he knew married Charlie, an engineer and they had moved to Atlanta, Georgia with his work. For a second time, Mrs. Henderson got up and went to get another photo, this time of Felicity's family. In fact, she brought back two, one of the family in Atlanta and one with the three grandchildren.

"These were taken on Alan's birthday back in March when we were all together. It was actually your father who took it." She handed him the two photos.

"They look lovely. Well, dad has always loved playing with the camera. Felicity hasn't changed a lot, I see, and her children look just like her."

"It's a shame that they live so far away as we don't get to see them that often." Jason could see the sadness in Mrs. Henderson's eyes and agreed with her. Long distances made family visits more difficult, especially with a young family. He didn't have to plan visits around children's activities but still found it difficult to get time to come home. Okay, so he might have had other reasons as well.

"Have you got anyone back in New York, Jason?" Mrs. Henderson's question caught him by surprise.

"Eh, do you mean girlfriend?" He wasn't sure. "If so, no, I don't have a girlfriend. Too busy at work, I'm afraid." He didn't think there was a need to mention Helen, as he had already decided to end his relationship with her.

"A shame it didn't work out between you and Julia though. You two were great together, and we all thought that you two would end up getting married."

"Yeah, I know, but we were so young back then," he wasn't sure what else to say.

"She is a nurse at the hospital now, so you might see her."

Jason nearly said he already met her but thought it best not to. Not yet anyway. It would only lead to a lot of questions that he wasn't ready for.

"I didn't know she was a nurse. Mom told me shortly before she died that she was engaged. Did she ever get married?"

The Hendersons looked at each other before Mrs. Henderson turned to Jason. She looked very serious, and he couldn't help but think that there was some bad news to come.

"So, your father hasn't told you?" Mrs. Henderson looked straight at him.

"Told me what? I have heard nothing. Did something bad happen?" He had a feeling it wouldn't be good news. Again, there was this exchange of looks between Mr. and Mrs. Henderson.

"Well, sadly it ended," and that was it. They wouldn't tell him why it had ended. Jason could feel that there was more to it but that it wasn't up for discussion tonight. Why is it a secret? Well, he realized he wasn't going to learn more about it tonight and made a note that he had to be careful on the subject when he was having lunch with her on Friday.

"So how long do you think you can stay, Jason?" now it was Mr. Henderson who had changed the subject. "I take it you can't be away from work for too long.

"Good question. I'm not sure how long I will stay as it all depends a bit on how dad is doing. As far as work goes, I can do a lot from here, but I will have to be back for a meeting on Monday. I was thinking of driving up Sunday evening and then, as soon as the meeting is done on Monday, I will head back here. However, I have told them it all depends on how dad is doing. I won't go if things have turned for the worse. After that, I intend to stay until I know dad is okay and he can cope at home. If he can't be at home, then until I have found alternative arrangements for him."

"Let's hope he will recover well enough to get back here, as things won't be the same without him and Duke around. Please let us know if there is anything that we can help with. I am happy to do some cooking and Alan can help if you need things moved."

"Thank you. Much appreciated. There is one thing that I would like to do while I'm here. The whole place looks like it could do with some attention. Now I'm not a gardening expert so maybe you could give me some advice? Jason looked at Mr. Henderson and carried on. "I might be taking on more than I can handle, but even if I only do a little, it will look better. Would you have any tools I could borrow?"

"That would be a good idea. Alan has most things when it comes to tools for working outside." Mrs. Henderson looked at her husband, "Isn't that right Alan?"

"Yeah, it's a guilty pleasure of mine, and I am sure we can

sort things out. Just let me know when you need me. Perhaps I should come and have a look and we could discuss what we could do."

"That's very kind of you." It was getting late, and Jason was beginning to feel the effects of the last two days.

"Thank you so much for a lovely evening and the lovely food. And thanks for looking after Duke as well. I'd better head back and get some sleep now. It's been a long couple of days." He stood up and looked at Duke. "Do you want to come with me?" Duke immediately got up and was standing right next to him, wagging his tail.

"I think that's a clear yes from Duke," Mrs. Henderson smiled. "Let us know how your father is doing, Jason."

"Will do. And once again, thank you for everything. Good night." He gave her a hug and shook Mr. Henderson's hand.

Jason wandered back towards the house with Duke right beside him but instead of turning in, they walked past it. The fresh air and the lovely smell of late spring had woken Jason up again. He had forgotten how peaceful it was here. You could hear the wind in the trees and no cars were driving past, no sound of music and shouting, all things he was so used to in New York, even at night. It was a clear evening with no clouds which meant he could see the stars. His thoughts turned to how he was going to handle it all. With hospital visits, work, and Duke, who would need a walk or two, he felt the need to have a sort of structure to the day. Despite his dad not being awake, Jason still wanted to visit him.

Once back at the house, Jason couldn't resist sitting down

on the terrace outside the kitchen. The stars were so clear to see and he was trying to work out which was which. His dad had once tried to teach him the names of the bigger ones, but it had never really interested him. Now he wished he had listened.

"Right boy, time for bed." he got up and headed in with Duke right behind him. Jason went to put him in his bed in the kitchen, but Duke seemed reluctant to get in it. Jason remembered seeing a dog bed in his dad's bedroom when he looked around the house last night. He went to pick it up and moved it into his room and before he could say anything, Duke had already jumped into it.

"Okay, you can sleep in here with me, but please don't snore."

*

The following day went as he had planned it. First a quick walk with Duke, then he had emails to check while eating a bit of breakfast. He made a couple of notes on things he needed to speak to Mrs. Anderson about later and by 9.30 am, he was on his way to the hospital. There had been no change, and the doctors were still satisfied with his dad's progress as far as Jason could understand. He stayed for a couple of hours and every time someone walked through the doors to the ward, he hoped it would be Julia. She had seen him briefly when he first arrived and given him a little wave but looked far too busy to stop and talk. Every time one of the machines his dad was attached to beeped, it was some other nurse that came and checked it out. Jason couldn't help thinking if Julia was trying to avoid seeing him, but it wouldn't make sense, as she had arranged for them to meet for lunch the next day.

Jason thought of what Mrs. Henderson had said the night before, or rather, what she hadn't said. He was pretty convinced that there was more to that story. Did her fiancé not turn up at the wedding; did he have an affair? Maybe one of them got cold feet. How could she be so unlucky? Jason thought of the day when they had parted almost ten years ago and how he had promised to stay in touch and come back to get her. Despite it being ten years, he could still remember how painful it had been.

He returned home at lunchtime feeling a little down, mainly because Julia had said she would see him that morning but didn't. He knew she was there as he had seen her but why had she not said hello? Maybe he had put his hopes up too high from the conversation they had the night before over messenger and maybe he should prepare himself for her canceling lunch tomorrow. Not once did it occur to him that she could have been busy. Right, somehow, he had to stop thinking of it and try to get some work done, starting with speaking to Mrs. Anderson.

He finished his work by five o'clock and was about to get ready to take Duke out for some fresh air when a message came through. It was Helen hoping that he had changed his plans and was on his way back to join her for the dinner that evening. A little lost for words, he replied, "not a chance," and left it with that. The fresh air did both him and Duke good. Dinner was easy as he had bought himself a ready meal that only needed heating. He spent the evening going through some of the paperwork on his dad's desk. It was nearly the end of the month and Jason wanted to make sure that there were no bills that needed paying. Everything seemed in order and just as he finished up he spotted a couple of letters addressed to Mr. F. Wild. He looked to see who the sender was and recognized the names. They were former work colleagues of his dad and both expressed their sorrow for the loss of his wife. Jason could feel the tears in his eyes and quickly put the letters away again. He went to get a beer and sat down to watch TV. This was something he hardly did in New York because he was rarely home in the evenings. As he sat there flicking through the channels, he couldn't get the letters out of his head. It brought back memories of the days just after his mom had died and it almost felt like it had happened yesterday, yet it was two years ago. There was a very nice photo of his mom in a lovely frame above the TV, and Jason couldn't take his eyes off it. With tears running down his cheeks now, he went over, picked it up, and put it on the table in front of him. There were so many questions he wanted to ask her, so many things he wanted to tell her, but all he could say was, *why*? What was all this about? He couldn't remember crying back then, so why was he doing it now? Why had those two letters turned him into this sobbing mess?

*

The alarm went off and Jason turned over to switch it off. Surely it wasn't time to get up already. He had only just gone to bed, or at least that was what it felt like. He took a closer look at the time, then remembered it was Friday and he was having lunch with Julia. Suddenly, he was wide awake, got out of bed, and went for a shower, but not before checking that she hadn't sent him a message and canceled their lunch meeting. He nearly thought lunch date but that could imply that there was more going on and he knew there wasn't and was pretty sure there never would be. That ship had sailed. Despite that Jason was looking forward to having lunch with her, but also felt nervous about it. What would come out of it? He hoped they could at least be friends again. Wishing for any more than that would be out of the question, and he only had himself to thank for that.

The morning walk with Duke took longer than he had planned, mainly because he couldn't stop thinking about the letters, he had found last night and his reaction to them. There had to be a reason for it, he thought. By the time he was back home, it was later than he had planned. He quickly scanned his emails while drinking coffee and then sent Mrs. Anderson a note saying he would be out until later in the afternoon. He didn't bother to tell her why, as it would only lead to a lot of questions. It would be easier to explain it when he saw her face to face on Monday and by then, he would also know how it had gone.

As if by magic, Dr. Peterson was standing by his dad's bed when he walked in.

"Morning Doctor. How is dad doing today?"

"Morning Mr. Wild. It's looking promising. The bleeding has stopped, and the swelling is slowly reducing. All signs that he is heading in the right direction, which is good news."

"That sounds like good news. Jason asked if Dr. Peterson thought he would be okay to go to his meeting.

"I don't see why you can't do that. If things keep progressing like they are, we will look to wake him up Monday or Tuesday."

"Really? You think it would be that soon?" Jason couldn't help but feel thrilled with that bit of information.

"Yeah, I think there's a strong possibility that we will start the process soon. So, if I were you, I would get the meeting done. Should there be anything while you are gone, we will, of course, contact you. Any other questions?"

Jason couldn't think of any and he thanked Dr. Peterson for his time, pulled a chair closer to the bed, and sat down. He took his dad's hand and sat like that for a while. At one point, he caught himself talking to him about his discovery the night before, about the letters and the tears. He took a quick look around to see if anyone else had heard it, but there was no one else in the room apart from the other patients. Feeling slightly embarrassed by it all, he checked the time and decided it was time to head home. Now what time had Julia said they should meet? He couldn't remember and got his phone out to check the message from the other night. Well, there was no need to do that as there was a new one from her telling him she would be at Benny's at 12.30. He definitely had to get home and sort out Duke. As he left, he told the reception lady that he would be back the next morning unless they felt he had to come in.

"Thank you, Mr. Wild. Have a nice day."

Now, should he walk and take Duke with him, or should he drive? The weather was nice and, from what he could remember, there used to be an outdoor seating area at Benny's. He decided to take a chance on it still being there and hoped that Julia wouldn't mind Duke being there, too.

"Come on Duke, let's go, we don't want to be late, do we" he had picked up Duke's leash and checked he had the keys on him and his phone and money. The clock in the kitchen went gong, which told him it was noon now. Plenty of time to get there on foot.

As he walked, he kept going over what he would say, and it wasn't until he turned the last corner that he suddenly had a thought. She never tried to contact him. Maybe she had had no intention of coming with him if he had come back. Maybe he had got it all wrong. This changed everything, and he found himself in doubt about what to do. Should he bring it up at all or would it be better just to forget about it? After all, she had moved on in life and so had he, so why open up old wounds?

As he got closer, he could see the café. It looked just like it used to, the same colorful front as he remembered. He was standing in front of the door, about to grab the handle to open it when a voice behind him said,

"So, you found it, okay?" He looked around and there, right behind him, she was standing. He hadn't spotted her coming across the street, as he had been so busy with his thoughts.

"Yeah, it wasn't that difficult. I'm pretty sure it's the same color."

"You wait till you get inside."

$$\{\,5\,\}$$

Jason opened the door and signaled to Julia that she should go in first. At the same time, he glanced across the room to see if the patio out the back was still there.

"I didn't get back in time to take Duke out for a walk first, so I brought him along. Hope you don't mind." Judging by the look on her face, he was pretty sure she didn't mind Duke's company.

"No, I don't mind at all, and it is lovely to see you again Duke," she bent down to give Duke a stoke on his head and he seemed pretty pleased to see her.

"And the weather is nice so we can sit outside." Julia walked in and Jason followed, with Duke right behind him. She took them right across the room and out into the courtyard. As he walked across the room, Jason had a quick glance around the place. Didn't look like anything had changed. Even the color scheme seemed the same.

"Doesn't look like it has changed a lot since I was here last. And it seems to be just as popular." They were now outside in the courtyard.

"Nope, it might have had a coat of paint, but that is about it." Julia had gone straight for the table in a sunny corner, away from the door. Jason was surprised but at the same time happy that there wasn't anyone else sitting outside at the moment. Julia carried on while taking her coat off, "I don't get why people want to sit inside when you have weather like this. Perhaps it's just me." She pulled out her chair and sat down.

"I think it's very nice to sit out here. There aren't many places where you can sit outside and hear the birds in New York, well apart from Central Park. Too much traffic for that." Jason pulled his chair out and sat down opposite her. He told Duke to lie down under the table in the shade so he wouldn't get too hot.

"I don't think I could live in a busy city like New York. Don't you miss the open space and fresh air we have here?"

Good question and something he hadn't really thought of. And it kind of answered one of his questions. She would never move to the city, and that's why she never contacted him.

"If I'm honest, I hadn't thought about it until now." He told her how he had walked straight past the house coming back from supper at the Hendersons'; how he had been looking at the stars and tried to remember what his dad had taught him. This was something you couldn't do in New York.

Now sat here opposite her, she hadn't changed a lot apart from looking more serious than he remembered. Was that because of him, or was it to do with the way life had treated her? He thought of what Mrs. Henderson had told him about the engagement and the sudden ending of it. Should he ask her what happened, or would that be too much? Probably better to wait for now.

"Who runs this now? Can't still be Benny?" Before Julia could answer his question, there was a loud noise coming from the door.

"Well, well, well, if it isn't the legend, that is Mr. Wild. Hi Jason, long time no see. What brings you back into town?" Mr. Jones, the café owner, was now standing next to their table, and Jason got up to give him a big hug.

"Good to see you too, Benny. You haven't changed a bit, and neither has this place."

"Nope, well apart from being a few pounds heavier, not a lot has changed." Benny pointed to his stomach which looked bigger than Jason remembered. "What brings you back here?" Benny glanced at Julia and wondered if it was her.

"My dad is in the hospital after a serious fall and Julia is the one looking after him. So, I thought I would treat her to lunch as a thank you," he hoped Benny would buy that and not ask further into it.

"Oh, sorry to hear that. Hope he gets well soon. Well, you are always welcome here if you need any help. So, what can I get you two?" Benny looked at them both with a smile. He was going to make a comment but decided he had better not. He, like most others back then, had been pretty sure that Julia and Jason were going to get married. They were so perfect for each other.

"What can you recommend?" Looking at the menu Benny had given him; he had recognized most of the things on it.

"I see even the menu hasn't changed." He looked at Benny and laughed.

"Well, I can recommend the salad, don't know if that is

something you like?" Julia had been quick to choose hers and handed the menu back to Benny.

"Make it two salads Benny, and can I have some water, please?"

"Me too" Julia added.

"Two salads coming right up" and Benny headed back to the kitchen with Jason watching him.

"Well, he has definitely not changed, and I am pretty sure the menu choice is more or less the same as it used to be."

"I told you so." Julia sat back in her chair and looked straight at Jason. "Can I ask you a question?"

"Of course, you can. Fire away." He took a silent deep breath. Her look had changed, and he wondered what was coming.

"How is your father coping at home?" What? Well, that wasn't what he had expected at all, not that he knew the question she was going to ask.

"What do you mean? You know he isn't at home." Jason was trying to work out why she wanted to know that. She knew he hadn't been visiting a lot in the last couple of years.

"Sorry for such a direct question and I know you haven't been home a lot, but I have to be honest that I was a bit shocked when I saw him. Your dad looks a lot thinner than I remembered, and that's why I asked. Are there any signs of him not coping on his own in the house? What's in the fridge and cupboards?" She felt bad about all the questions but if she was right in her thoughts, Jason needed to talk about what had happened - not just this week but in the last two years. He looked like he had the world's problems on his shoulders. What had happened to the happy and always smiling Jason that she remembered?

Jason hadn't planned to talk about his father, or at least not straight away. He was trying to work out how to answer her questions, but before he could, she carried on.

"Sorry about all this, but as you well know, your parents meant a lot to me. So, seeing him now like this has concerned me. I know that a loss can change people, but still. And before you say anything, I'm not blaming you for not being there." She reached out and put her hand on his in a sort of comforting way. Jason was lost for words. Not only wasn't he prepared for those questions, but Julia holding his hand as well. It was just as well that there was a table between them, otherwise, he would have given her a big hug. That would have been overstepping the line. He pulled himself together.

"Difficult to say. There wasn't a lot of food in the house when I arrived." After a pause, he told her exactly what he had found the other night. Everything from the lack of food to his mother's slippers and the unopened letters addressed to her. He stopped short of telling her about his discovery last night and the meltdown he had. How was he going to explain that he had been crying his eyes out over some letters? No, it would be far too embarrassing and personal to talk about. Even though he had known Julia most of his life he wasn't ready to share that kind of personal stuff with her yet. In fact, he wasn't sure he would ever be ready for that.

"If I am honest, the house looks like mom is away on vacation and will come home soon. I have no idea where to start or whether I should leave it until dad comes home;

if he comes home?" Jason could feel his eyes filling up and looked away.

Julia looked at him and couldn't help feeling sorry for him. Despite promising herself that she had to keep a distance and not get personally involved, she couldn't help it. She reached out and took both his hands. Jason looked up and for a few seconds, he couldn't take his eyes off her.

"Take it easy, Jason. It sounds to me like your dad hasn't moved on yet. Maybe he needs you to help him and is waiting for you." She thought of taking it further by asking him about his feelings but thought it might be too much for now.

"Really? Mr. Henderson said the other night that whenever he spoke to dad about it, dad would say he was waiting for me. Do you really think that could be the case?"

"Jason, she wasn't just his wife, she was also your mother. I think it is very likely that he wants you to have a say in what to keep and what to let go. In some ways, you are lucky if that is the case. Many people in the same situation don't get a say on things like that."

"Well, it isn't easy when he lives here and I'm in New York."

"I know. Sorry, I didn't mean it like that. I was only stating facts. Of course, I know you are busy. Your dad told me so not long after the funeral." Julia backed off a bit. The way he had said it made her realize he had used work as a way of coping with his mother's death.

"What were you talking to my father about?" Jason immediately regretted the way he had said it.

"Don't worry, I ran into him at the grocery store, and I asked him what you were doing now. He looked a little sad, which was understandable, but told me how proud he was of what you had achieved. He only hoped that you would have a little more time off so you could come and visit him more often."

"Really?" Jason could feel his stomach turn. All those phone calls he hadn't replied to and all the promises about visiting he hadn't kept. Before he could say any more, Julia pulled her hands back as the waiter came through the door with their food.

"This is looking good" Jason felt a sense of relief. He hadn't intended the lunch to be all about his relationship with his dad. The food would be the perfect chance to change the subject.

"You wait until you taste it. It's so amazing." Julia took the first mouthful.

"You're right, this is amazing. Funny, I don't remember ever having this here before."

"That's because we always had burgers back then. You used to call salads rabbit food if I remember rightly." Julia couldn't stop laughing.

"Yeah, but I wasn't the only one," pointing his finger at her with a big smile. Somehow, the combination of her laugh and the food had him feel more relaxed.

"So, how is life in New York? Got yourself a girlfriend?" Julia couldn't help herself. He was bound to have a girlfriend. She couldn't figure out why she wanted to know, as it didn't really matter to her. It was his life and had nothing to do with her. Jason on the other hand nearly choked on a lettuce leaf when he heard the question.

"Nope, haven't got time for that. I'm far too busy with work to have time for a social life." He didn't mention Helen, as that chapter was soon to be history and it would only lead to more questions on the subject.

"Really, how can a handsome young man like you not have a girlfriend? And what happened to Jason that couldn't get enough of parties and watching movies?" She couldn't quite believe that he had given all that up. They had similar tastes in movies and music, or at least they used to.

Jason couldn't help but smile. It was the way she looked at him with her head tilted a little to one side, just like she used to back in the day.

"Handsome young man!" He smiled. "Well, who says I'm not going out? In fact, I still don't spend many evenings in. I have a lot of receptions, conferences, and work dinners now." For a second, he thought of telling her about his promotion plans but decided not to.

"Okay, but don't you do movie nights?"

"Movie nights are only fun if you are together with someone." That was the truth. He had tried a couple of times with some of his girlfriends, but it hadn't been the same; not like what he and Julia had. For a start, you had to like the same kind of movies. "When I went to see dad this morning, I was lucky enough to see Dr. Peterson. He had just been checking up on dad. As you know I have a meeting back in New York on Monday, so I asked him about dad's progress. Now before you say anything, I will only go if dad is okay, and I intend to come straight back Monday evening. Dr. Peterson was very positive and said that if he carried on improving, they would be looking to wake him up Monday or Tuesday."

"I know. He told me yesterday when he checked in on him in the afternoon. I am sure it will be fine for you to go for a couple of days." Julia couldn't help but feel a little concerned. She could still remember the day ten years ago when he had promised her, he would be back.

"Thank you and I promise you I will be back." He had noted that she had sounded sad when she said it. Time to talk about something else. "Now that's enough about me. What about you? What have you been up to, apart from gaining a degree in nursing? I seem to remember mom telling me you got engaged." That's it, he'd asked now and was watching her closely to see how she reacted. The second he had said it, Julia had looked down at her plate.

"Yes, I got engaged." The way she said it made Jason feel that there was more to come, but she said nothing.

"What happened? Wait, you don't have to tell me anything. I shouldn't have asked. Sorry." Now it was his turn to reach out and touch her arm. It was clear that he had touched on a very sore subject.

"It's okay, just a bit hard to talk about. His name was Peter, and we got engaged just before he left for Afghanistan. A week before he was due to come home, he broke off the engagement and I haven't seen him since."

"I am so sorry to hear that, Julia. Did he give a reason for it? Sorry, you don't have to answer – not really any of my business." He felt so stupid having asked that last question. He had no right to ask her, and it was pretty clear that whatever the reason was, it had hurt her deeply. At the same time, he felt anger toward Peter. Why would he treat her like that?

"That's okay. It was very hard. I had just finished my nursing degree, and we were going to plan our wedding once he had returned. Instead, I packed up, moved back in with my parents, and now I work at the hospital here. Not sure what I would have done without mom and dad. They have been a big help to me."

"How are they? And your sister too. I forgot to ask about them." He felt he had better move on for now.

"They are fine. Mom and dad haven't changed a lot, well apart from getting older. Dad is semi-retired now. My sister married Tom. Do you remember her boyfriend from school? They have two children now and live in Fort Valley."

"Yeah, I remember Tom."

A waiter came and asked if they had finished and if they wanted coffee. Jason looked at Julia.

"Coffee?"

She shook her head, and he turned to the girl.

"Yes, thank you, it was delicious, but we will pass on coffee". He asked her to bring the bill and Julia began searching her bag for her purse.

"What are you doing? This is on me" Jason looked at her with a firm but caring smile.

As they got up, Benny came out of the kitchen.

"Everything okay, guys?"

"Yes, very delicious and I will definitely be back again soon." Jason shook Benny's hand.

"Glad to hear my friend. Say hello to your old man from me."

"Will do when he wakes up." He turned to Duke, "Come on, old boy, time to get going again." They waved goodbye to Benny and headed back out onto the street. Jason looked at his watch, then turned and looked at Julia.

"Did you walk here?" He knew her parents' house wasn't that far away. It would be a slight diversion back home, but he didn't mind that as long as Julia was okay with it.

"Yes, why?" She couldn't help but wonder what he was going to say next.

"Would you mind if we walked with you?" It was bugging him that he still hadn't said sorry to her as he had planned. He knew it would only get more difficult the longer he waited.

"No, not at all. Why?" she looked at him with a suspicious smile and started walking. Jason did a quick look around to see if there was anyone close by. As luck would have it, the street was more or less empty, so he was safe. Not everyone needed to hear what he was about to say to her.

"Julia, there is something I have been meaning to say to you, something that I am not very proud of." There was no way back now. He didn't dare to look at her.

"Okay. You better say it then, or do I have to guess?" Julia had a feeling about what he was going to say, but there was no way she would go back to what they had. After what happened to Peter, she had made a promise to herself that she would never put herself in that position again. It was simply too painful.

"I'm sorry for what I did to you all those years ago. Leaving you behind was one thing, but then not coming back as I promised. I'm really sorry about that. I hope you can accept my apology and we can move on as friends, but I can understand if you feel that is impossible." He slowly turned his head to see her reaction and at the same felt an enormous relief that he had said it. It felt like ages before she said anything, and he was beginning to regret even bringing it up. Had he done the wrong thing?

It wasn't quite what Julia had expected him to say. Why did she even think he would try to get back together with her?

"We were too young back then to know what was right and wrong. And let's face it, I didn't go looking for you either, but that doesn't stop us from still being friends now."

"Are you sure? I mean, I can totally understand if you don't want to?" Her answer surprised him and at the same time made him relieved.

"Jason, you are a good guy and we've had a lot of fun together over the years. Life took us in different directions back then and that is okay with me." Before she knew it, she stuck her arm under his. "You were my best friend back then, and that hasn't changed."

"Thank you. You have no idea how happy that makes me. I am not proud of what I did back then and if there is anything I can do to make up for it, please let me know. Right now, I could really do with a friend to help me through all this." Jason wasn't sure what to make of her holding on to his arm. It felt so natural, and he just wished they could have carried on walking

"You have already done a lot by reaching out. I've missed having you as my friend and I'm here if you need me. But this is something you and your dad will have to work out together."

As they turned the corner and were almost outside her parents' house, Julia let go of Jason's arm.

"Thank you." He looked at the house. "This brings back memories."

"Yeah, I know. Let's not go there, okay? Happy to be friends and that's all." However tempting it would be, Julia knew she couldn't get back with Jason. She could see that the last bit of conversation hurt him a little. It would be so easy just to forget everything she had been through and go back to what they had. But no, she had to stay strong and resist the temptation of falling for his charm again. There was no way that she could or would let herself into anything that could end up hurting her again. It had happened twice now, and that was enough.

"I know, and I am very grateful that you are even talking to me." This was true. She could have said no to being friends, but she hadn't.

"Look, I'm here to help and I know that both of you will get through this okay."

"Thank you. Anything that can help will be much appreciated." It was tempting to give her a big hug, but he knew it would be wrong.

"I am working tomorrow, so I might see you at the hospital."

She gave him a little squeeze of a hug before heading in. Jason stood for a few seconds and watched her close the door behind her. He couldn't help but wonder how things would have turned out if he hadn't gone to New York.

"Well, no good at thinking of what could have been old boy. We can't change the past. Come on, let's go home."

6

Jason was sitting out on the patio with a cup of coffee, thinking of Julia. It had been so nice to chat with her and he felt so much better now that he had finally apologized. He couldn't stop thinking of her smiling face with lovely brown eyes. She still did that thing where she put her head a little to one side, which made her look sweet. He could still hear her laughter ringing in his ears. However, there was something a little different about her, something about her eyes. They looked more serious or sadder than he remembered, and he had a feeling that he hadn't heard the full story. And maybe he would never know the full story. Julia had made it very clear to him that they could only be friends now. Better than nothing, he thought, and it was more than he could have dreamed of considering what he had done to her all those years ago. It also meant that from now on, he didn't have to worry about bumping into her at the hospital whenever he was visiting his dad.

Jason dosed off for a bit with a smile on his face but was woken by a new message on his phone. It took him a couple of seconds to work out where he was - he'd only been sleeping for about ten minutes. The message was from Helen begging him to come back for the show on Saturday evening. Jason could feel the frustration and anger growing. Couldn't she understand he needed to be here? He thought of Julia and compared her with Helen. They couldn't be more different. Helen could only think of herself, Julia was so helpful and caring even though he hadn't treated her that well in the past. What a fool I have been, he thought and wrote a quick reply saying that there was no way he was coming back for Saturday. He nearly carried on saying that he would be back Sunday evening but thought that could wait until he was sure. It would only encourage her to send more messages, which he didn't really want.

Jason checked the time and decided that he better get some work done. First, he had to call Mrs. Anderson, as he had promised her an update. She must have been sitting waiting for his call as she answered before it had a chance to ring. Before Jason could say anything, she had asked how his father was.

"He's doing okay according to the doctors. They are talking about trying to wake him up Monday or Tuesday next week."

"That is fabulous news, Jason. Does that mean that you won't be coming into the office on Monday?" She felt slightly disappointed with the prospect of him not making it to the interview, not because she thought he should but because she had planned to make him a cake and some cookies over the weekend to take back.

"No, quite the opposite I'm aiming to be with you Monday morning but will head straight back here after the interview.

I really would like to be here when dad wakes up." He was trying to stay calm, but on the inside, he felt a mixture of happiness, frustration, and nerves. And before he knew it, he was telling Mrs. Anderson all about his lunch with Julia and the message from Helen.

"Who is this Julia?" Mrs. Anderson had sensed that Julia meant something special to Jason, but she had never heard him mention her before.

"She is an old friend. We grew up together." Jason stopped short of telling her they had dated in the past.

"Good to hear you have someone to talk to." Mrs. Anderson had a feeling there was more to it but decided that now wasn't the time to ask more questions about Julia.

"Yeah. What do I do if dad doesn't wake up or if he can't talk or recognize me?"

"I'm sure your father is going to be fine. You have to try to stay positive Jason. By the way, Mr. Patterson came in earlier and asked how you were doing. Would you like me to let him know you will be here for the interview? He said they were more than happy to reschedule it if you couldn't make it Monday."

"That's alright I will call him in a minute. Think it's only right that I speak to him. I don't want them to treat me differently and if I can't make it, it's just bad luck, or maybe not meant to be. I want to be sure that he is okay with me being stuck here for a while. Can't remember when, if ever, I last spent so much time away from the office."

"I'm pretty sure he'll be fine with that. With your job, it doesn't really matter where you are sitting. By the way, I'm not sure how many other candidates they have. You might be the only one. The only other one from here would have been John Jackson, but he is moving back to Montana as we speak. If there are others, they're not from within the company." Mrs. Anderson had overheard a conversation earlier about the interview and candidates but kept it to herself. She knew Jason was the only candidate.

"Yeah, I heard about John. He sent me a message earlier in the week, something to do with his mother being ill and the family ranch in financial problems." He and John were very similar in the sense that they had started at the company at the same time. They had both arrived in the big city quite young and, for the first year, they had shared an apartment. When the new position came up, they had talked about the fact they both were keen to take it on and agreed that should one of them get it, it wouldn't change their relationship. A couple of days later John had to rush back to Montana because his mother was ill. He had rung Jason a few days later to say he had withdrawn his application. This surprised Jason as he knew how much John had aspired to be Head of Investment. When Jason had asked if he was sure, John had just said that things weren't good at home, and he needed to spend some time there. Jason had at the time found it difficult to understand that there could be anything so serious that he would give up an opportunity like this.

"Maybe you should give John a call? I'm sure he could give you some advice, seeing as he has just been through a similar thing with his mother. Although I spoke to Tracey, his PA, and she said that John's mother was doing better.

Well, anyway, enjoy your weekend. Have you got anything nice planned?"

"I am seeing my old school friend Andrew tomorrow. He is the son of dad's neighbor, and we were inseparable growing up. It's been far too long since we last saw each other so we have a lot to catch up on."

"That's good. You will have a lot to talk about." One thing Mrs. Anderson had discovered, which very few others knew about Jason, was that he appeared to be a happy, confident guy, but deep down, he was a very sensitive man. After his mother's death, Jason went from being very outgoing and happy to stay at work. He stopped going out and only left the office if it was work-related. It had taken her many hours of talking over a long period to get him to open up a bit. They had talked a lot about his mother and his childhood, but he had never mentioned any names of friends from the past.

"Yeah, I'm looking forward to it. I hope he can help me fix up the house a little. It needs a few small repairs done and the place could do with a tidy up too."

"That's great. Hope you have a lovely weekend, and I will look forward to seeing you on Monday. Let me know your travel plans and don't forget that you can always phone me if you need to talk, okay?"

"Thank you. If all goes to plan, I will drive back to my apartment Sunday evening and be in the office first thing Monday morning."

There were a few emails to sort before he decided to call it a day. He grabbed a cold beer from the fridge and headed for the couch next door. As he passed the stack of mail addressed to his mother, he stopped for a second, debating if he should or shouldn't look at them. In the end, he decided it wouldn't hurt to have a closer look at them and picked them up. He got himself comfortable on the couch and started to sort through the letters. Most of them were just junk mail that could be thrown out straight away. He was down to a small handful and now he was debating whether he should or shouldn't open them. One had caught his eye, well in fact there were two. The address on the front was handwritten and when he turned them over, they were from the same person, a G. Smith. Jason spent some time trying to work out who G. Smith could be, and then he remembered. Yeah, it could only be her. It had to be Grace Smith: his mother's old school friend. They had been friends since they were very young. But why did she send letters to his late mother? Did they forget to tell her what had happened? The date on the stamp told him they had been posted after his mother had died. There was really only one thing for him to do and he went to get a knife from the kitchen so he could open them neatly. Once back on the couch, he had to decide which to open first. Was it any of his business to know what was in the letters? Not really, but then again, it would only be fair to let Mrs. Smith know that his mother had passed away.

Just as he was about to open the first one, he remembered he had to call his boss. Although it had gone past five o'clock and it was Friday, he decided it would be okay to call Mr. Patterson now.

"I'm sorry for disturbing you this late on a Friday. I have only just finished speaking to Mrs. Anderson. We have been sorting a few things out. I'm so grateful that I have her. Not sure how I would manage my work without her."

"Don't worry Jason. I'm glad you called me. First, how is your father doing?"

"He seems to be fine. The doctors are planning to bring him around next week. And that's really the reason for the call. I'll be heading back to New York Sunday evening and will be in the office for the interview Monday morning. But I won't be staying. I'll be heading straight back here once the interview has finished. I want to be here when my dad wakes up. I hope this is okay with you."

"Jason, that's good news about your father. And don't worry if you can't make it. I'm more than happy to postpone your interview if you feel you need to be by his side." Before Jason could reply, Mr. Patterson told him how he lost both his parents when he was thirty.

"I spent all my time working and socializing. Never had time to visit them and then one day it was too late. Take the time you need, Jason. To this day I regret not spending more time with my parents."

"Thank you. And thank you for the offer, but I would like to get the interview done now if you don't mind. I don't want special treatment over the other candidates."

"That's okay. Now, should you get the job, don't forget that it doesn't start until September. And I see no reason why you couldn't stay with your father through the summer and work from there. You might have a few meetings where you will need to be in the office, but the rest I think you are more than capable of doing from where you are now."

"Are you sure that will be okay? I mean it would be a great help. Dad and I have a lot of things we need to sort through."

"Yes, I'm sure. I know how dedicated you are to your job. I made the same arrangements with John Jackson when his mother fell ill and it's working well for him, so I see no reason why it shouldn't work for you. You two are very alike in the way you work. Maybe you should call him."

"That is very kind of you and yes, I will give John a call. We have already spoken a bit, as he asked me for my opinion on something to do with the family ranch."

"Good. Now I will see you on Monday. Have a nice weekend."

"Thank you, Mr. Patterson. See you Monday." Jason couldn't quite believe what had just happened. His boss had basically told him to spend the summer with his father. John had told Jason about how supportive Mr. Patterson had been to him when his mother got ill. Maybe it wouldn't be a bad idea to have a chat with John over the weekend.

Now these letters and what to do with them? Something told him it would be a good idea to open them. He picked one up which according to the franking was sent before last Christmas. As he unfolded the letter with his shaking hands, he was trying to remember when he had last seen Grace Smith.

"Dear Alice, my dearest friend. I haven't heard from you for quite a while now. I hope you are okay. Wondering if you have moved and forgotten to tell me or if something has happened to you. I won't write again. If the dear Lord thinks we should get back in touch, he will make sure you get this. With all my love. Grace."

Poor Grace - she didn't know what had happened. Jason picked up the other letter and could see that it had been posted the year before around October, so it couldn't be a Christmas letter. His heart sank when he read it. Grace wrote to let Alice know her husband had died a month earlier after a long illness. Jason did a quick count on his fingers and worked out that Grace's husband had died about four-five months after his mom. He could feel his eyes filling up. There was only one thing to do, but how? He had to let Grace know the reason she hadn't heard from her friend, but how? And what would he say? He couldn't just phone up and say *sorry, but mom died*. Perhaps Julia would know what he should do, and Jason reached for his phone. He quickly found Julia's number, but just as he was going to press call, he decided against it. He could ask her tomorrow at the hospital. One more day wouldn't make a lot of difference.

He read both letters again, wondering if and when to try and call Grace. All he had was her address on the back of the envelope which meant he could write to her. Then he remembered a little book his parents used to have. It was full of all the important addresses and phone numbers. Now, where would it be? Jason went to look on the little shelf by the phone as it would be the most likely place for it and, sure enough, there it was. Judging by the handwriting, it must have been his mother that kept the book up to date. It was definitely her handwriting throughout. He ran his finger down through the alphabet and found S. The first entry was the address and phone number for Mr. and Mrs. Smith. Okay, so now he had both an address and a phone number. Should he or shouldn't he try to phone her? Or should he send her a letter? But what would he write? In the end, Jason decided he had nothing to lose and dialed the number.

The phone rang a few times, and Jason began to wonder if it was the right number. She could have moved or, even worse, she could have died.

"Hello." Finally, a lady answered the phone.

"Hello is this Grace Smith?" He thought he better make sure he had the right one before telling her his reason to call.

"Yes, who's speaking?" she sounded suspicious now and who could blame her? A strange man calling her on a Friday evening.

"Hi, this is Jason Wild - Alice and Frank Wild's son." He hoped she would remember him.

"Oh, hello Jason. So nice to hear from you. How are you? And how are your parents? I haven't heard from them and was wondering if something had happened to them."

Jason took a deep breath and began to explain everything. His mother's death, him not being home and now his father was in the hospital and how he had found the letters. Once he'd finished, the phone went quiet, and he wasn't sure if she was still there.

"I had a feeling that things weren't right but weren't sure what to do. Jason, thank you so much for letting me know. I'm so grateful that you took the time to call me. And poor Frank, I hope he will be okay soon. If only I had known, I could have visited him. We could have helped each other."

"Yeah, I know," he stopped for a moment. He had an idea that he wanted to run by her.

"Do you still drive?"

"Yes, why?" Grace sounded very puzzled about his question, and Jason, now he had time to think about what he had in mind, began to doubt it would be a good idea. Too late to go back and it wouldn't hurt to ask he thought.

"I'm just thinking that it might be helpful and good for dad if he saw someone who knew mom well." What had he just said and where was all this coming from? For a start, he didn't know if his father was going to be able to speak or recognize him, or anyone else for that matter when he woke up. Even worse, he might not wake up at all. He wished he had run the idea by Julia before making the call. But something deep inside him was telling him this could be a benefit for everyone, not least for his father, but also for Grace.

"Please don't feel you have to. I don't even know if he will ever wake up."

"I'm sure he will be fine, Jason. And I think it is an excellent idea. I would love to visit him. We've always got on well, but I'm not sure I'm up for the long drive." Grace was trying to think how long it would take her. At least a couple of hours, if not more. It had been a while since she had done any long-distance driving like that. The last time was when she visited Alice nearly four years ago. After the family vacations together stopped, the two of them carried on meeting up once or twice a year. Then when her husband got ill, and it got too difficult for her to leave home for any length of time, their meetings stopped. Grace's husband suffered from an aggressive form of dementia, which meant he couldn't be left alone. And because of his frustration and anger, she had avoided taking him out in public.

"I'm sure we can work something out. Maybe there is a train you can take, or perhaps I could come and collect you?" Now that Grace seemed to be in on the idea, he wasn't prepared to give up just because of driving issues. There were ways around that.

"Are you sure you want to do that? Tell you what, let me think about it and I will get back to you. How long are you home for?"

"I'm heading back to New York on Sunday evening, but only for a day. I've got an important meeting Monday morning, which I need to go to. Will be back late Monday." Jason decided just to call it a meeting. There was no need to say more right now as it would only lead to even more questions.

"However, it all depends on how dad is doing over the weekend. And after that, I plan to stay here for the summer to make sure dad is okay."

"Okay, I will let you know over the weekend. It would be good to see you both again, and I would love to put some flowers on your mother's grave at the cemetery as well."

Cemetery! The one thing he hadn't thought of. Jason felt a cold shiver down his spine and, for a second, he didn't know what to say. Not once had he thought about visiting his mother's grave. What was worse, he had no idea where it was in the cemetery. What was he going to do? Somehow, he managed to pull himself together.

"Okay, I will wait to hear from you." He avoided

answering the bit about the flowers and hoped that Grace didn't notice anything.

"Jason, thank you so much for calling. It has been really nice to speak to you even though it was sad news. But at least I now know why I hadn't heard from her."

"Yes, I'm really sorry that we forgot to tell you. There were so many things to do at the time."

After hanging up, Jason looked at the letters from Grace. He was glad and relieved that he had spoken to her. From his memories, she had always been a lovely and caring lady and he was trying to think when he had last seen her. The two families used to regularly visit each other and go on vacations together. This all ended when his dad and Mr. Smith argued over something. Jason had no idea what the arguments were about, but since then, they had only seen Grace on quick visits. He looked her address up on Google to see how long it would take to drive to hers. Just under two hours and in fact, it wasn't far from his route to New York. He could actually call in to see her on Sunday. It would add less than 30 minutes to his journey, plus the time he spent with her.

Now she had mentioned the cemetery. How was he going to show her the grave when he couldn't remember where in the cemetery it was? The day of the funeral was very much a big blur for him, and he wouldn't have any idea where to look. Somehow, he had to find it before Grace came to visit. He was so busy trying to work out how he was going to show Grace his mother's grave that he nearly jumped off the couch when his phone went ping as a new message came through.

"Thank you for lunch today. It was nice to catch up with you. Hope you're okay." J." For a moment, Jason completely forgot about the whole cemetery problem. Instead, he was busy trying to work out what to reply.

"Yeah, I'm okay. It was good to catch up. Btw you remember I told you about the letters that I found? I have just spoken to one of mom's old friends." He didn't go any further for now as he wanted to see what or if she would reply. It didn't take long before he received a reply, but not in form of a message. No Julia phoned him.

"Sorry, I thought it would be easier if I phoned you. Tell me what you found out." She sounded so excited that it made him smile. And before he knew it, Jason had told her everything, including the bit about the cemetery.

"I have no idea what I'm going to do, but somehow I will have to find moms grave."

"Jason don't worry about it. I can show you where it is." Julia had said it without thinking what it would mean.

"Are you sure?" He was both surprised but also glad that she offered to help him out.

"Yes, of course, I will. That's what friends are for. I will see you at the hospital tomorrow and we can arrange something if you like. Okay?"

"Thank you." Her offer rather touched him but didn't really surprise him as that was the kind of person Julia was. Always helpful.

"You're welcome. Good night, Jason."

What a day it had been. Duke was standing looking at Jason.

"Oh, is it time for a quick little walk before bed, old boy?" Jason got up and picked up the dog leash, not that he would need it.

"Right, let's get a bit of fresh air," and the door closed behind them. The stars were so clear this evening. They walked past a house that looked like it could do with a makeover. Looked like it had been empty for a while. Jason was trying to remember who used to live there when he was growing up and he could picture the boy but couldn't remember his name. Jason and Andrew spent little time with him, as he always wanted to be the one who decided what they should do. Wonder what happened to him?

As he returned, he sat down on the veranda out the back and looked at the stars for a while. He thought of the day's events: it had been good to see Julia away from the hospital and it had almost felt like the old days. They had laughed at things, and only once had he felt he might have gone too far. It was when he had asked about her fiancé. She hadn't looked at him when she told him what happened, and he had a feeling that she hadn't told him the full story. It wasn't really any of his business, but why not say it how it was?

7

Why won't that noise stop? Jason kept tossing and turning, trying to get away from it. But instead, it just kept getting closer and closer.

Beep, Beep, BEEP!

He finally opened his eyes and realized that it was his alarm going off. Having turned it off Jason laid back down and took a couple of deep breaths trying to relax. What a night it had been. His body felt like he had been running a marathon. All Jason could remember of the nightmare were two ladies that had chased him, but who they were, he didn't know. He was trying to think who they could be and why? And what did it all mean if it meant anything at all? In the end, he gave up and went for a shower.

That's better. Now a quick walk with Duke before breakfast would get rid of the rest of it. As they were heading out, Mrs. Henderson was out in front of their house, and she waved to Jason.

"Morning. Hope everything is okay." She gave Duke a pat on the head.

"Yeah, everything is fine. How about you?" She sounded

so happy this morning, and he was wondering what would come next.

"Andrew called yesterday and said he would come over a bit later, probably around lunch. Are you still free to see him?" She looked so excited that Jason couldn't help but smile. He wasn't sure whether it was because Andrew was coming home or the fact that he and Andrew would meet up again.

"No, not a problem at all. I plan to head to the hospital after breakfast so lunch or after would be fine." He paused for a second. " Tell you what, I will take him out for lunch if that's okay with you. We have a lot of catching up to do and I'm looking forward to it." He knew Mrs. Henderson too well. She would only insist on doing lunch if he wasn't careful, which would be very nice, but it would also mean that they couldn't speak freely - not that he had anything to hide. Jason felt the need to just be on his own with Andrew. The only way to make sure of that would be to go some-where else.

"Yes, that's fine. I will let him know."

Jason could see she was slightly disappointed and felt bad. Maybe it had been a while since she had seen Andrew.

"Hey how about we come back for coffee and cake later?"

"I can do that. I will see you later." Her eyes had lit up when he had suggested the cake.

"Good. Thank you, Mrs. Henderson. Just tell Andrew to come over when he gets here. If my car is here, I'm back from the hospital." He gave her a wave and started walking.

Back home, it was time for some coffee and a bite to eat

before going to see his dad. Just as he was about to bite into his toast, his phone rang and without thinking, Jason picked it up and answered.

"Jason Wild speaking."

"When are you coming back? Are you planning on staying there forever?" The voice was so loud that he didn't need to hold the phone to his ear to hear what she was saying.

"Morning to you too, Helen," and he regretted not looking before answering. He was already running a bit late because of the chat with Mrs. Henderson earlier.

"You haven't answered my question." She was still speaking rather loudly.

"Well, give me a chance. I have told you several times now that my dad is seriously unwell and therefore, I need to be here." For a second, he wondered if he should tell her about the plans for Sunday evening. Maybe that would get her to calm down and back off for a bit. "Now I am hoping to make it back to New York tomorrow evening. I got a meeting Monday morning in the office, but I will head straight back to here afterward."

"That is not long. I could really do with having you here now. We have several dinner invitations coming up and I need you to be there." She had changed from shouting to sounding desperate, and Jason knew he had to be careful not to fall for it.

"I will let you know when I get back. Perhaps we could meet up on Sunday evening?" This was risky and not what he really wanted or, in fact, needed, but he realized it would be best. The sooner he could face up to it and tell her face-to-face that it was over, the better. It wouldn't be easy, he knew that, but it was only fair. He looked at his watch. It was 9.30, and he wanted to get to the hospital.

"Sorry, Helen got to go now. I need to be with dad when the doctor comes to see him. I will let you know what is happening tomorrow morning." He quickly hung up on her before she could say anything else.

*

Jason walked through the doors into the hospital feeling relaxed. He stopped at the shop to buy a paper. Not that he really read it, but it gave him something to look at while he was sitting at his dad's bedside. He had even started to do the crosswords at the back of the paper. The lady at the checkout commented on how happy he looked.

"Thank you, just looking forward to seeing my dad." He headed for the doors at the other end of the entrance hall. As he walked toward his dad's bed, Jason did a quick scan to see if he could spot Julia, but she wasn't there. Feeling a little disappointed, he pulled the chair round to the bed and sat down.

"Morning dad." Julia had said that talking to his dad was good and could help stimulate him. The first few times he had done it, it had felt strange, but he had kept it up and it had now become part of the routine. He opened the paper and one of the first things he saw was half a page on some local businessman who had died. Jason didn't recognize the name, but it didn't stop him from reading it. From what he could work out the man had been in a coma for a couple of months. Jason looked up at his dad. Would his dad ever wake up again? Would his dad ever speak to him again? Would he be able to recognize his own son if he woke up and would he be able to come home? Would his dad be depending on daily help? Would it mean that he had to move back home? He had his job and life in New York.

Jason was so taken by his thoughts that he hadn't heard Julia entering the room. She could see Jason was thinking and he looked so serious.

"Hey, daydreamer." She was standing right behind him and saw the paper; Jason looked around to see who it was.

"Oh morning. I didn't see you come in." He quickly closed the paper and got up. Her face was lit up with a lovely smile which automatically made him smile.

"I noticed. You seemed to be somewhere else. What are you reading?"

"Oh, just read about that businessman who died, and it made me think that it could be happening to dad too." He had said it without thinking.

"Jason your dad is different and I'm pretty sure he will be fine. What the paper doesn't say but everyone knows is that the man didn't live a healthy life and he had underlying health issues." Julia pointed to the paper.

"Oh. No, the paper didn't mention that, but still, I can't help thinking that dad might not wake up again." He looked at his dad and then back at Julia. What he really could do with was a big hug from her, but he knew it wouldn't be the right thing to do. She had clearly stated the day before that they were only friends.

"I know but you have to try and keep thinking positive here." Julia could see Jason was struggling, and she had to fight back the urge to hug him.

Jason knew she was right, but it wasn't that easy. He couldn't just switch his brain off from thinking the worst would happen.

"Do you think he will remember me? Will he be able to speak to me?"

"Jason, the doctors had a look at your dad this morning. He is doing great, and the plan is to wake him up on Monday or Tuesday."

"Really?" He remembered the conversation he had with the doctor the day before about the plans for the coming week.

"Yes. And they mention your plans, which is why they might wait until Tuesday so you can be here. And then we will know the answers to all your questions. Until then you have to stay positive. I know it is hard but trust me it is for the best."

Do you think he will wake up?" Jason was looking her straight in the eyes.

Julia quickly pulled the curtains around the bed to give Jason some privacy. He was obviously finding it difficult today, which could be a delayed reaction to it all. She also wanted to avoid any of her colleagues seeing them talking. When Jason's dad was brought in, she had spoken to him using his first name, Frank. This led to a few questions about how she knew him and then when Jason showed up, a few of her colleagues asked about her history with him. It appeared they all thought Jason was a good-looking guy, and some had even asked if she knew whether he was single.

She went and got an extra chair and sat down.

"Jason, I can't tell you how he will be when he wakes up, but I can tell you, he is in the best hands here and all the tests are looking good."

"I know and I'm sorry for asking, but I just can't stop thinking about what I will do if he can't talk or even recognize me. There is so much I want to tell him." Jason could feel his eyes filling up; he turned his head to look at his dad and to avoid Julia noticing.

"Jason, I know this is difficult, and trust me, you are not the first one to experience this, but you have to try and stay positive." Julia took his hand and looked straight at him.

"I know. Thank you for listening" His eyes caught hers and for a second it felt like time had stood still and he would have agreed to anything she said.

"Now tell me more about Grace." Julia let go of his hand and went to check the machine as it was beeping. Jason told her all he could remember about Grace and her family and how nice it had been to talk to her again.

"I've looked up where she lives and it isn't far from my route to New York, so I'm thinking of visiting her tomorrow if I go."

"What a good idea and yes, you are going. I will look after him while you are gone, so you don't have to worry about him." She smiled and nodded toward his father.

"Thank you." He was pretty sure he had detected a minor disappointment in her voice when he mentioned New York. Could he blame her? "Julia, I know what you are thinking, but I promise you I will be back Monday evening. I have no option but to go, as it is a very important meeting." He reached for her hand, and to his relief, she didn't object.

"I know, and I know it's none of my business."

"Well, I can't blame you for thinking what you are thinking." He wasn't sure what else to say.

"I'll be fine. I'll see you when you get back. Now I better get on with my job." Julia went to pull the curtains back. Hearing that Jason was going to New York had affected her - but why? It was his life, and he was free to do what he wanted.

"Julia, thank you" now it was Jason's turn to look her straight in the eyes. "I will speak to you before I go tomorrow."

Back home, Jason felt the need for some fresh air to clear his brain, and the best way to do that would be a walk with Duke. Just as he was heading out, he could hear the house phone ringing and wondered who that could be. For a second he just wanted to leave it. If it was important, they would phone again but then he changed his mind and rushed back in.

"Mr. Wild speaking." He was preparing himself for the caller not being there.

"Is it you Jason? It's Grace here."

"Oh, hello how are you? Sorry, I have just come back from

the hospital." Hearing her voice made him thankful that he answered the call.

"Oh no, is everything okay with Frank?"

Jason could hear she sounded concerned.

"Yeah, everything is fine. Actually, he is doing so well that they are going to wake him up next week."

"Oh, that is great news. I was just calling to see if it would be okay with you for me to come next weekend to visit him?"

"Of course, it is. Would you like me to come and collect you?"

"That's very kind of you to offer Jason, but I have spoken to a distant relation of mine who lives halfway between me and your father. She has said that I'm welcome to stay with her and that would break up the journey and make it easier for me."

"That sounds like an excellent idea. Well, I have been doing some thinking myself. As you know, I am heading back to New York tomorrow and I have been looking at the map. Your place isn't that much of a detour for me, so I was thinking if you were home that I could call in to see you. Would that be okay with you?"

"I would like that, Jason. We can then talk about the weekend. I shall look forward to seeing you. Would you like supper?"

"Yes please, but don't do too much. I'm not sure what time I will set off yet. Would it be okay with you if I call you when I leave here?"

"Yes, of course, you can. I will head to the store later today and get a few simple things. It will be nice to eat with someone for a change." Grace already had a few ideas of what she would do. One thing she liked was making dinner for guests, but it wasn't that often now she had the opportunity to do it.

"Okay. I shall look forward to seeing you tomorrow. Bye for now." Duke hadn't moved from his side, and Jason gave him a pat.

"Come on boy, let's go for a walk. We'd better remember to ask if our friends next door would look after you while I'm away. Don't think you would enjoy the long drive or the big city." Jason spotted the extra car in the Hendersons' driveway and as he walked past, the front door to the house opened.

"Well, well, well, how are you, my friend?" Andrew came running out of the house and before Jason could say or do anything, Andrew wrapped his arms around him and lifted him off the ground.

"Good to see you, Jason. It has been far too long. How are you?" Andrew did one of those quick up-and-down looks at Jason. "You look pretty good for your age, I would say," and he laughed.

"Hey, you don't look too bad either." Jason couldn't help but smile. Apart from having filled out a little, Andrew looked pretty much like Jason remembered him.

"Oh well, it's so good to see you, my friend." They were so busy greeting each other that Jason hadn't seen Mrs. Henderson come out as well.

"Any news on your father, Jason?"

"Yes, and no, in a kind of way," Jason explained what Julia had told him earlier.

"That is good news. Fingers crossed he will be fine and can come home to you soon," she was looking at Duke now.

"Oh yeah, about Duke. I have to get back to New York tomorrow afternoon but will be back late Monday evening. Would you mind having Duke while I am away?"

"Not a problem, Jason. Just bring him over when you are ready."

"Thank you, Mrs. Henderson. Oh, by the way, I'm going to visit one of my mom's old friends on the way." Jason explained how he had opened the letters, which then led to him getting in contact with Mrs. Smith.

"She is planning to visit us next weekend. Hopefully, dad will be awake by then and able to talk." Jason could feel the doubt creeping in on him again.

"I'm sure he will be fine Jason and what wonderful news about Mrs. Smith. It will be good for your father to see some friends. I'm pretty sure I have met her. Am I right in thinking you used to go on vacation with them?"

"Yeah, that's right, we did until Mr. Smith and dad argued over something."

"Okay, enough of this. Mom, I will be back later once Jason and I have finished catching up." Andrew knew his mother too well. If they didn't get going soon, there would be a strong chance that they wouldn't go at all. He gave his mother a quick hug.

"I will make sure we will be back for cake later Mrs. H." Jason gave her a little hug and then turned to Andrew.

"I have already promised her this as I'm taking you out for lunch."

"Well, we better be going then." Andrew rubbed his stomach. "But let's start by taking Duke for a walk." Andrew gave Jason a pat on the shoulder, and they headed off.

"Sorry about that, but you know what my mother is like."

"Yeah, I know, but she means well. So, what have you been up to all these years?"

Andrew told Jason how he had trained as a car mechanic and then took over the repair shop in Preston from his father-in-law.

"Well, you always enjoyed messing around with grease and engines, so that doesn't come as a surprise. Business going well?"

"Yeah, I can't complain. Taken on a couple of lads to help me. And I look after this one too." They were back at the house now and standing next to Jason's dad's car. It wasn't that old, and Jason had noticed that there weren't any dents or scratches on it. He had been trying to work out whether it was because his dad was still an excellent driver, or he just wasn't using it.

"Well, I can only hope he will be able to drive it again, not that I know if he did before. It doesn't look like it gets used a lot."

"Trust me, your father is still an excellent driver, much better than many people at his age." They were now in the kitchen and Jason reached for a couple of glasses.

"Would you like some water?" He filled one glass up and offered it to Andrew.

"Thanks". Andrew took the glass and downed the water in one.

"Your mom told me you got married. Which one did you end up with?" Jason's memory of Andrew was that he always had a string of girls following him. He couldn't remember Andrew not having a girlfriend, but he couldn't remember any of their names. They never hung around long enough for him to get to know them.

"Actually, not one from around here. Her name is Amy, and she is a nurse, but not here in town." Andrew put his glass down. "Did mom also tell you I have a son called Colin? He is nearly two now."

"Yes, she mentioned she had a grandchild called Colin and I have seen pictures as well." Jason couldn't help noticing how happy Andrew sounded when he talked about his family.

"What about you? Have you got married and all that?" Andrew knew the answer from his mother, but it wouldn't hurt to hear it from the man himself.

"No, I haven't found the one and if I am honest, I got too much work on to be worrying about that at the moment."

"Come on, you must at least have a girlfriend?"

"Well, there is or was one, but she doesn't seem to think it is important for me to be here right now."

"That's a shame, sounds like she isn't the right one for you. Don't worry, you will find one. You are far too good-looking to not get a catch. Maybe you already have met the right one." Andrew, like so many others, had thought that Julia and Jason would have gotten married.

"Hey what would you say to lunch at Benny's?" Jason

was feeling a little uncomfortable with the direction their conversation was taking, and he hoped that by suggesting lunch, the subject would change.

"What a great idea, just like old times. I haven't been there for a very long time. Is it still Benny running it?" Andrew knew what Jason was trying to do, and he decided to leave the girlfriend subject for now.

"Yep, and trust me, it hasn't changed." Jason grabbed his keys, "I'll drive."

Jason parked right outside Benny's Café and, as he turned the engine off, he looked at Andrew with a smile.

"Are you ready for a trip down memory lane?" He opened the door and got out.

"I see what you mean. This has definitely not changed, well not on the outside. Pretty sure that is the same color." Andrew kept looking at the front of the café as he was getting out of the car. Jason was holding the door and let Andrew walk in first. Before he could close it behind him, a loud voice was coming from the kitchen door.

"Now who have we got here?" Benny had spotted them getting out of the car and was now making his way across the room with a big smile.

"Hi Benny, you remember this man?" Jason shook his hand.

"Of course, I do. How could I forget him? How are you, Andrew? Long time no see." Benny gave Andrew a handshake and then turned to Jason. "You haven't been here in years and now two days in a row? You must have missed me." Benny had put his hand on Jason's shoulder and gave him a friendly pat

"Yeah, I brought my partner in crime with me today. Now, where would you like us to sit?" Jason looked around to see where there was a free table, but before he could make a move, Benny pointed toward a quiet corner table.

"Look, your regular table is free and waiting for you. Take a seat and I will bring the menu over. I bet you I know what you will order?"

"You might be right, but it would be rude not to have a look." Jason gave Benny a smile and headed for their old regular table in the corner.

"Doesn't look like a lot has changed here?" Andrew was busy looking around as he followed Jason across to the table.

"I know but I kind of like it." They had reached the table and Jason sat down.

Benny soon returned with the menu.

"Who was his partner yesterday?" Andrew looked at Benny and was trying to work out who it could have been.

"Well, all I can say is that it was a lady friend," Benny gave Andrew one of those looks and Andrew had a feeling who Benny was referring to. He didn't say anything but instead turned his attention to the menu Benny had given him.

"Wow, this definitely brings back memories." Andrew recognized most of the meal options. Jason was right when he said nothing had changed.

"Shall I give you a little time to decide?" Benny didn't give them a chance to answer as there was a table that needed him.

"Nice to see that it's still a popular place to come." Andrew looked at Jason. "You didn't mention anything about your company yesterday. Who was she?" He could see that Jason was trying to avoid eye contact with him. Well, well, well, he thought to himself, it would explain the way he reacted earlier.

"If you insist on it. Yes, I had lunch with Julia here yesterday, but it was purely as a friend helping a friend and nothing more. She happens to be the nurse in charge of dad's care." Jason could feel the heat in his cheeks and hoped that Andrew hadn't noticed it.

"Okay. Of course, she works there. How is she?" Andrew put the menu down as he had decided what he was having. He wondered how much she had told him. Before Jason could answer, Benny had come back to take their order. They both went for a burger and coke.

"I knew it. Just like the old days," Benny laughed as he headed for the kitchen.

"So, how was it seeing her again?" Andrew was looking directly at Jason.

"Well, it was a bit of a shock when she answered the phone." Jason told him how he had called the hospital on his way from New York the other night, "I had no idea that she was working here at the hospital or even that she was a nurse now." He told Andrew about the meeting at the hospital and their lunch meeting the day before.

"What a coincidence she should be in charge of your dad's care." Andrew couldn't help but think that the universe was trying to say something. Not that he was a big believer but what were the chances of this happening?

"Yeah. It was uncomfortable to start with. Now we've

had a chat and cleared the air, and she has offered to help me out, for which I am very grateful. I'm still a bit shocked I think."

"Well, I think I would be too. Glad to hear though that you two are talking." Andrew couldn't help but smile and thought this could be just the thing that both of them needed.

"It is nothing more than that, trust me. She has made it very clear that she doesn't want to be any more than a friend."

"Please tell me you didn't ask her for more?" Andrew was a bit surprised. Surely Jason hadn't been that foolish.

"No, of course, I didn't. I just said it felt like the good old days and she told me that we shouldn't go there again. That's all." Jason felt it was time to change the subject and told Andrew all about the letters he had found.

"Two of the letters were from one of mom's old school friends. She lost her husband a few months after mom died. I decided it would only be fair if I told her what had happened, so I phoned her. She was so pleased to hear from me, and she is actually going to come and visit dad next weekend. I just hope he will be awake by then."

"I'm sure he will be fine and what brilliant news, Jason. Why did your father not open those letters?

"I have no idea. It looks like he has touched nothing that belongs to mom. Oh, by the way, the place looks a bit overgrown and there are a few smaller repairs needed on the house, so I was thinking of spending next weekend giving it all a once over."

"Sounds like a good plan." Andrew was still thinking of Julia, and whether she had told Jason the full story.

"Was Julia happy to see you? What did you talk about, apart from your dad and his problems?"

"Well, she seems happy, although I feel that there is something that I haven't been told about. Before mom died, she told me that Julia was engaged. When I asked your parents about it the other night, your mom told me he broke it off just before returning home. Now I told Julia that I had heard she got engaged and all she said was *'correct, but it didn't work out'*. Why do I feel that there is more to that story, that there is something I haven't been told? Do you know what happened?" Jason looked at Andrew, hoping he, as his best friend, could give him a straight answer.

"Yes, she was engaged to a man called Peter, who was in the armed forces stationed abroad. They were going to plan their wedding and all that when he returned. A week before he was due to return and leave the forces for good, he was involved in an accident and died. As you can imagine, Julia was in quite a bad way for a long time afterward. I know she doesn't like to talk about it; she doesn't want people to feel sorry for her."

"Oh god, that must have been so hard for her." Jason felt sick hearing this. Poor Julia.

"It was, and it took her a while to get over it I'm not sure if that is something you can get over. The strange thing was that most people didn't think they were suited to each other, but what do I know?"

"Really?" Oddly somehow that last comment made Jason feel better.

"Two burgers for two handsome men," Benny had arrived with their lunch.

"Thanks, Benny. This looks delicious." Andrew took a bite of his burger and, as he was chewing, he gave Jason a thumbs-up sign. They ate in silence.

"So, you are planning to do some gardening while you are here? What do you know about gardening? Don't you live in an apartment? Surely you don't have anything like that in New York. Andrew could remember how Jason's mom had tried to educate them both on gardening when they were young. Unlike Jason, Andrew had found it very interesting.

"Come to think about it, not a lot." Jason used the napkin to wipe his mouth. It hadn't crossed his mind that he knew absolutely zero about gardening.

"Well, luckily for you, I do, and I will be happy to help. Have you got any tools?"

"Not sure, but dad must have some. I also asked your dad if I could borrow some of his."

"He did mention that. Look, I have an idea. Why don't I bring the family along next weekend? Mom would love to look after Colin, and you could meet Amy. We could get mom to make a BBQ in the evening?"

"That sounds like a good plan." Jason hadn't really thought that far ahead.

"I mean that is if you still plan to be here?" Andrew couldn't quite work out the look on Jason's face.

"Oh yes, I will be here. My boss told me yesterday that

he could see no reason why I couldn't work from here, so we agreed I will be based here for the time being. I just hadn't thought that far ahead. But seriously, I would be really grateful if you could and would help me. And I would love to meet Amy and Colin."

"Wow, that is good news. It will be good to see some more of you. Let's have a look at the place when we get back and see what needs doing" They carried on chatting about the old days and Benny came over to join them after the lunch rush was over. Benny and Andrew were trying to update Jason on all the things that had happened since he had moved to New York.

It was mid-afternoon by the time they got back to the house.

"Hey, why don't I go and get dad and we can all three have a look at the place." Before Jason could say anything, Andrew had gone across to his parent's house to get his dad. The advantage of having Mr. Henderson with them was that he knew what the place should or would look like if Jason's mom had been there. Standing there looking at it all while waiting for Andrew and his dad, he realized he had no idea where to start and what to do.

"Afternoon Mr. Henderson. It's very kind of you to give me some advice."

"Afternoon Jason, think it's time you just call me Alan. Anyway, Andrew was talking about doing some gardening?" Mr. Henderson turned his head and looked around.

"Yeah, I wanted to tidy the place a bit before dad

hopefully comes home and there are a few things to do on the outside of the house as well."

"Tell you what, I think it's an excellent idea, Jason. Your father is going to like it. He was only talking last week about how it all had become a little too much for him. He has never been as keen as your mother was on gardening."

Andrew told his father about his idea for the coming weekend and Alan could only agree with it.

"Let's have a look and see what we have." The three of them spent the next half hour wandering around discussing things.

"Well, I think a day would make a lot of difference here. If you don't mind, I will draw up some plans during the week, so we all know what we need to do. Right Andrew, your mom has made a cake so we better all three get back and have some coffee." Alan then turned to Duke, "Think she has a treat for you too."

*

Jason spent Saturday evening in front of the TV, not really watching what was on. If someone had said to him the previous weekend that he would spend the following weekend at his dad's house, he would have told them that there was no chance of that, especially with the interview coming up. He had gone to work Tuesday morning feeling pretty good about life and looking forward to the prospect of a promotion. Not at one point did it cross his mind that he would be back here, and he would meet Julia again. One phone call was all it took to completely change his plans. Some would say it changed his life. Looking at it now, he was in some strange way glad that it had happened, though perhaps not as serious as it had been. Of course, he would rather have seen his dad at home. Seeing him lying in a hospital bed, unable to communicate made Jason feel guilty. How could he have let it get so far?

Until two years ago, Jason would visit his parents every couple of months, but since his mother had passed away, he had only been back a few times. It had taken him a long time to come to terms with the loss, and he had used work to control the pain. Looking back, Jason now realized that it had been a very selfish thing to do. It couldn't have been easy for his dad, either. And then there was Julia. Meeting up with her had been awkward at first, but after a couple of days and lunch, things were a lot better. In fact, after yesterday's lunch, he felt things were almost back to where they had left off ten years ago, but only as friends. Nothing more than that. Julia had made that pretty clear and after what Andrew had told him earlier, he could understand why. However, it didn't stop him from thinking of her, her smile, and her voice. But why hadn't she just told him the truth?

Then there was the week ahead: tomorrow he was going to visit Mrs. Smith and see Helen; Monday he had the interview. All three things could have a big impact on what was to come. The one thing he wasn't looking forward to was seeing Helen, but he knew he had to, and the sooner, the better.

It was getting late and with a long day ahead of him, it would be good to get a decent night's sleep.

*

A quick walk with Duke, then some breakfast, and he was ready to head to the hospital. Not that there was a lot he could do there, but Jason felt good just being there next to his dad. And maybe, if he was lucky, he would see Julia. He stopped at the shop in the entrance hall to get the paper, not that the Sunday paper had a lot in it, but it gave him something to do while he was there.

Julia had been busy with a new patient who had come in overnight and was very unwell. She had to make sure that there was a nurse in that room all the time. It was now time for a brief coffee break and as she walked past the door to the room where Jason's dad was, she spotted Jason sitting next to the bed reading the paper. She couldn't help but smile. It was nice to see that he was more relaxed now when visiting and it brought back memories. For a split second, she thought of how nice it could be if they picked up where they left off but quickly stopped herself. No, she couldn't go there again.

"Morning you two. How are we today?" She couldn't help but laugh at Jason's reaction. He jumped up and spun around like someone had spotted him doing something he shouldn't.

"We are fine, well I am and he's not complaining," he gave her a big smile.

"That's good then. So, when are you heading back, Jason?" Julia went to check the machines and made a few notes on the board at the end of the bed.

Jason wasn't sure what she meant.

"Well, I am hoping to leave this afternoon, and I will call in on Mrs. Smith on the way. She is insisting on giving me supper. The meeting tomorrow morning should be finished around lunchtime so I will leave as soon as I have had a bite to eat. With a bit of luck, I should be back here around seven. Why?" He had left one little detail out that he didn't think she needed to know about. There was no need to get Julia involved in his meeting with Helen this evening.

"Okay, well everything looks fine here, and don't you worry Frank, I will take good care of you while he is gone." Julia had turned to face Jason's dad and pretended to sort something out. She didn't want Jason to see how much it hurt her that he was leaving. And the stupid thing was that he was a free man and could do what he wanted, so why was it bothering her so much?

"Do you always talk to your patients?" Jason had noticed she often spoke to his dad and was wondering whether she just did it because she knew him or if it was something she did to all of her patients.

"Yeah, an old habit of mine, but it also keeps them real. Just because they can't speak doesn't mean we can't talk to them. Well, have a safe journey Jason, and I will look forward to seeing you on Tuesday." She had put her hand on his shoulder and given him a gentle squeeze. It almost felt like a tiny hug. Or was he reading too much into it? Whichever way, it stunned him a bit.

"Thank you and I will look forward to seeing you too." He gave her a smile and watched her leave the room.

Reunited

*

By mid-afternoon, the car was packed, and Jason was ready to leave. He had checked that all windows and doors were closed and locked. All he needed to do now was to take Duke across to the Hendersons.

"Hey boy, sorry I have to leave you, but I promise you I will be back in a couple of days. In the meantime, you're staying with Mrs. Henderson." Duke was looking at him with some rather sad eyes and Jason felt so guilty leaving him behind, but he had no choice. There was no way he could take him with him to New York.

"Hope your meeting goes well, Jason. Drive careful and we will see you tomorrow evening" Mrs. Henderson had that look in her eyes like she was sending her own son off out into the world.

"Yeah, I will be fine. Now not sure what time I will get back, but I will let you know when I am leaving. Don't wait up for me." He couldn't help feeling rather touched by her concern.

"Not a problem. Jason," she had reached out for his hand, "would you mind letting me know when you have reached your apartment? I know it sounds silly, but it would make me feel better."

"Not a problem." Jason gave her a big hug, and he was on his way. As he headed out of town, he thought of what Mrs. Henderson had said. In a strange way, he felt rather emotional about it. She had acted just like his mother would have done, and that couldn't really surprise him as he had spent a lot of time in her company as a child.

Grace's address was in the GPS and a quick look told him that he would be there in just under two hours, so he had better let her know.

"Hi Grace, I have just left and should be with you around five. Hope that is okay with you."

"Perfect Jason. I will have food ready for you."

"Thank you."

As Jason got closer, he recognized the area. A few things had changed, but otherwise, it looked just like he remembered it and he had no trouble finding Grace's house.

He had hardly touched the doorbell before the door opened.

"Hello, Jason. It is so good to see you." She had put her hand out but changed her mind and went straight for a big hug.

"Goodness me, you haven't changed a lot, still a handsome young man. Come on in."

"Thank you and here I bought you some flowers". He had debated with himself whether to get something and decided that you couldn't go too wrong with some flowers.

"Thank you. Now please come on in." She closed the door behind him. Jason did a quick glance around the bit he could see. It all looked like he remembered it.

"I hope you don't mind if we eat in the kitchen, as there are only two of us. It makes it easier. Let me just find a vase for these pretty flowers."

"Fine by me," and he followed her through to the kitchen.

They spent the next hour talking about what Jason had been up to. And of course, Grace wanted to know about his mother and her passing. At first, Jason felt a little uncomfortable talking about it, but after a little while, he told her everything he knew from the last time he had seen her right through to the day of the funeral, including the run-in with his dad.

"Jason, that happens in other families as well. Don't be too hard on yourself and I am pretty sure that once your father wakes up, he will understand."

"I hope so. Let's just hope he wakes up and can talk to us." That thought was still playing with his mind and Grace could see he was worried. She reached out for his hand.

"I am sure he will be fine, Jason. He is a strong man."

All this talk about his parents had rather put a damper on his otherwise good mood and he decided to change the subject.

"So why did the vacations stop?" Jason had never discovered the real reason. He remembered asking once but was told that the Smiths were very busy and therefore didn't have time to see them.

"I am not 100% sure what started it, but my husband and your father were two completely different people and I think in the end it was politics that did it. Democrat versus Republican. The final straw was an election year and after that, your mom and I decided it wasn't worth it any longer. However, we still kept in touch on the phone and when I visited my relatives, we would meet halfway, just her and me."

"What a shame. I remember the fun vacations we had together. It was never really the same after they stopped."

"Your mom and I both tried to keep them under control when we were together, but in the end, it just got silly. Anyway, we can't change what happened and I have nothing against your father, so I intend to come and visit him." She smiled and took Jason's hand. "When do you think he will be ready to see me?"

Good question, he thought; now what do I say?

"Well, the plan is to wake him up tomorrow or Tuesday. I'm not sure how long that will take and what state he will be in if he comes around. Think the best thing would be for me to let you know what is happening regularly and we can take it from there. Does that sound okay with you?"

"That is a good plan. I will wait to hear from you. There is nothing here stopping me from going now that I'm retired."

"I can't promise that I will call every day, but I will give you an update when I have them." He looked at his watch, "now I'd better get going, as I still got a little way to go. It was very nice to see you, Grace, and thank you so much for dinner." He gave her a hug before heading for the door.

"Likewise, Jason. Drive safely and let's hope I will see you next weekend. I will bring some flowers to put on the grave." She was standing at the door, waving him on his way.

Jason had kept it together enough to wave to her as he drove off. Once out of sight he pulled over and took a deep breath. Grace had mentioned the grave again, which had made him feel a bit sick. Should he call Julia? No, don't be silly. Pull yourself together. Julia had said she would help him with it, so there was no point in thinking about it now. He started the car again and headed for the main highway.

Just before joining it, Jason pulled over to check his phone. It was on the back seat and in silent mode. He hadn't actually looked at it since he arrived at Grace's. There were a few messages from Helen, who seemed to be keen to speak to him. She hadn't forgotten he had mentioned coming back to New York today. Right, time to get this sorted once and for all, and he dialed her number. It didn't take her long to answer and after the usual complaint about him not answering straight away, he finally got a word in.

"Sorry. Just stopped for gas and realized that my phone was in my jacket on the back seat and on silent. Anyway, I hope to be back at my place around nine. Could we meet at the bar on the corner?"

"Why don't I come to yours?" He could hear she was disappointed, but the last thing he wanted was for her to come to his apartment. That was far too risky.

"Sorry I haven't been home for a week and don't know what state it's in. Besides, I could do with a drink when I get there. I will see you at the bar at nine. Got to go," and he hung up.

As he walked through the door, he spotted Helen at the bar. She was so busy chatting with some guy standing next to her that she didn't notice Jason coming in. Part of him felt a bit disappointed that she didn't even look like she was waiting for him. Not quite what he had expected after their conversation only a couple of hours ago. He headed towards her and still, not once did she look in his direction.

"Well, I made it on time." He was now standing right behind her and was waiting to see what reaction he got. Helen turned round to see who it was, and it was as if someone had flicked a switch.

"Oh, you're here. I have missed you so much," and she threw herself into his arms. The guy she had been chatting with looked so confused as to what happened that Jason almost felt sorry for him. At the same time, he thought Helen could make a good actor.

"Trust me, you don't want to know," Jason half-whispered to the confused man and then turned his attention to Helen.

"Come, let's go and sit down." He had spotted a table that was free in the corner and headed towards it. Helen followed him while busily trying to find something in her bag. As they reached the table, Helen pulled out a piece of paper that looked like it had a list of things written on it. This rather surprised Jason, as he couldn't remember ever seeing her with a piece of paper in her hand.

"I have so much to tell you, Jason. First, we have been invited to three things next week, and then there is a big show coming up the following weekend, which we will need to attend." She started to read from the list on the paper. And to no surprise, it was all things to do with her work and her so-called friends. Jason had also made a note that not once had she asked him how his dad was doing.

"Oh, shall I get us a glass of wine?" she was waving to the bartender to get his attention. That's it. Jason had had enough, and the sooner he could get this done, the better.

"No, thank you. That won't be necessary." The tone of his voice had somehow got through to Helen and for once she stopped talking and looked puzzled.

"Are you okay, darling?"

"Helen, we need to talk." He was trying his hardest to stay calm and be gentle, but before he could say more, she had the diary up on her phone.

"I know. We have so many things to plan, and we need to book that vacation."

Jason had reached his limit now and he couldn't care less how the next bit sounded. He just needed to say it and get out of this place.

"Helen, I am heading straight back to the hospital tomorrow afternoon after my meeting, and I will be based there over the summer so I can help my dad."

"You are what?" She shouted so loud that all the people sitting around them could hear her. "Why are you doing this to me? You never do anything for me."

That last bit was definitely not true, but he decided not to comment on it. There was no need to add fuel to the scene she had created. Instead, he pointed out that not once had she asked about his dad. If she had, she would know he was still in a coma and seriously ill.

"So, why do you need to be there? Surely the hospital has nurses to look after him?" She was now trying her hardest to press out a tear.

"Look, this is my dad we are talking about. He is my family, and I am sorry if that doesn't fit into your plans. I think it's best if we take a break for a while until I know what is happening back home."

She looked at him with eyes that if they could kill, he would be dead by now, but he didn't care. He'd had enough. He got up and put a few dollars on the table.

"Here, buy yourself a drink. I wish you all the best," and headed for the door. As he passed the guy she had been chatting with, he couldn't help it:

"She is all yours now, my friend."

Once outside, he took a deep breath and hurried toward his apartment. He wanted to get away from the bar as quickly as possible, in case Helen decided to come running after him. Not that he thought it would happen, but just in case. He reached his apartment fairly quickly and, just as he was about to lock himself into the building, he decided to walk a bit further. There was this half-open square just down the street, which he had never actually been in. It wasn't that big but a nice little green space, and to his delight, there were a couple of benches you could sit on. He sat down and looked up to the sky to see the stars, but to his disappointment, he couldn't see any because of all the streetlights. Ah, of course, the light pollution. He had never really thought about what it meant until now. A message came through on his phone and his first thought was that it would be Helen sending him some sort of message, so he ignored it. Then suddenly he thought it could have been the hospital sending him a message, and he quickly pulled out his phone from the inside pocket of his jacket. It wasn't either the hospital or Helen. No, it was, in fact, from Julia. His heart was pumping faster as he was trying to open the message and he couldn't help but smile when he read it.

"Hope you made it safely to New York. See you on Tuesday. X," it read. He thought for a little while about what to reply.

"Yep, just back. Visited Mrs. Smith on the way." He pressed send and then almost immediately wrote "I can't see the stars here," followed by a sad emoji, and clicked send again. A message came back almost instantly. "Well, that's one of the advantages of living here" and a smiley emoji. Jason could only agree with her.

*

Before heading to bed, Jason packed a couple of bags of clothes and left them by the door. That way, he could soon be on the way when he returned from the office tomorrow. Then he did a last quick look around to see if there was anything else he thought he would need, not that it mattered that much, as he would be back for meetings occasionally. One thing he did realize was how sterile his apartment was compared to his dad's house. There were no pictures of his parents either. The walls were more or less empty, with only a couple of abstract posters he didn't even know who had created. Some friends had given them to him. The apartment looked more like a hotel room than a private apartment. No, this wasn't really a family home, and he decided that when he returned later in the year, he would have to do something about it, and he headed for bed.

Jason woke up just before the alarm went off, feeling rather confused, and it took a little while before he worked out where he was. He quickly reached out for his phone to check for messages, and, to his relief, there weren't any. That could only mean that his dad was fine, and it had just been a bad dream. All he could remember of it was walking into a room and seeing many people around his dad's bed working very hard on something. Julia had come across to say that it would be best if he waited outside, and she had put her arm around him.

Despite there not being any messages from the hospital, Jason decided to make a quick call to check that his dad was okay. It was still very early, and he apologized for the early call; he came up with some sort of excuse that he was heading to a meeting and just wanted to check how his dad was doing. The nurse informed him that his dad had had a good night, and everything was fine.

"Thank you," and then thought how stupid it must have sounded. Who sets off for a meeting just after six am? Why couldn't he just have told her the truth? Why try to hide the fact that he was really concerned about his dad?

After a quick shower, he checked everything was ready by the door for when he returned from the office. Jason wanted to get out of the city as quickly as possible once he had finished work. All looked to be okay, now it was just a matter of picking up his workbag and heading for the office.

There were hardly any people on the street this early, so he decided to take the subway. This time in the morning they were half empty, so it would be easy to get a seat and today was no different. As he was sitting there staring out of the windows, watching the city slowly wake up, he thought of the interview. What would life be like if or when he took up the new position? He wasn't sure exactly what it would be, but there would be some traveling involved both within the U.S. but also abroad. He would probably not have a lot of time to get back to see his dad. How would he feel about that? This was definitely not something he had taken into consideration when he applied for it.

He stopped to pick up some coffee before heading through the main door and passing the security guy, who smiled.

"Good morning, Mr. Wild. Hope you have a lovely day."

"Morning" Jason nodded and headed for the elevator. As he stepped out of the elevator on the third floor, he looked around to see if anyone else was in this early. It looked like he was the first one, which suited him fine, and he headed straight down to the far corner where his office was.

Mrs. Anderson had left a few things for him to look at and sign off. He sat down and started to work his way through it, and soon it was all done. Then he checked his emails and once that was done, he didn't really know what to do. The day had been marked for the interview, so Mrs. Anderson hadn't booked or planned anything for him. He checked his phone. Nothing there either, not even from Helen, which surprised him a little. He had kind of expected a call or at least a couple of messages from her by now, but not a word. Think that just proved my point, he thought to himself. He looked at Julia's messages. Her brief message asking if he had arrived okay just showed how much she cared even though they were only friends. That was the kind of person she was, always very caring for others. He remembered how she would always help his mom when she was at their house back in the day. Getting back in touch with her was one of the best things that had happened to him in a very long time. Now it was up to him to make sure they stayed in touch. Jason was so caught up in thinking about Julia that he hadn't heard Mrs. Anderson calling him.

"Morning daydreamer. How are you today?" she stood right in front of his desk with a big smile and a basket that had a lovely smell.

"Oh morning, sorry, just thinking of old times." He wasn't going to say what or who he was thinking of.

"Whatever it is, it must be nice because it has been a long time since I have seen you smile like that. Would that have something to do with your father?" She was pretty sure there were other things behind it as well but didn't say it.

"Well, I was thinking of dad and how it will go when they start to wake him up," he paused for a second, and then carried on, "By the way, you shouldn't get any more calls from Helen. I ended it last night."

"Well done. She was never right for you, too caught up in herself, I would say. There will be someone out there for you, trust me. And maybe sooner than you think." She looked at him closely to see what reaction she got and smiled.

"I know," he smiled. "What's in the basket?" He was desperate to divert the conversation over to something other than his failed girlfriends.

"Oh, I nearly forgot. I have made you a cake and some biscuits to take back with you today. Thought you might like a little treat."

"That is very kind of you. Thank you so much."

"That's okay. So, are you ready for the interview?"

"I think so. Once it's done, I will head home and get my bags and leave." He stopped for a second. "Mary, am I doing the right thing?"

"What do you mean, Jason?" Mrs. Anderson went to close the door so they could talk in private. She had learned over the years that when Jason called her Mary, he wasn't talking to her as her boss but more as a friend.

"Well, you know, going for this position and all that. It won't give me much time to visit my dad, will it?"

"No, probably not unless you make sure you take time off to do it." It was Mrs. Anderson's turn to stop for a second, "forgive me for saying so, and please don't take this the wrong way, but you don't know what the outcome of your father's illness is yet or how you two will get on. Just for the record, I'm pretty sure he is going to be fine. So do the interview now and should you get the job, you can always turn it down."

She was right. There was a risk that his dad wouldn't wake up or, worse, maybe even die. And what if his dad didn't want to see him? But then again, if everything turned out well with his dad and he wanted to spend more time with him, was this the right job to go for? He felt like his head was about to explode and he had no control over it. Mrs. Anderson could see he was struggling.

"Jason, take a deep breath and try to relax a bit. Everything is going to be okay. Things have a way of working themselves out."

He did as he was told and after a little while, he could feel the tension ease a bit.

"You're right. I will do the interview. I lose nothing by doing that."

"Maybe instead of the new position, they could offer you something where you could work from there. I think that's what is happening with John Jackson. And you have proved this last week you can do it. Have you thought of that?"

"Actually, when I spoke to Mr. Patterson last Friday, he suggested that I work from dad's house for the summer and just come into the office for the odd meetings. And yes, they have made that arrangement with John. I'm meant to call him and have a chat about it. It's on my to-do list this week."

"That is good. I saw Tracey last week, and she told me all about it. Maybe this is the start of something new for you." She paused for a second. "But I will miss you if that happens."

The phone rang and Mrs. Anderson answered it from Jason's desk.

"Just one moment Mr. Patterson," she pressed a button on the panel and turned to Jason.

"Mr. Patterson is saying that if you want to, they can see you at 9.30. Someone has dropped out, and he knows you need to get back to your father."

Jason looked at his watch: 30 minutes to get ready. Well, he had nothing else to do, so why not?

"Yeah, I can do that."

"Hello Mr. Patterson, yes, Mr. Wild will be there at 9.30." After putting the phone down, she turned back to Jason.

"Can I just say that no matter what the outcome is from this or what you decide to do, I'm so proud of you Jason."

"Thank you." Jason got up and went around his desk to give her a big hug. "I couldn't have done it without you, especially after mom died."

"Right, get yourself ready and head on up. I got work to do." She was feeling rather emotional now and was trying hard not to show it. The phone was ringing, and she quickly pulled herself together and went out to answer it.

Jason took one last look in the mirror to make sure he looked okay, then wrote a quick message to Julia to tell her that if anything happened with his dad, they should phone his PA. She could get hold of him if needed. Then he picked up his little leather folder and headed for Mr. Patterson's office but left his phone behind.

*

Jason looked at his watch as he entered his office. Just gone 11.30, so he had plenty of time. Mr. Patterson had walked out with him after the interview and thanked him for coming. Then he asked Jason if he could have a quick word with him before he left. They arranged to speak just before lunch.

"How did it go?" Mrs. Anderson looked up as he walked back into her little office a couple of hours later. Jason was one of the lucky ones that had two offices in one. You entered through a door in the glass wall into a smallish room where Mrs. Anderson's desk was and then through a second door into his office.

"Good, I think. Any phone calls for me?" Jason felt pleased with how the interview had gone but had no idea if it was good enough. And for once, he didn't really care. He had done his best and that was all that mattered. Now he could turn his attention to his dad which meant he needed to get home.

Jason picked up his phone before sitting down and, for some reason, he felt nervous to see what messages there were. Why? Surely if something had happened to his dad, they would have phoned Mrs. Anderson as he had instructed them to. There were a couple of missed calls from clients, but none of them had left any messages. Then there was a message from Julia and his heart started to beat faster.

"Got your message. Everything is fine here. Don't worry, and I will see you tomorrow." She had finished it with an X, which made him very happy. Now, should he tell her that he would be back earlier, maybe invite her over? Wait - what did she actually mean when she signed off with an X? Jason sat down and read her message again. Just thinking of her made him happier and he couldn't wait to get back to see her. He was pretty sure that her X was a way of showing that she still had feelings for him. Maybe there was hope that he one day would gain her trust again. In the end, he wrote a reply:

"Thank you. Meeting has finished, just sorting out a few things and then I will be on my way. X."

Didn't take long before he had a reply.

"That's good news. Btw Dr. Peterson says they will try to wake your father up tomorrow morning. Would be good if you could be here. X."

This was indeed good news. Jason quickly replied that he would be there and then went to tell Mrs. Anderson the good news. He knew from his conversation with the doctor a couple of days ago that they planned to do this but somehow it just became real.

Jason looked through what Mrs. Anderson had put on his desk, then made a couple of calls. A half-hour later he had finished. He quickly gathered his things and was ready to go when Mrs. Anderson reminded him that he was seeing Mr. Patterson first.

"Oh, nearly forgot that in all the excitement. He wanted to have a word with me before I left."

"I will send you a list of things for next week. I have moved a couple of online meetings to next week as I think you will have enough to do right now." Although Jason was keen to try to work as normally as possible, he had to admit that she was probably right. Mr. Patterson knocked on the door; he had overheard the conversation.

"I will agree with Mrs. Anderson, Jason. I'm not expecting a lot from you this week. Focus on your father."

"Thank you." Jason didn't really know what else to say.

"Jason, I just wanted to thank you for taking time out to come in today. The board will make their decision either Friday or Monday. I will call you as soon as I know the result. Have a safe journey back and keep me posted on how things are going." Mr. Patterson reached out to shake Jason's hand and left.

Mrs. Anderson got up and gave Jason a hug. "Now you can share this with others"; she pointed to the basket she had given him and smiled.

"I will and promise I will call you later. Well, I better get going." Jason had picked up the basket and was about to leave.

"I think I better take you for some lunch first. You got a long drive ahead." Mrs. Anderson quickly closed down her computer, then grabbed her bag. Suddenly Jason could feel he was quite hungry; not really a surprise as he hadn't eaten anything so far today.

After a good bit of lunch, Jason was ready to leave.

{ **10** }

Finally, Jason had left the city behind him, and the road ahead looked pretty clear. The city traffic hadn't been too bad, mainly because it was still early afternoon. If he had waited another hour, things would have been different. The GPS had the estimated arrival time as 6.45 which was much earlier than Jason had hoped for. It meant that he would have time to call in at the hospital on the way home, which somehow felt very important to him. Strange how things can change you, he thought as he was driving along. He had gone from seeing his dad less than five times over the last couple of years to now feeling he needed to see him every day, despite his dad not being able to communicate with him. Jason dialed the hospital number.

"Hello, Mr. Wild. How are you?" Most of the receptionists knew who he was by now.

"I just wanted to say that I have left New York and plan to stop in to see dad on my way. Aim to be there before seven o'clock this evening."

"That is fine, Mr. Wild. I will let the nurses know that you're coming."

"Thank you."

Next on the list were the Hendersons. Although he had arranged with them that Duke should stay until Tuesday, he decided he wanted to pick him up tonight. The house wouldn't be the same without Duke around. There was something special about that dog: it was almost as if Duke could understand his feelings. And he wouldn't be on his own.

The sun was shining and there wasn't much traffic, which made the journey a lot easier. Jason looked at the fuel gauge and decided that it was best to do a pit stop soon. He wouldn't make it the entire way anyway and he could do with some coffee. As he walked out of the shop with his coffee and a chocolate bar, he noticed a car pull in. It drove straight past him at a slow speed, and he noticed it had a wheelchair in the back but didn't really think any more of it. Soon he was back out on the interstate with the radio playing good music. The news bulletin came up and it was all about a court case against someone who had shot and wounded a couple of people. They talked about the life-changing injuries that the two victims had suffered. Jason remembered the car with the wheelchair in the back. Life-changing. Jason thought about his dad: what if his dad had suffered brain damage? Would he need a wheelchair? Jason's head was spinning, and he pulled over. He got out of the car and walked around trying to gain control again.

Why was he always thinking that the worse would happen? Dr. Peterson had told him they were pretty confident that his dad would be fine. Of course, no one could be one hundred percent sure until his dad was awake. Somehow, he had to snap out of these negative thoughts. Should he call

Julia? Jason looked at the time and decided that she would still be at work and therefore not be able to answer right now. Instead, he looked at his phone to see if there were any work calls, he could make. That would get him thinking of other things. There was nothing. Well, the best he could do would be to get back in the car and keep going. The sooner he could get to the hospital, the better, he thought. Just as he was about to get in, a message popped up from Julia.

"Just finished work. All is good here. X." She had finished with a smiling emoji. Just what he needed. Of course, everything was fine. Why wouldn't it be?

"Thank you. Got just under two hours to go. X." He jumped in the car and headed back on the road.

Finally, he passed a road sign telling him he had just five miles to go. He had spent the time thinking of all the things he and Julia had done in the past and the time had flown past. As he parked near the entrance to the hospital, he looked at his watch - just gone seven. That wasn't bad he thought and got out of the car.

"Evening Mr. Wild. You made it back." One of the nurses was just checking the monitors his dad was attached to.

"Yeah, I am back. How is the old man?" He went across and took his dad's hand.

"Evening dad, I am back as promised."

The nurse made a few notes and then turned to Jason.

"All looking very well and set for a wake-up tomorrow. Any questions?"

"Thank you and no. Julia mentioned earlier that they would start the process tomorrow but not at what time." The minute he had said her name, he regretted it. Up to now, he had managed to keep their history out of any conversations with any of the staff. Dr. Peterson knew, but only that they had grown up together.

"That is correct. She will be here tomorrow to oversee it. The doctors normally come around nine." The nurse smiled as she left. Her conversation with Jason had just confirmed what they all knew: there was a history between the two of them.

Jason didn't stay for long. It was never his intention, he just needed to see his dad was okay. It had been a long day and a lot of driving. Jason hadn't had a lot to eat all day, so he stopped to pick up a pizza for dinner. Once home, he quickly dropped his bags in and went across to collect Duke, who was very pleased to see him.

"His head has been hanging a bit. I think he missed you, Jason. Glad you are back. Did it all go well?"

Just for a split second, he was about to tell them all about the interview and how he most likely would end up with the job but managed to stop himself.

"Meeting went well and finished earlier than we thought, which was good. It meant I could escape New York before the traffic got bad. I popped in to see dad on my way home too and the good news is that they will try to wake him up tomorrow morning."

"That is good news. Please keep us posted, Jason."

"I will. Now come on Duke, let's head home. It has been a long day." As he got outside, he turned to Mrs. Henderson, "I will let you know how it goes later tomorrow."

Reunited

That was close, he thought on his way home. If he had told Mrs. Henderson about the interview and his feelings about it, there was no guarantee it wouldn't leak out and others would hear about it, including Julia. Jason wanted to tell her in person when the time was right and that wasn't now. He knew it was wrong not to tell her, but right now he needed her as a friend. Besides that, he wasn't sure if he would take the job, so why risk the friendship?

*

Jason reached out to turn the alarm off and couldn't believe it was already time to get up. It felt like he had only just gone to bed and on any other day, he would have stayed in bed, but not today. Today was a big day and a day where he hoped to get some answers to all his questions. He swung his legs out and sat on the side of the bed, feeling both excited and nervous. It reminded him of his school days when he did exams. He was never very good before them but somehow always managed to do very well. Today was no different, he thought. He looked at Duke, who was still in his bed looking unimpressed at being woken up early.

"I know. It was a bit of a short night old boy. You carry on sleeping while I have a shower."

Once dressed, he headed for the kitchen to make coffee, and as he passed the door to the living room, he saw all the photo albums on the table. Last night, he had taken one album out to look at and before he knew it, he had them all out. By the time he finished, it had gone past midnight. Both his parents had been keen photographers, and there were seven or eight albums full of pictures stretching from when they first met right up to a few months before Jason's mom died. And some loose ones hadn't made it into an album yet. It had brought back a lot of memories for Jason and at one point, he had tears running.

There were some beautiful photos of his mom and he realized how much he really missed her, her laugh, and their talks. He could really do with her advice now.

There were a couple of albums which were all photos of him and his friends which of course also included Julia. Everything from when he took his first steps, school awards, and birthday parties. Jason hadn't seen a lot of them before. He had spent some time thinking of all the things he and Julia had done together over the years.

There wasn't a lot of writing in the albums, only important notes like the place, date, occasion, and names. Judging by the handwriting it had been his mother that created the albums and that would explain why there were some left unsorted.

While the coffee was brewing, Jason went to put them all back where he had found them and made a note to himself that he would get another album so he could sort the rest out.

After a quick walk with Duke and a bit of breakfast, Jason was ready to head to the hospital. For a second he wondered whether to ask the Hendersons to let Duke out in case he would be gone most of the day but decided that if that was the case, he could always call them later. Last night the nurse had said that the doctors would be there around nine and Jason really wanted to be there.

As he walked through the doors of the hospital, Jason felt anxious about the outcome of the day, just like when he did exams. Would his father wake up? How long would it take for him to wake up? Would he be able to talk and understand what they said? Would he recognize his own son? Would he be pleased or angry to see him? So many questions and no one could tell him the answers. All he could do was wait and see what happened. Hopefully, by the end of the day, some of them would have been answered, if not all of them.

Just before entering the ward, he took one last look at his phone and then turned it off. When Mrs. Anderson had suggested it to him the day before, Jason had told her he would put it on silent. He had never, ever turned his phone off before. But now, standing outside the doors to the ward, he didn't hesitate and turned it off and put it back in his pocket. Today was going to be all about his dad and nothing else, not even work. Jason pressed the button for the door and walked in just as Julia came out of the office.

"Morning, that is what I call good timing. We are about to go and see your father now." Despite Jason promising that he would be back, part of her wouldn't believe it until she saw it. He was looking rather nervous, she thought, and Julia could feel her cheeks getting red. She gave him a big smile. "Come let's go and see what they have to say." Julia nodded her head in the way of his father's bed and Jason followed her.

"Morning." Jason felt nervous and at the same time weak in the knees, seeing her smile. She looked so happy.

"You will both be fine. Come and take a seat. Can I get you a drink?" Julia pointed to the chair next to his dad's bed.

"Coffee would be nice - thank you." Jason sat down as he was told to. Julia returned together with Dr. Peterson and another colleague.

"Here you are." She handed Jason his coffee.

"Thank you." Jason was trying very hard not to show his nerves, but his hands were shaking so he quickly put it on the small table next to him.

"Morning, Mr. Wild. As you know we are starting the process of waking up your father." Dr. Peterson was quickly scanning the folder he had in his hands before carrying on. "We can't say how quickly it will happen but if everything goes according to plan, it shouldn't take too long. Every patient reacts differently to this process, and it also depends on the level of damage the brain might have had. Now you might find your father a bit confused to start with when he wakes up, which is normal, but I feel pretty confident that he will be fine. Any questions?"

"Thank you, doctor," Jason had loads of questions, but he knew they wouldn't be able to answer them now, so there was no point in asking them.

"Dr. Hanson here," Dr. Peterson turned to his assistant, "will be here or close by to observe your father together with nurse Taylor. If you have any questions, just ask them. I'll be back a bit later to see how things are going."

Both the doctors and Julia headed back to the office. A

few minutes later, Julia returned and sat down next to Jason. She had pulled the curtains around the bed.

"So, what is happening now?" Jason was a little confused as it didn't seem like they were doing anything to his dad.

"We have already stopped the medicine that was keeping him asleep; now it is just a question of time. One of the first signs a patient is waking up is that they start to move their fingers. Now you can stimulate this by holding your father's hand."

Jason couldn't stop looking at her, so caring and thoughtful she was. If only she could stay with him, but he knew she had other things to do.

"I got to go and do a few things, but I'll keep an eye on both of you, okay? And should there be anything, just press the red button here and we will come straight away." Without thinking about it Julia put her arm around his shoulders and gave him a little squeeze. It just felt like the most natural thing to do. Jason looked at her but didn't say anything.

"You are going to be fine Jason and so is your father, I promise you." Julia knew she might have promised more than she could deliver but felt pretty confident that Jason's father was going to be fine. There was nothing medical that showed anything else. It hurt her to see Jason like this, even after what he had done to her years ago. Now she had to re-focus and be professional, as she had other patients to look after.

"Okay?" She went to pull the curtains back.

"Julia. Thank you." That was all Jason could say. He watched her walk towards the door. One monitor did a beep which brought his attention back to his dad. As instructed,

Jason took his hand and then did something he hadn't done since he was a child. He started to pray. He wasn't sure what to say, so he just kept repeating the same thing over and over again.

Suddenly Jason felt something in his hand, or was he just imagining it? No, it was real. There was definitely some movement in his dad's hand. He panicked and pressed the button Julia had shown him.

"Dad, can you hear me?" Jason was now standing up and leaning over his dad. He could see the eyes moving, but they didn't seem to open. Julia came in together with Dr. Hanson, who was now standing on the other side of the bed. Julia was standing next to Jason and took his hand. She didn't really care if anyone saw it.

"Jason, it's okay, just let Dr. Hanson check him out." She gently pulled Jason back a bit so Dr. Hanson could do his job.

"Mr. Wild, can you hear me? Open your eyes, Mr. Wild." Nothing happened at first and Dr. Hanson repeated the questions and squeezed Frank's hand. Meanwhile, Jason looked at Julia with great concern.

"Is he okay? Why isn't he opening his eyes?"

"He's fine, Jason, just give him a little time." She gave Jason's hand a little squeeze and looked calmly at him. "This is normal, everything looks normal," Julia had scanned all the various machines that Frank was attached to.

Jason looked at his dad again and after what felt like a very long time, he finally opened his eyes. That was it. Jason couldn't hold back the tears any longer. He kept trying to wipe them away, feeling rather embarrassed about it. He was a grown man; he couldn't cry in public. Julia handed him a tissue and put her arm around him. He could no longer resist so turned around and gave her a big hug and whispered to her.

"Thank you for being here with me."

Julia could feel that she was getting emotional as well. Now was this because Frank had woken up or was it Jason and his reaction? She had to admit to herself that Jason's hug felt good. Jason let go of her and turned to his dad, who was looking rather confused. You could see he was trying to say something but couldn't because he still had the tube down his throat.

"Mr. Wild, I am Dr. Hanson, and this is nurse Taylor and Jason, your son. You are in hospital as you had a fall at home and hit your head. We will take this tube out now and then you should be able to speak." Dr. Hanson turned to look at Julia, who had managed to pull herself together.

"Could you get the things we need?"

"Yeah, will be right back," and she returned a moment later with a small trolley and Dr. Peterson.

"Jason, I think it would be best if you pop over to the lady at reception while we just sort this out. It won't take long." Julia had hold of his hand again and gave it a little squeeze.

"Okay." Jason turned to his dad, "I will be right back, dad."

She was right. It didn't take them long, and they had even managed to raise his dad's head a little bit.

"Right Frank, here you have Jason who, if I may say so, has been very concerned about you. I will get you some water." She looked at Jason, "Would you like a top-up?"

"No, thank you, but a glass of water would be good." Jason wouldn't take his eyes off his dad. He took his dad's hand and kissed it.

"Hi dad, you have no idea how pleased I am that you are awake. How are you feeling?"

Frank looked confused at Jason and then in a very quiet voice said: "What happened? And why are you here?"

"You had a fall and knocked yourself out, dad. And you broke your hip too. Mr. Henderson found you in the morning, as he could hear Duke barking. He then phoned me, and I came straight home."

"How long have I been asleep?"

"It all happened last week. Because you hit your head, they kept you asleep to give your brain a rest."

Julia came back with water for both of them.

"Now Frank, let's try to sit you up a little more. I have put a straw in your water, so it is easier for you." She pressed a button on the side of the bed and the head end slowly moved upwards.

"I won't take you too far. Is this comfortable?" she readjusted his pillows and was holding the glass so he could take a sip.

"Thank you. That was nice. You are very kind." He paused for a second. It was clear he was trying to remember something.

"Julia. How could I forget your name?" he reached out and took her hand.

"Good to finally see you awake, Frank. How are you feeling? Have you got any pain?"

"I feel like I have been in a boxing match and my head is hurting a little and I feel very tired, but Jason tells me I have been asleep for a while."

"That is correct, but that is a different kind of sleep. I will get you some painkillers."

Frank turned his head and looked at Jason with a smile. "You got a good one there son. She's a keeper."

Before Jason could say anything, Julia had returned with the medicine.

"Dr. Peterson is just looking at all your notes, then he will come in to see you and talk about what is going to happen next."

"Thank you, Julia. I was just telling Jason...." He was stopped by the doctor, who was now standing at the end of his bed. Jason felt a big relief as he had a feeling his father was about to make both him and Julia embarrassed.

"Good morning, Mr. Wild. Good to hear you are speaking. Now that you are awake, we need to run a few tests and also try to get you out of bed to see how you move. So, the plan is that the nurses will help you try to stand up a bit later today. It won't be much more than that today, as we have to take it slowly. Then we will run a few tests in the next couple of days, depending on how you are doing. I want to make sure that we haven't missed anything in terms of why you had the fall. It's still a bit of a mystery and we may never know the reason. You will then be moved to a ward where they can help you get mobile again and build up some strength so you can get home. How does that sound?"

"Well, I will try my best, doctor. Can I take this nurse with me?" he pointed and smiled at Julia.

"Well, you won't move until tomorrow at the earliest, so you will have her for another day. Any questions?" Dr. Peterson looked at both Jason and his dad and before his dad had a chance to say anything, Jason quickly replied: "Thank you, Doctor."

"You're welcome. If you have any questions, just ask the nurses." Dr. Peterson reached out, shook both Frank's and Jason's hands, and left.

"Well, I better get back to my other patients, too. Just press the button if you need anything. Okay? I will come and check on you in a bit." She turned to Jason. "Now I know you have been waiting to speak to your father, Jason, but maybe not too much today." She then turned to Frank, "I think it would be good for you if you had a little rest before we try to get you out of bed."

Jason stayed with his dad for about an hour. They didn't really talk about a lot. Frank kept dozing off and, in the end, Jason looked at the time.

"Better get back to Duke and you better have a rest before they start chasing you out of bed."

"Okay. Thanks for being here, Jason." Frank was holding Jason's hand and had tears in his eyes.

"I will be back tomorrow dad, don't you worry. I am staying here with you for the summer." He bent over and kissed his dad on the forehead.

"What about your work?" Frank looked worried.

"I can work from here. Might have to go back to New

York for a couple of meetings but will only be gone for a day or two and only if I know you are okay. Now, would you like me to bring anything in tomorrow?" Jason knew his dad liked to do crosswords and made a note to get some on the way home.

"I don't know. Don't feel like reading."

"Well, I will bring your reading glasses and what about a paper? You could always do the crossword at the back of it."

"If it isn't too much trouble for you."

"Not at all, dad. I will see you tomorrow and remember to be nice to all the nurses," he waved to him as he left. Part of him felt rather sad having to leave, but another part of him was desperate for fresh air and some time for himself. He pressed the big square button for the doors to open and just as he was about to walk out, someone grabbed hold of his arm.

"You are leaving without saying goodbye?" Julia was standing next to him outside. The doors to the ward had closed and for a moment it was only the two of them. His body was longing to throw his arms around her, but he resisted it.

"Oh, sorry, just in need of fresh air, and I need to get back and let Duke out."

"Just kidding. What are you doing tonight?"

"Nothing, as far as I know. Why?" He was rather puzzled by the look on her face.

"Just thought you might like some company. Shall I bring some food?"

"That is very kind of you. You have always been so

thoughtful, Julia," and he would have carried on, but the door opened again.

"Well, I will let you know later how your father gets on with getting out of bed. Shall we say seven o'clock?"

"Yeah, that will be fine. Thank you. See you later."

{ 11 }

Duke was very pleased to see him when he opened the door. It was almost as if he knew there was good news.

"Hello to you too. Fancy a quick walk before lunch?" Duke was out of the door and waiting before Jason could grab the leash just inside the door.

"Come, let's just go and see the Hendersons first so I can tell her the news about dad."

Just as Jason was about to knock on the door, it opened. Mrs. Henderson had seen him come home and was waiting for news.

"How did it go? Is he okay?"

"Everything is fine. Dad is awake, and it looks like he is going to be okay."

"Oh, that is really good news Jason. We have been thinking of him all morning," and before he could say or do anything she gave him a big hug. "You must be so relieved. When can we visit him?"

"Not sure. I will find out tomorrow. They need to run some tests and then move him to a different ward. I will let you know as soon as I know more. Now I better take this boy for a walk before I have to get some work done. I will speak to you tomorrow once I have seen dad." Jason knew he had to get going quickly otherwise he could end up being stuck there for lunch. Not that there was anything wrong with that, but he just needed some time to himself right now.

"Okay, we will wait to hear from you. Please let your father know we are thinking of him."

"I will. Now better be going. See you tomorrow."

The quick walk turned into just over an hour and just what Jason needed. There were so many things running around in his head, and he was finding it difficult to focus on any of them. For a start, it was an enormous relief that his dad had woken up and looked like he was going to be okay. But why had he fallen in the first place if there was nothing wrong with him? Could it happen again? Then there was his dad's comment about Julia being a keeper. Why did his dad seem to think that they were still an item? Surely, he would remember they broke up. Did this mean he had forgotten everything? And what was worse, Jason hadn't managed to correct him. And then there was Julia, who had been very caring and even told him she would come over this evening. What was that all about? Did this mean she wanted it to be more than just friendship? Still, it would allow him to warn her about his dad's thinking about her. And on top of all that, there was the promotion to think about. Jason was pretty convinced it was his if he wanted it, but was that what he wanted now? It would mean even more work and travel, which would lead to less free time to see his dad.

By the time he walked in through the door he was feeling rather hungry. Jason looked at his watch: Nearly 2.30

pm already. No wonder his stomach was complaining. He quickly made a sandwich and while eating it, he looked at his phone. It had been a silent day on the phone front, he thought, and then remembered that he had turned it off when he had entered the hospital this morning. Well, that was a first for him, nearly a whole day without a phone. He smiled and turned it on. Suddenly, he had plenty to do, but before starting on any of it, he called Mrs. Anderson to let her know the good news of the day. She was very pleased to hear it and laughed when he told her he had only just switched his phone on.

"Good to hear you took my advice." Mrs. Anderson then went through all the things she had sorted for him. There were a couple of things she needed him to check before she could send them, but she assured him it wouldn't take long. If there was one thing Jason had full confidence in, it was Mrs. Anderson's ability to do her job. He knew he could trust her and that things got done. She had been his assistant since he started in the company ten years ago.

"Thank you so much for all your work, Mary. Not sure what I would have done without you."

"You would have found a way through it, Jason. Now, before I forget, Mr. Patterson called in about an hour ago to hear if there was any news. Will you contact him, or shall I?"

Jason looked at the time. He still had a few things to do before Julia turned up, and he was hoping to get a little rest as well. The last 24 hours had been rather emotional and drained him of energy.

"Would you mind letting him know dad is fine? He is

awake but needs to undergo some tests, so not out of the woods yet."

"That is not a problem. And I will tell him you will get in touch when you know more."

"Thanks, that would be great. Now I better get a few things done and then I'm having a rest before seeing an old friend this evening. I will catch up with you tomorrow."

"Okay. Sounds interesting. Have a good evening and I will speak to you tomorrow." Mrs. Anderson decided not to comment any further on the last bit about an old friend. She knew him well enough to know that he would fill her in when he was ready. However, it was nice to know that he had connected with some old friends, so he wasn't sitting there alone.

Once he had sorted out the emails, he turned his attention to a couple of text messages from Helen. It surprised him it had taken her this long to get in touch with him. Now, should he or shouldn't he look at them? His first thought was just to delete them, but that wouldn't stop her from sending more of them, so he decided to have a quick look and then delete them.

Helen was begging for him to meet up with her so they could try to sort things out. She wrote something about them both working so hard lately that they had forgotten each other and all they needed was a nice vacation away from work. Not once did she mention anything about his dad, which made Jason very cross. He thought for a second about whether or not to reply.

"I'm not in New York at the moment and don't know

when I will be back. Currently working from here. I'm very sorry if you can't understand this, but it is over. I wish you all the best for the future. Goodbye." After he had pressed send, he deleted her number. There was no need to keep that number any longer, as he had no intention of getting back with her.

Suddenly, he remembered Mrs. Smith. He had promised to update her when he had news and quickly dialed her number. While he waited for her to pick up the phone, he went to get a glass of water and headed outside to sit in the shade.

"Hello?"

"Hello Grace, it is Jason here."

"Oh, Jason, how are you? Any news? I've been thinking of your father today. Wasn't it today they would try to wake him up?"

"Yes, it was, and that is why I am calling you. He is awake now, and it looks like he is going to be fine." Jason told her what had happened in the morning.

"I am so glad to hear that. So do you think it will be okay if I come and visit at the weekend?"

"I can't see why not. They are running some tests on him tomorrow and then we will know more. How about I give you a call tomorrow once I have seen him and spoken to the doctor?"

"That would be okay with me. I have spoken to an old friend who lives almost halfway between me and your dad. She says I'm welcome to stay with her, which will break up the journey."

"Sounds like a good plan. Any problems just let me know and I will come and collect you. I don't want you to feel you have to drive if you don't feel you are up to it."

"I know Jason. You are like your mother, always willing to help, but you have enough on your hands, and I haven't seen my friend for a long time. I will be fine."

"Okay. Now I haven't told dad yet that I have spoken to you but I'm pretty sure he will be pleased to see you. He doesn't know that I have opened the letters and I'm not sure how and when to tell him."

"Don't worry about it, Jason. Things have a way of working themselves out. The truth is, I had been thinking of calling them when you phoned me, so you don't need to say anything for now."

"Let's say that for now, then. I will call you tomorrow and let you know the latest, and then we can arrange the weekend." Mrs. Smith was right. There was nothing he could do about the letters, and it probably didn't matter, anyway. The important bit was that his dad was awake and seemed to be okay. Everything else would sort itself out somehow.

"That would be great. Looking forward to hearing from you. Bye, bye."

He looked at his watch, just gone past five, which gave him enough time for a little rest before Julia would be over. A message just came through from her: "Will be over around 6.30ish, bringing food to cook. Is that okay?" He smiled and replied, "Fine by me."

*

Julia put the bag with her shopping on the table. "I thought we should test your cooking skills." She laughed when she saw Jason's face, "Did I say something wrong?"

"My cooking skills are not great. Can't say I do a lot of it."

"Really, but what do you live on then? Fast food?" It didn't really surprise her that he didn't cook, but on the other hand, he looked too fit and well to be living on take-outs.

Jason didn't really want to tell her the truth as that would involve Helen. She was definitely history now.

"Well, we have a good canteen at work and, as you can see, I seem to survive." He gave her a big smile. "Anyway, what have you brought with you?" he peeked in the bag to see what was in it.

"Oh, fairly simple things, some salad stuff and a few things to make an omelet. Hope that is good enough for you. I wasn't planning on cooking all evening."

"Sounds perfect to me. What do you need me to do?" Jason wouldn't know where to start.

"Right, I'm sure you can handle the salad. Difficult to go wrong there. I will do the omelet." Julia quickly emptied the bag and started to find what she needed. It surprised Jason a bit to see how she seemed to know where everything was.

"Looks like you know where everything is and just as well, because I wouldn't be of any help." He grabbed the lettuce and tomatoes and went to wash them.

"Have you forgotten how much time I used to spend in this kitchen?" Back in their senior years at school, Julia would often come by so they could do homework together.

And that often led to her helping Jason's mom with the cooking.

Jason found a bowl for the salad and once he had finished, he suggested they had a glass of white wine with it, which Julia agreed to.

"Cheers," she raised her glass and smiled.

"Cheers and thank you so much for doing this and for looking after dad."

"That's what friends are for, and it is my job to look after him as long as he is on my ward. By the way, we got him out of bed this afternoon. He did really well, and I don't think it will be too long before he will be ready to come home. Of course, it depends on what or if they find anything when they run the tests tomorrow."

"Oh, so you think he will be ready to come home soon?" Jason wasn't sure why that surprised him. It was what he was hoping would happen but deep down he hadn't dared to think that it would, and definitely not that soon.

"What's up? You look shocked. I know he has surprised us all, but I think it is great news." She looked straight at him. There was no escape.

"Sorry, I have just been so busy thinking of whether he would pull through that the thought of him actually coming home soon hasn't crossed my mind. I have even told my boss that it could be quite a while before dad was ready to come home."

"Oh, I see. Well, just because he can come home doesn't mean he is ready to live on his own." She was a little puzzled by his reaction.

"What do you mean by that?"

Julia reached out and put her hand on his. "Nothing serious, but he might not feel that confident living by himself for a while, especially if they can't find a reason for his fall."

"Oh, I see. Well, the good news is that I have arranged with my boss, that I will be working from here this summer. Hopefully, that will give dad plenty of time to settle. And as a bonus, he will have me here. Now, enough about that. This was delicious Julia, thank you so much for this. I owe you one now, but it won't be home cooking." He raised his glass to her and for what seemed like a long time, but probably was only a couple of seconds, they just looked at each other. It almost felt like they were locked in, at least that was how Jason felt it.

"Oh, have you told Mrs. Smith the news?" Julia broke the silence.

"Yeah, I called her earlier, and she was so pleased to hear dad had woken up and is planning on coming to visit him next weekend. I told her I would call her later tomorrow when we know more and then we can plan it. She has a friend that lives halfway between here and her, and she plans to stay there for the night. I have offered to collect her, but she insists on driving herself. The next thing will be to tell dad she is coming. Not sure what I am going to tell him, feel it's a bit too soon to start the whole debate about mom and the letters and all that."

"Shouldn't think it would matter when she comes now. I think he is ready to see people and it will probably help him in his recovery. Eventually, you will have to talk to him about your mother and the letters and all the rest of it. If you don't feel ready now, why don't you just say that she called?"

"That was what Mrs. Smith suggested. Funny enough she had been thinking of contacting mom and dad as she hadn't heard from them, but I beat her to it."

"There you are. But at some point, you will have to talk to him about your mother. I have always been a big believer in telling the truth."

That last comment made Jason feel a bit uncomfortable. He knew she had always been one for telling the truth and it made the whole situation a lot more complicated. Yes, he should talk to his dad about the letters, but it wasn't just the letters that were on Jason's mind now. Julia didn't know the real reason for his meeting in New York the day before, and he was afraid that if he told her, he would lose her again. Seeing her and spending time with her had made him feel so much better. Yes, she had and was helping him with his dad and all that, but there was more to it than that. He felt happier and more relaxed than he had done for a long while. But was he being fair to her? She had already been through so much in terms of relationships that it would be fully understandable if she cut him off again, even if they were only friends.

"I know but seeing as I haven't really understood why dad and I fell out, or shall we say I have stayed away, I don't feel I can approach the subject yet."

"Well, you got to do what you feel comfortable with, but eventually you will have to talk to him about it."

"Hmm," he just remembered something else that Mrs. Smith had mentioned.

"Something else on your mind?" Julia recognized the look on Jason's face, and it usually meant something was bothering him.

Jason took a deep breath: "You know that Grace asked me if I could tell her where mom's grave is in the cemetery? I didn't want to tell her that I can't remember where it is and that I haven't been there since the day we buried mom. It's something that I am not very proud of saying but it's the fact." He kept fiddling with the mat on the table and avoided looking at her.

"Jason, this is not something to be ashamed of. You are not the first person that this has happened to, and you won't be the last. What did you say?" Julia reached across the table and took both his hands. As he looked up, she could see he was trying to hold back the tears.

"I just said that it was difficult to explain." He looked down at her hands. They felt so soft and warm, and he could happily stay sat here holding on to them all evening.

"Jason don't forget I was there too, and I know where it is. In fact, I have been to see it since that day. I know that might sound strange to you. You know how your mom always had an open mind and you could talk to her about anything. Well, I used to do that with her too, and when Peter left me, I went up and sat by her grave for a while. I'm more than happy to show you where it is."

He looked at her and was trying to picture the day of the burial, but it was all very fuzzy. He couldn't remember a lot from that day apart from arguing with his father and leaving quickly. If only he knew what the argument was about.

"I didn't know you spoke to mom about things." Julia was right about his mom. She was always positive about things, and she never told you what you should do. Somehow, her presence was enough, and whatever the problem was, it sorted itself out. Jason could no longer hold back the tears.

They just sat there for a while, still holding hands. Jason stroked her hands with his thumbs, and Julia didn't seem to mind. None of them said anything.

"What I can't understand is why I can't remember what we argued over. I wish I knew so I could apologize to the old man. Whatever it was, it has kept me from coming home to visit him." Jason looked at Julia, hoping she could tell him what it was all about. After all, she was there and had heard part of it.

"Sorry, I can't help you with that. All I heard was you shouting that you hated him, and you didn't want to see him again. Pretty harsh words, but probably something you said in the moment but didn't really mean deep down."

"Yeah, not nice at all, and no, I definitely don't mean it."

After a little while, Julia let go of his hands, got up, and cleared the table.

"What can I do? I mean, dad seems glad that I am here, but it feels like there is still something between us that keeps pulling us apart. I deeply regret what I have said and done, but how can I get my dad to understand it if I can't remember what it was all about?" Jason was still sitting at the table.

Julia had almost cleaned everything and, as she put the last dish away, she looked at him.

"I'm not sure, but maybe if you try to tell him what you know and be honest and tell him you can't remember what started it all. You might find that he remembers, if not all of it, maybe some of it. I know it's not going to be easy, but in order for you both to move on, I think it is important that you get to talk it through with each other." She had returned to the table and was standing next to him with her hand on his shoulder.

"Come, let's go and sit down on the couch. It's a bit more comfortable unless you have had enough of me and want me to leave." Julia knew that wouldn't be the case, but somehow, she had to try and lighten his mood a bit.

If only she knew he could never get enough of her, he thought and got up. Then he remembered the photo albums.

"Come, there is something I would like to show you." He headed in next door and went straight to the drawer and pulled out all the albums before sitting down next to her.

"What's all this?" Julia took one and opened it up.

"I was looking through some of the cupboards and drawers last night and found all these albums. As you probably remember, my parents were very keen on photography. I never really knew what they did with them all until now."

"These are lovely Jason, lots of great memories. I don't think my parents have many from my childhood. I can't remember ever seeing them with a camera." She kept turning page after page, with lots of beautiful pictures, all so organized.

"Well, have a look at this one," and he handed her the one that was all about him and his friends.

Julia didn't really know what to say. She just kept turning pages and looking at them. Occasionally she looked at Jason with a big warm smile and lent sideways towards him. He couldn't resist but put his arm behind her and she didn't object to it.

"If there is any you would like, I am sure we can find the right negative and get a copy. They are all organized in a box in the drawer," he pointed to the drawer.

"I would love that, but do you think that would be possible? Where can you get that done?"

"I might have to do a bit of searching online, but pretty sure it will be possible." He gave her a little squeeze.

"Okay, I would love that but maybe we can do that another day?"

"Sure, not a problem. You know where they are now."

They looked through all of the albums and talked about some of the memories and people in the photos. In the end, Julia looked at her watch.

"Gosh, have you seen the time? I better get home and get some sleep before I've got to go to work again." Julia got up and started to stack all the albums up ready to put them back.

"Don't worry about that, I will sort that out," Jason had got up too. "Thank you so much for coming over and for the dinner. I owe you one now." He went to get her jacket.

"Jason, it has been a lovely evening that went far too

quickly. Come here." She gave him a big hug and a kiss on the cheek. "I will see you tomorrow," and left.

{ 12 }

"Morning Frank. How are you feeling today?" Julia had arrived early for work, as she wanted to make sure she could be the one getting Jason's dad ready for the day. Some of her colleagues had smiled at her and commented on her allocation of jobs for the morning, but she didn't care. Frank was like family to her and that was that.

"Good morning. I have to be honest and say I'm a little nervous about what they might find."

"I'm sure everything is fine, Frank. You have already had some scans and if there was anything nasty, I'm pretty sure that would have shown up. Now, would you like to have a shower this morning?"

"Is that possible with this thing?" Frank pointed to the stand with the bags.

"Yes, of course, it is. Come, let's take you to the bathroom."

Frank was back by his bed 20 minutes later feeling refreshed but also tired. Julia had just got him back into bed when Dr. Peterson popped his head in through the curtains.

"How are you feeling this morning, Mr. Wild? I see you have had a shower."

"Yes, this very kind nurse insisted that I should have one, and I thought it was best not to argue with her."

"I wouldn't have either. I will be back after lunch to let you know what they have found if they find anything."

"Thanks, Doctor." Frank was looking at Julia. She could see he was nervous so she took his hand and reassured him he would be fine.

"Could you let the son know in case he would like to be here too?" Dr. Peterson scribbled a few things in the journal.

"Yes, I will," she gave Frank's hand a gentle squeeze as she looked at him. "I take it you would like Jason to be here?" Julia was pretty sure she knew Frank well enough to know that he would want Jason to be there, but the question had to be asked.

"Of course, I want Jason to be here." Frank gave her a smile.

A porter turned up to take Frank to the scans.

"I will call him now. See you when you get back" Julia gave him a wave and headed for the office.

*

"Just five more minutes." Jason turned off his alarm and turned over, covering his head with a pillow. Suddenly, he woke up to the telephone in the kitchen ringing and quickly jumped out of bed.

"Hello," he tried not to sound too rushed. Who would call this early in the morning? No one had called on that phone in the time he had been here apart from Mrs. Smith and that was only because Jason had asked her to.

"Morning. Are you still in bed?" Julia had been trying to get hold of him via his cell phone, but without luck. It surprised her a bit, as it was nearly nine o'clock. The Jason she knew wasn't one for sleeping in, even after a night out.

"Sorry I have overslept. Is dad okay?" Jason's heart was racing partly because he had rushed out of bed but was also worried that something had happened to his dad. Surely that could be the only reason for her to call. He looked at his phone and could see a few missed calls from the hospital and a couple of messages from her.

"No, nothing has happened. I was just going to tell you that your father has gone down for the scans now and Dr. Peterson says he will speak to you both at two o'clock this afternoon if that is convenient for you. I thought you might like to know so you could plan your day. And before you say anything, I asked your father, and he says he would like you to be here when Dr. Peterson comes."

"Oh, thanks for letting me know. Yes, in that case, if dad doesn't need me to go with him, I will get some work done first. Are you going to be there?" He hoped she would say yes. How was he going to cope without her if the doctor had bad news?

"Yes, don't worry. I will be here and no; he won't need you. I will let him know you will be in this afternoon." Julia had already put herself down to be sitting in when Dr. Peterson was going to speak to them. There was no way she would miss that one. "Oh, and by the way. Thanks again for a lovely evening." Seeing all those photos last night brought back some wonderful memories, and she would be a fool if she didn't acknowledge that she still had feelings for Jason. But was she ready for it?

Jason could hear she was whispering that last bit, probably because she didn't want everyone around her to hear it.

"My pleasure. I will always enjoy your company and thanks for bringing the dinner."

"That's okay. I will see you at two o'clock." She could carry on talking to him, but work was calling.

"Okay, see you," and hung up. As he was walking back in to get dressed, he couldn't help but smile with happiness.

*

Jason parked the car close to the entrance and grabbed the bag with the paper, a crossword magazine, a couple of pencils, and his dad's glasses. He'd just gotten out of the car when his phone rang. For a second he thought of just turning it off but then decided to check who it was first.

"John Jackson. What a surprise. How are you, and how is Montana?" Jason had been meaning to call John but hadn't managed to find time to do it yet.

"All well here. How are you and how's your dad doing? And did you go for that interview?"

"Dad seems fine. He is awake now, which is good, but still in the hospital. Yes, I did it on Monday but don't know the result yet. How's your mom?"

"Glad to hear he is better. And I'm sure you'll get that

new position. Mom is fine. She has to take it easy for now. The ranch is a slightly bigger issue, not helped by my brother wanting to do it all himself." John quickly explained in a few words what was going on at Jackson Ranch, especially the part with the bank.

"Yeah, Mr. Patterson mentioned something about the manager. Let me know if there is anything I can help with."

"Will do. How long are you staying with your dad?"

"I don't know, but probably for the summer. Mr. Patterson said I should. In fact, he told me to speak to you about working away from the office. How long do you plan to stay in Montana?" Jason was pretty sure he had heard that John was moving, but it wouldn't hurt to hear it from the man himself.

"I'm moving back here. It's not official yet but working on it. What is Helen's view on you being away from the city?" John was pretty sure he knew the answer.

"Well, she didn't take to it too well, so we have ended it, or should I say, I have ended it. She didn't seem to understand that my dad being rushed to the hospital was more impor-tant than discussing where she wanted to go on vacation. What about Melissa? Is she moving to Montana?" There was no way that Jason could imagine Melissa living in Montana. She and Helen were very similar.

"No, she is not coming and if I'm honest I am relieved. In fact, mom's illness has saved me from making one of the biggest mistakes in my life."

"Same here."

"Tell you what, why don't you come and visit us here at the ranch once your dad is well enough?"

"Would love to, but it won't be for a little while. I might bring an old school friend with me if you don't mind." The minute he said it, he realized it would lead to even more questions from John and he really needed to be with his dad now. A quick glance at his watch told him he had five minutes.

"Friend? Sounds interesting? This wouldn't be a lady friend, by any chance?"

"Yeah, but it's complicated. Look, I have to go now. Can I call you later in the week?" It was far too complicated to tell John all about Julia now. He really needed to be with his dad.

"Sure, looking forward to hearing more. Look after yourself, Jason." John couldn't help thinking how similar they were. They had started at the company at the same time, they had fallen for the same type of girls and now they both had to go home because of a parent being unwell.

*

Jason headed to the ward, smiling at everyone he met on the way, and looking forward to seeing his dad. Or was it more than that? Frank was sitting in a chair, looking at the door and waiting for Jason to turn up.

"Hey, look at you dad. You look like you are ready to walk out of here if it wasn't for all that." Jason pointed to the stand on which there were a couple of bags hanging with some sort of fluid.

"Not sure I would make it much further than the door at the moment," Frank gave him a smile.

"Here you are, something to keep you entertained for a bit." Jason handed him the bag. "Sorry I'm a bit late, but my colleague, John called. He is back home in Montana because his mother is unwell."

"Thank you, son. What time is it? Julia says the doctor will come and see me at two o'clock." All Frank could think about was what the doctor would tell him. What if it was bad? Surely there had to be something wrong for him to fall like that. He thought of Alice, Jason's mom. Maybe she would still be here if they had checked her out. And the thought of her brought a tear to his eyes, which he quickly wiped away, hoping that Jason didn't see it.

"I know he is. That's why I came now and not this morning." Jason pulled a chair over closer to his dad. "Let's hope he has some good news," and as he said that Dr. Peterson appeared with Julia right behind him.

"Afternoon Mr. Wild. Have you recovered from this morning?" Dr. Peterson looked at the notes, did a scribble, and then looked at Frank.

"Feeling a bit tired, but otherwise fine, doctor." Frank tried not to sound too nervous.

"Yeah, sorry about that, but the sooner we get it all done the sooner you can go home." He looked at the papers he had in front of him. "The good news is, I don't think there is a lot wrong with you. All the results are looking good. We still don't know the reason for the fall, but I suspect that a combination of having not had enough fluid and possibly tripping over your own feet is the cause. Your blood results when you came in showed us you were slightly dehydrated, but that is really all we have found. So, going forward, we will have to make sure that you drink plenty and are mobile enough to go home. Do you live on your own?"

"Yes, dad is living on his own, but I will stay with him for now." Jason looked at his dad, "I will in fact stay for the entire summer or as long as dad needs me."

Frank didn't know what to say and felt rather overwhelmed by it all. Jason took his hand. "My boss has offered me the opportunity to work from here this summer."

On one hand, Frank was full of joy at the thought of having Jason home, but he couldn't let him do it. What about his job? How could he possibly work from here when his job and office were in New York?

"Son, you don't have to. I will manage, I have up until now. I don't want you to lose your job just because of me."

"Dad, I won't lose my job and I'm not going anywhere until you have fully recovered." His dad's reaction slightly surprised Jason, and he felt lost at what to say next. He looked at Julia for help.

"What a surprise Frank. It will be nice to have Jason here for the summer." Julia couldn't quite believe what she had just heard. Was Jason actually going to stay? Perhaps this was a sign of better things to come. Just looking at him filled her with happiness, something she hadn't felt for a long time. And for a split second she thought about what it could lead to, but then had to pull herself together. No, she had to be careful not to rush into anything. One thing was what he had just told them, another was what was really going to happen.

"But before you can go home, we need to give you some physio so we can make sure you are stable on your feet. This will sadly mean that you will move to another ward where they have all the gear and expertise." Julia had kneeled in front of Frank and was focusing only on him.

"Will you come with me?" Frank had taken hold of her hand.

"Unfortunately not, but I promise I will come and visit you every day."

"Promise me that," he gave her a smile. Frank had always liked Julia, even after she and Jason had split up. She had been like a daughter to both him and his wife.

"I will. Now would you like to get back into bed and have a rest?"

"Well, I wish you all the best, Mr. Wild. I will leave you in Miss Taylor's care and she will sort out your transfer. Any questions?" Dr. Peterson nodded to both of them and left.

Julia helped Frank back into bed before she left to get him a glass of water. Now they were on their own again, Frank took hold of Jason's hand.

"Son, you don't have to stay. I have managed up to now and besides that, I have Duke to keep me company. I know your work is important and keeps you busy. That's why you haven't been home a lot."

"That's not the only reason dad. Losing mom hit me

harder than I realized, and I didn't know how to handle it or what to say to you. So, I pretended that work was very busy. I'm really sorry about that. The risk of losing you has made me realize that there is more to life than work, and that's why I'm staying here for now. It was actually my boss that suggested I worked from here. He pointed out that most of my work is done either via email or over the phone and that can just as easily be done from here. There will be a couple of meetings that I will have to attend, but other than that, I'm here and I'm looking forward to spending the summer with you. We have a lot of catching up to do." Jason could feel the tears coming. He had said it now and hopefully, his dad would understand and forgive him.

"I hope you can forgive me for not being home more often. I am so, so sorry, dad." He couldn't hold back the tears any longer.

"That's okay, son. I know I haven't been very good either, but that's all in the past. Let's look forward now, but promise me you won't lose your job because of your staying here?" Frank had tears running down his cheeks too. Jason bent over and hugged his dad, "I love you, dad."

Neither of them had seen Julia standing by the door. She had watched it all and now headed across to Frank's bed. Before saying anything, she quickly pulled the curtains around the bed and was now standing next to Jason with tears in her eyes. Jason stood up and looked at her.

"You okay? What's wrong?" He nearly put his arms around her but thought better of it. Although he had a feeling that they were getting closer, he didn't want to push it.

"Nothing's wrong. I am just so pleased that you two have talked."

"I know and it is my fault it has taken so long. But that is about to change with me staying here for the summer." Jason looked at Julia.

"That is good news." Julia could feel her cheeks getting red. She still couldn't quite believe that he was going to be here for the summer. Was she really hearing it right? Could this really be true?

"Hey son, it's not all your fault. Let's draw a line under it and instead enjoy that we have each other. If your mom was here, that's what she would tell us."

Jason noticed the sadness in his dad's voice and reached for his hand.

"Dad, we all miss mom, but we have the memories. She wouldn't want us to be sad. Isn't that right, Julia?" Jason didn't really know what else to say.

"Yes, we all miss her Frank, me too, but Jason is right. Alice wouldn't want us to be sad."

Us, yeah; he was pretty sure that was what Julia had just said. All Jason really wanted to do right now was to give her a big hug, but he managed to control himself.

"Frank, I have a favor to ask you. Last night, Jason showed me all the photo albums you have." The minute she had said it, she realized it would create a lot of other questions, but there was no way back now. Before she could carry on, Frank took hold of both Jason's and Julia's hands.

"I'm so glad that you two have worked things out.

You belong to each other. Mother always said that." Frank couldn't stop smiling and was looking from one to the other.

"Well, let's not get ahead of ourselves here, dad. We are just friends." Jason looked at Julia and hoped she wouldn't take it the wrong way. Why did she mention she had been at the house the night before?

"Yeah, Jason and I are still good friends, despite what has happened. Now when you are back home again, I would like to come and visit you. I don't have many pictures of me growing up at home, so I would love to have some copies of the ones you got. Jason says he can find a place that will do it. Would that be okay?"

"Of course, it will. You are always welcome in my house." Frank tried to sit up a bit more.

"You know you can adjust the bed with these buttons here." Julia gave him the remote to adjust the bed.

"Right, I better get back to work. Here is a jug of water: try to drink some. Once you are drinking enough, we can remove this." Julia pointed to the stand and then pulled the curtains back.

"I will try my best. Thank you, Julia."

To avoid any more questions about his relationship or lack of with Julia, Jason decided it was time to tell his dad about Grace.

"I had a surprise phone call yesterday. You will never guess who?"

"Don't know. I don't get many calls. Who was it?" Frank couldn't think of anyone that would call him. Apart from Jason, the only other family he had was his cousin. She lived in Florida, but she would normally only call around Christmas.

"A Mrs. Smith, one of mom's old friends. She told me she had written twice but had no response, so she finally decided to try and call instead." This wasn't quite the truth, but it didn't matter right now. The main thing was that Jason had mentioned Mrs. Smith and now he was looking to see how his dad reacted to the news.

"Oh, what did she want?" The news didn't seem to impress Frank.

"Well, I told her what had happened, you know, with mom and now you. She then told me she had lost her husband, not that long after mom died."

"Really?" Frank's face lit up and Jason felt he could detect a certain amount of surprise, which was a good start.

"Yeah. Now she has asked if you would like her to come and see you. She seems very keen to get back in touch. What shall I say?" All he could hope for was that his dad would say yes, not that it mattered, as Jason was under the impression that Grace would come, anyway.

"Well, it wouldn't hurt to see her. It wasn't her that was the trouble back them." Frank had always liked Grace and was trying to remember when he had last seen her.

"Okay, I will let her know. I promised to give her a call tonight." Jason wondered whether to ask what the issue had been but then decided that it wasn't really his to know.

"Well, I better get back to Duke. By the way, the Hendersons are keen to come and visit you too. Would you like to see them?"

"That's kind of them. Tell them to come tomorrow afternoon. I am too tired now." Frank was looking at the controller for the bed.

"That's okay. I will tell them, and I will come and see you in the morning." Jason got up, bent over, and kissed his dad on the forehead: "Love you, dad."

"Love you too, son. How do I put the head down a bit?" Frank was trying to work out which one to press. Jason looked at it and pointed to the right one. Once he was sure his dad was comfortable, he gave him another hug and left.

As Jason left the hospital, he heard someone calling his name and turned around. Julia was half walking, half running towards his car.

"Glad I caught you before you disappeared."

"What's wrong?" he immediately thought something had gone wrong.

"Nothing's wrong. I just wanted to tell you how proud I am of you. Well done for opening up to your father. I know it couldn't have been easy for you."

"Thanks. No, it wasn't easy, but it kind of just happened. I'm happy that I have got it off my chest but also sad. We have wasted nearly two years just because I am, or was so, selfish."

"We all learn from our mistakes, Jason. Now, is it really true that you are staying for the summer?"

"Yes, it is. Why?" Was that why she had run after him?

"I just wanted to make sure I heard it right. Well, I better get back in." She leaned forward and kissed him on the cheek. "Call me if you need to talk." Jason watched her head back in through the doors. Completely lost for words, he got in his car and sat for a while trying to work out what had just happened and what it all meant.

{ 13 }

The sun was shining from a clear sky and all you could hear were the birds busy chatting with each other. Jason took an extra deep breath of the fresh air as he headed out on a walk with Duke. This was just what he needed to clear his head. It had been a rather emotional visit to the hospital, but not in a bad way. His dad got the all-clear from the doctor, which was a big relief. He had said sorry to his dad for the way he had behaved over the last two years. Now they could both look forward to spending the summer together. And then there was Julia. She had spent most of the time he was there together with them despite being on duty. Jason was pretty sure that she had gone beyond her duties, but he didn't mind. It had been nice to have her there.

About six houses down the road Jason noticed a new sign had appeared outside a house. As he got closer, he could see it was a "For Sale" sign. He had walked this way a few times and not seen the sign before so it must have just gone up today. Jason stopped to take a closer look at the house. It looked like it had been left empty for a while and looking closer he could see that both the ground and the house hadn't had a lot of work done for a long time. How had he not noticed this before? He'd been walking past it nearly every day. Jason was trying to think of the family who used to live there when he was young, but all he could remember was a little boy who neither he nor Andrew liked. He did a quick scan up and down the road to see if anyone else was out as he quite fancied having a closer look at it. What did it look like inside, and how big was it? And why was he so keen to know all this? In the end, he decided to ask his dad about it first.

Jason carried on walking and thinking about what had happened earlier at the hospital. His dad's reaction to him staying for the summer had confused and disappointed him at first, but then he realized with Julia's help that it had been a lot for his dad to take on board, too. And then there was Julia's reaction to the news of him staying. She had definitely sounded happy. He could still see the smile she had given him. If he wasn't mistaken, she was getting closer to him. Last night when they had sat on the couch looking at the photos she had rested up against his shoulder, just like she used to back in the day. Was there really a chance that they could get back together? His phone rang. He tried to ignore it. They could leave him a message if it was important. It rang again and this time he did a quick glance at it and saw it was Mrs. Anderson. It had to be important for her to call again, and he quickly answered.

"Hello, Mrs. Anderson. How are things looking in New York?" He was trying to work out what would be so impor- tant at this time of the day for her to call. They had sorted a lot out before he had left for the hospital.

"Okay, and with you?" And before Jason noticed it, he had told her all about his conversation with his dad. She had this magic way of getting him to talk without asking him directly.

"I'm so pleased you have spoken to him, and I'm sure he will be pleased to have you around. It must be a little confusing for him right now. On a different subject and the reason for my call, Mr. Patterson is asking when it would be a good time to speak to you. I think he has some news to tell you. Shall I ask him to call you now?"

"What news?" Jason generally did not know what she was on about. He had been told the result of the interview wouldn't be until Friday so it couldn't be that.

"You know what I'm talking about. Are you free to speak to him now?"

"Not sure I do but yes, I can give him a call now. Or shall I wait until I'm home? Just out walking the dog at the moment. Why don't you tell him I will call him as soon as I'm back home?" He looked at his watch. "I'll be about 30 minutes."

"Think he is going somewhere a bit later so probably better to do it now. Now promise me one thing, Jason. Don't say yes straight away. Ask if you can think about it. You need to be 100% sure it is what you want. Have you spoken to John Jackson yet?"

"Wait do you think it's about the interview? I was told I wouldn't hear anything until Friday. Don't worry, I won't rush into anything right now. And yes, John called me this morning. We had a nice chat and I'm calling him back later in the week." He couldn't help but smile. It was clear Mrs.

Anderson was trying to protect him from doing anything he might regret later.

"I just think that you have so much going on right now that you can't think clearly. If you were to take this new position, it would mean you will be away a lot more. And is that really what you want now?"

"I know. I will have to think about it. Look I will call Mr. Patterson now."

"Thank you. Speak to you tomorrow. Take care, Jason."

Judging by the way Mrs. Anderson had spoken, Jason could only assume that he had got the job. Could it really be true? His thoughts immediately turned to Julia. If he said yes, it would definitely be the end of any chance for him to get back together with her. What was he going to do? Well, he had promised Mrs. Anderson not to rush into saying yes despite it being the post he had aspired to for so long. He needed time to think about it and also talk to someone about it. But who? Then he remembered John and he knew he would give him some good advice. And even better John didn't know Julia as a person so her history wouldn't affect him. Well, it was time to find out. He dialed Mr. Patterson's number.

"Hello, Mr. Patterson: Jason Wild here. Mrs. Anderson informed me you would like to speak to me."

"Thank you for calling Jason and yes that's correct. But firstly, how is your father doing?"

"He is doing well," Jason told him about the progress but decided not to mention that his dad was likely to come home within a week.

"That is good to hear, and it must be a bit of a relief for you knowing he is going to be okay."

"Yeah, it is, but we still have some way to go. He isn't very stable when walking and he has lost rather a lot of weight." On one hand, it was nice that his boss was concerned and interested in his dad's progress but right now Jason just wanted to know why it was so important that they spoke today.

"I know and please make sure you take all the time you need. There is no need for you to be here at the office to do your work. Mrs. Anderson tells me that you are getting a lot done from there and she also said that you are planning to come to New York next week."

"That is correct. Most of it I can do from here without any problem, but I have a couple of things that will require a physical meeting and that's why I will be in the office one day next week. This is of course providing that it all goes well with dad."

"Good to hear. Well, I have some news for you too. We have decided to offer you the job as Head of Investment if you want it."

"Oh, thank you. That's a surprise." Jason tried to sound really surprised.

"I know, and I also know that it might be a lot to think about right now with all the other things you've got going on. So, we are willing to give you a little time to think about it, but we would like to make the official announcement Friday next week. Maybe you and I could meet when you come in and you can let me know then."

"Thank you. Yes, that would be okay with me." Jason

didn't know whether to be happy or sad. It was the news he had been waiting for but was it really what he wanted now?

"Good. When you know what day let me know. Have a lovely weekend."

"Will do." Jason was surprised he wasn't feeling happier with the news. After all, it was what he wanted. Or was it?

"What am I going to do, Duke?" The news had left him with a dilemma. On the one hand, he had got the dream job he had been aspiring for since he started at the company. It meant that he would have to head back to New York by the end of the summer. Now if the offer had come to him a couple of weeks ago, he would have said yes straight away without even considering a life outside the city. But now, having been here for just over a week it had reminded him how nice it actually was here, how much he really loved it and how much he missed the quieter life. If only mom was here, he thought and looked up to the sky. She would know what to do. Who could he speak to apart from John? Julia was definitely out, as it would only turn her away from him and hurt her at the same time. He couldn't do that to her. Then there was his dad, but they had only just mended their relationship and his dad thought highly of Julia, so he couldn't really discuss it with him either. What about Grace? Would she be the one to talk to?

It reminded him he had to call Grace when he got home. Hopefully, it wasn't too late. Jason looked at his watch: nearly five o'clock. She would probably be sitting waiting by the phone by now.

"Come on Duke, we better get home." He walked faster

and soon they were outside the Hendersons' house. Jason decided he had time for a quick stop to give them an update on what had happened and that his dad would love to see them the following afternoon.

"I will let you know where he will be. The plan is that he is moving out of the ICU, but I don't know where to yet."

"Thank you, Jason. Is there anything we can bring him?"

"Don't think so, but I will let you know once I have been to see him in the morning. Now I have to get home, as I promised to call Mrs. Smith as well. I will pop in tomorrow when I'm back from the hospital." Jason headed back to his dad's house before Mrs. Henderson could ask any more questions.

He gave the front door a push with his foot as he took his coat off and headed to the kitchen. He had left his office work on the kitchen table and for a second he thought of doing a bit more but decided against it. It had gone past five and no one would expect him to work now. Instead, he grabbed the phone and a beer and headed in next door there he dialed Grace's number. She must have been sitting right next to the phone as she picked it up straight away.

"Hello, Jason. How is your father?"

"He is fine and looking forward to seeing you. And sorry I haven't got round to call you before now, but I had some work stuff I had to deal with."

"Don't worry about that. I'm just glad to hear that he is doing okay and that he would like me to visit him. So, when will it be best for me to come?"

As he had arranged with the Hendersons to visit his

dad tomorrow afternoon, he suggested she could come the following day, which was Friday.

"I think I can get to you by ten o'clock. Would that be okay?"

Now what Grace said next made Jason freeze.

"I would also like to go to the cemetery first if you don't mind, Jason."

Jason didn't know what to say. He felt like someone had pumped all the air out of him. Somehow, he pulled himself together.

"That will be fine, we can do that," and he hoped she hadn't spotted the delay.

"Thank you, Jason. I will see you on Friday. Let me know if I need to bring anything."

Jason was staring at the photo of this mom on top of the television. His head was a mess. How was he going to show Grace his mom's grave when he didn't know where it was and not only that but how would he react when he got there? He remembered Julia had mentioned she knew where it was. Could he ask her to show him? Well, what was the alternative? Him walking around looking for it himself? No, he didn't fancy doing that. There was only one thing to do. He dialed her number and just hoped she wasn't working one of those long shifts.

Julia didn't have time to even say hello before Jason asked if she had a minute.

"Yes. You okay?" Julia knew something was up. It was the tone of his voice. It had been a long day: she had stayed on as she wanted to finish a couple of reports and was now looking forward to getting home. She had planned to call Jason later on, but it sounded like he needed her now.

"Would you like me to come over now? I'm just on my way home from work."

"I have just spoken to Mrs. Smith, and she has asked me to take her to see mom's grave. What do I do?" Jason wasn't really listening to what Julia said.

"Okay. That is not a problem. I have told you I know where it is, and I can come with you if you like. When is she coming?"

"I think I would like to see it before I take her, not 100% sure how I will react if you know what I mean."

"That's okay. We can do that. When is she coming?"

"Friday morning."

"Well, in that case, it will either have to be now or tomorrow afternoon. Which do you prefer?"

Jason thought for a second. If he waited until tomorrow, he knew he would spend the night thinking of it.

"Is it too late to do it today?"

"No, it isn't. I will be with you in a minute," and she hung up before he could change his mind.

Jason hadn't moved, and he was still holding the phone in his hand when Julia let herself in. This has really hit him, she thought and sat down next to him.

"Okay?" she took his hand and Jason turned his head to look at her. She could see the fear in his eyes.

"Look, I know it won't be easy for you and we won't rush it. Come, let's find some flowers outside we can take with us."

"You have always been so kind to me, even though I haven't treated you well at all."

"Come here, your old softy," and she gave him a big hug that for Jason seemed to last forever.

"Right, come on." She got up, reached out to take his hand, and gently suggested he got up. They headed outside to pick a few flowers that were growing along the house.

"I will drive." Julia unlocked her car while Jason locked the house.

He didn't say a word on the short trip to the cemetery. Julia parked the car close to the entrance. Jason did a quick look around and it looked like they were the only ones there. They stayed sat in the car in total silence. Julia wanted to give him time. There was no point in rushing it. Meanwhile, Jason was trying to picture the day of the funeral, but it was still all very blurry for him.

"Let me know when you are ready." Julia put her hand on his and he turned to look at her.

"Thank you." He took a deep breath and opened the door but stayed sat in the car for a few more minutes before getting out.

"Right, let's do it." He took a deep breath and got out.

Julia picked up the flowers from the back seat and they slowly headed towards the corner of the cemetery where Julia knew the grave was. Jason kept looking around to see if he could see it. His legs felt very heavy. Suddenly Julia stopped.

"Here we are," she pointed to a stone with the name 'Alice

Helena Wild'. Jason stood like he was frozen to the spot. This was it. He fell to his knees.

"Mom, I am so sorry for all that I have done. I know I should have taken better care of dad and I should have been here to see you too. Please forgive me." The tears were running down his face now, but he didn't care. Julia kneeled next to him and put her arm around him. After a little while, she handed him the flowers and looked at him.

"Here, do you want to put them down, or shall I?"

He looked at her and took the flowers.

"Thank you." He gently put the flowers by the stone, then touched the stone with his eyes closed and said a prayer before standing up again.

"Thank you for being here with me. Not sure I would have been able to do it on my own." He was looking straight at Julia's lovely, warm eyes and reached out for her hands.

"Jason, I wanted to be here and I ..." she didn't finish but instead leaned forward, put her arms around him, and gave him a kiss. Jason put his arms around her and buried his head in her shoulder. They stood like that for a while, saying nothing.

After one more look at the grave, they slowly walked back to the car, holding hands.

Neither of them said a word on the way back to the house. Once they were inside and the door was closed, Julia took hold of Jason's hand.

"Jason, I'm sorry if I overstepped earlier. I know we are just friends, but I couldn't hold it back any longer."

"Julia, you have no idea how much I have been wanting

to do the same thing ever since I saw you that first day at the hospital last week. I know you said you only wanted to be friends and I respect that, but I can't help it. I'm still in love with you."

"Well, I still love you too, but it is so complicated with you in New York and me here. My experience is that long-distance relationships don't work." She had put her head on his chest, and he put his arms around her. What could he say? She was right, and with the new job, it would be even more complicated. How was he going to tell her about that? After a little while, he loosened his grip on her and lifted her chin so he could look into her eyes.

"I know." He nearly let on that he knew what happened with her engagement but thought it best not to. "Maybe there is a way around it which we haven't seen yet. Anyway, I would like to take you out for dinner tonight as a thank you. Would that be okay?"

"That would be lovely, Jason. Where?"

"Well, one minor problem. I don't know any places other than Benny's. Don't get me wrong, I like Benny's, but I was thinking of something more like a restaurant. Do you know of any nice places?"

"I know there is a very nice restaurant in Preston which is about 20 minutes away. We could try to call them?"

"Great, let's find the number." Jason got his phone out and googled the place.

"Wait, I can't go dressed like this. Have I got time to get home and change?"

Jason put his arms around her. "I will pick you up in 30 minutes," and gave her a quick kiss on her forehead.

Half an hour later, Jason parked outside Julia's parents' house. One thing he hadn't thought of was the chance of it being one of Julia's parents opening the door when he pressed the doorbell. What was he going to say? And more to the point, what were they going to say to him? Well, too late to back off now. He got out of the car and headed up the path to the front door. Just as he was about to press the door-bell, the door opened and Julia appeared, looking amazing. He did a quick glance over her should and to his relief, there were no signs of her parents.

"You ready to go?" He could have kicked himself. What a stupid thing to say. Of course, she was ready. She was standing there in front of him.

"That's what I call good timing. And yes, I'm ready." She gave him one of her lovely smiles and they headed for the car. As he opened the car door for her, he couldn't help but comment:

"You look amazing."

"Thank you. You don't look too bad either."

*

It was very late by the time Jason parked outside her parents' house again. He turned the engine off.

"Julia, thank you for a wonderful evening. I have to be honest and say it's been a long time since I have had an evening like this."

"Me too. Thank you for the meal tonight, Jason. I better get in and get some sleep, as I have to work tomorrow morning." She leaned across and gave him a kiss.

"I will see you at the hospital tomorrow. Good night."

"Good night." Jason didn't take his eyes off her until the door closed. He started the car and drove home. What a day it had been!

{ **14** }

The sun was shining, and the birds were busy with their morning communication. Duke's tail was wagging as well, and even Jason was feeling happy despite all the things that had happened the day before. It had been a day of various difficulties, but looking back, it had all been worth it despite giving him another problem. He and his dad had spoken a bit about what had happened in the last two years. There was a new job for him back in New York if he wanted it, and why wouldn't he? After all, this was what he had worked so hard for over the last few years. The hardest bit of the day had been seeing his mom's grave and his reaction had surprised him. Jason was so grateful that Julia had offered to go with him. There was no way he could have done that on his own. And what about Julia? She had kissed him and told him she still loved him but that it could never work. And she didn't even know about the job offer. Her decision was based on his current job. Basically, Jason had now found himself at a crossroads. He could turn one way and take the job or turn the other way and stay with Julia. If only there was an option where he could have both.

Jason was trying to think who he could speak to, who

could give him some advice on what to do, and then remembered the conversation he had with John the day before.

"Hey John, would you be free to chat this afternoon? Have something I need to run by you. Jason." He pressed send and all he could hope for was that John would have some bright idea about what he should or could do.

As he was passing the house that was for sale, Jason couldn't help but stop and look at it again. It was clear to see that it needed some work done from the outside, but what was the situation on the inside? He still hadn't remembered the name of the boy that used to live there. He looked at the sign and felt very tempted to call and ask for more information. But why would he do that when he had no intention of living here?

After a quick shower and breakfast, he headed to the hospital. Jason wanted to be there when his dad moved to the new ward so he could meet the new team that would look after him.

"Morning dad. You got out of bed early today. Looking good." Jason bent forward and hugged his dad. "And you have lost your wires."

"Yeah, Julia says it's up to me now to make sure I drink enough. You are just in time, she has just gone to the office to finish a few things, then I will be on the move. How're things at home?"

"Good timing then. It's all okay. Duke and I went for a walk this morning."

"You seem very happy this morning." There was something

different about Jason this morning, but Frank couldn't quite work out what.

"Why wouldn't I be? It's a beautiful day out there. Duke and I were listening to the birds as we did our morning walk. Hey, who used to live in that house that's for sale? I have been trying to remember his name."

"What house is for sale?" Frank was rather puzzled as he wasn't aware of any houses being sold on his road. Then Jason remembered that the sale sign only went up the day before so his dad couldn't have known about it.

"Oh, sorry that one that looks like it hasn't seen a person for a long while. The sign went up a couple of days ago."

"Oh, that one. Well, it was Johnson's back when you were young. I think the son was Patrick. They moved away not long after you went to New York. After that, a couple moved in but sadly the husband died about a year later in an accident and we rarely saw her. Your mother did try to get her to join in with some of the things she did, but the lady wasn't interested. She kept herself to herself. I think they moved here because of her husband's work and not sure she ever really liked it here. Then, about a year ago, she fell ill and died. Alan and I think there were some family issues or disputes which meant that the house couldn't be sold. Let's hope some nice people buy it. Seems such a waste to leave it empty."

"Yeah, it does. Do you have any idea what it looks like inside?"

"No, not really. Well, apart from it used to be a nice house similar to ours and was built around the same time, but I suspect that not a lot has been done to it since it was built. Why all the questions?"

"Oh, just wondered, that's all." There was something about the house that Jason couldn't explain or more to the point, he rather wanted to keep to himself for now. And before either of them could make any further comment on it, Julia appeared.

"Morning Jason, and how are you today?" She did a quick glance at him but avoided eye contact.

"I'm fine and you?" He smiled at her and tried not to look at her. As his dad had already commented on how happy he looked this morning, Jason didn't want to add fuel to that.

Frank looked at them both and had his thoughts but said nothing. It would be so nice if his son could settle down. Then he remembered something that Alice, his late wife, had said. "One day, Jason will see that he belongs with her." Thinking of Alice made him feel sad.

"Why are you looking so sad, Frank? I thought you were looking forward to moving?" Julia had spotted Frank's face had changed.

"Well, you're not coming with me." Frank didn't want to give the real reason, so he quickly came up with some excuse.

"I promise you I will visit. Now let's get you over into this chair. Oh, and Jason, before I forget," she turned and looked at him, "Could you bring in some clothes and some footwear for your father to wear?"

"Yeah, that shouldn't be too difficult. You will have to let me know what you want dad, okay?"

Soon they were on their way, and it didn't take long to

reach the new ward. Once Julia had handed over to the new nurse, she turned to Frank and told him she would look in on him once she finished work. While the new nurse was welcoming Frank, Julia turned to Jason, gave his hand a little gentle squeeze, and whispered: "I will see you later." She left before he had time to say anything. Jason's heart was pumping, but he had to try and stay calm so his dad wouldn't notice anything.

The nurse offered to help Frank back into bed, but he asked if he could sit in the nice chair that was between the bed and the window.

"I have spent so much time in bed the last couple of weeks. Feel I need a change."

"That is not a problem. Just let me know when you are ready for a rest. But be careful not to overdo it."

Before the nurse went to get them both a drink, Jason asked what kind of clothes he should bring in for his dad.

"Just what your father would wear daily. Part of the rehab is to make sure that he can get dressed. Oh, and a pair of shoes, but they must be non-slip and not slippers."

The ward was up on the first floor and where Frank's bed was, there was a good view out over the town. They spent some time talking about what they could see. In the end, Jason thought he better remind his dad about Mrs. Smith's visit the following day.

"You know Mrs. Smith is coming tomorrow. I spoke to her yesterday, and she is really looking forward to seeing you." Jason stopped. Should he or shouldn't he tell him about her wish to see the grave? "She asked me to do one thing."

"Okay, and what was that?" Frank looked at Jason.

"She would like me to take her to the cemetery to see moms grave."

"Oh, are you going to?" Frank had turned his head and was now staring out of the window.

"To be honest dad, I don't think I have an option."

"Oh. Do you want me to explain how to get to it?" Frank kept staring out of the window. He didn't want Jason to see he was struggling to hold back the tears.

"No need, dad. I panicked a bit and called Julia because I couldn't remember where in the cemetery the grave was. And just for the record, I'm not very proud of that. However, Julia was very kind and came with me late yesterday afternoon."

"Hmm. She did. Did it look okay? I normally go every Saturday to check."

Jason could see he was struggling but somehow, they had to talk it through.

"Dad, I know it's difficult for you, but I do think we need to talk about what happened that day. And let me make one thing very clear: I'm not proud of the way I behaved that day. I can't remember what happened and what I said, all I know is that it wasn't very nice, and I am truly sorry. I hope you can forgive me."

"Son," Frank finally turned his head and looked straight at him, "We were both in shock and not thinking straight. And we both said things we regret. You've no idea how many times I have wanted to go and see you in New York." He stopped and turned his head to wipe a tear away before carrying on. "But I was afraid that you would push me away.

As I said yesterday, let's draw a line under it and look to the future now." He reached out to take Jason's hand. Jason could see the tears in his eyes, which made it even harder to hold his own tears back. He pulled his chair closer so he could give his dad a hug.

"Dad, you have no idea how much this has bothered me over the last couple of weeks. I thought I would never be able to tell you how sorry I am. I promise you that from now on, I will be here for you."

For a little while, they sat in silence. Jason had his arm around his dad's shoulder.

The nurse came in to ask if Frank wanted a rest before the physio would be in to assess him after lunch.

"They are keen to get a plan made for your rehab."

"Might be a good idea, dad. Don't forget you got visitors coming this afternoon. I will pack a bag for you and get the Hendersons to bring it in this afternoon. Sounds like you will need it." He gave his dad a kiss on the forehead. "And I will see you tomorrow. Don't forget we will be in a bit later in the morning - not sure what time she will get here. And you better be dressed." He didn't mention that he and Grace would be visiting the cemetery first.

"Thank you, Jason." Frank turned to the nurse, "Might be a good idea for me to have a little rest."

Jason dropped in to see Mrs. Henderson on the way home to tell her where they would find his dad and asked if they would be kind enough to take a small bag of clothes in for him.

"I will head home and pack it."

"Of course, Jason. I'll come and get it when we leave."

*

Jason spent the afternoon speaking to a couple of clients; he replied to a few emails and went through some notes with Mrs. Anderson that she had sent him. He also needed her to arrange for a meeting in New York one day in the coming week. He had suggested that it should be Wednesday which meant he would drive up Tuesday evening and return to the house late Wednesday evening. As a backup plan, they reserved Thursday and Friday just in case things didn't quite go to plan with his dad.

Then it was time to have a quick glance at what had happened in the news. His phone rang and without looking, he reached out and answered it.

"Jason Wild speaking."

"Julia Taylor speaking," was the reply he got, and he immediately apologized. Julia found it so funny, and she was laughing so much that she found it difficult to speak. Finally, she pulled herself together.

"What are you doing tonight?"

"Hopefully seeing you." Jason hoped it didn't sound like he was desperate.

"I was hoping you would say that. Just popping home for a shower and a change of clothes. Had a rather busy day today."

"Okay, what do we do about dinner?"

"Let's discuss this when I get to you. Will be with you in 45 minutes." Before Jason had a chance to reply she was gone.

Right. Time to log off work, pack the office away, and then a quick change. Suddenly, he remembered he had arranged earlier in the day that he would call John. Should he delay that? No, better not. John had mentioned in his reply that he was busy but still happy to chat later in the day. Instead, Jason sent Julia a message saying he had forgotten that he had to speak to one more client, so no rush. He dialed John's number while tidying up the kitchen table that had become his temporary work desk.

"Hi, Jason. How's it going?" Jason couldn't help but think John sounded so happy.

"Good and thanks for taking time out to listen to me."

"No worries. I take it you have heard from Patterson and that's why you want to talk?"

"Yeah, kind of why I'm calling," Jason explained the situation. Everything from his dad's situation, the visit to the cemetery, Julia, and the dilemma with the job offer.

"I know how much you wanted that position as well. What made you change your mind? And have you regretted it?"

"Firstly, congratulation on getting it. You should be proud of yourself. In terms of me pulling out of the race, my mother was in the hospital, just like your father, so I had to rush back here. We had no idea how it would end. Then I discovered the problems that the ranch was in and thought that while I was here, I would help my brother out with some support. I then bumped into an old friend who made me realize that life is not all about work or dining out. She, her name is Maria, made me see that I grew up in a lovely part of the world and somehow it just felt like I was in the right place. I was back in New York for a meeting and realized that I was done with the city, the noise, and the rush on the subway. And I also realized that my family is important to me: I want to be closer to them, especially my parents, as they aren't getting any younger. It made me start to think of alternative job opportunities. And if I'm honest, it sounds like your situation is very similar."

"Really?" Jason was speechless. Not only had John made it sound so easy, but he had also connected with an old girlfriend.

"Yeah, funny how you and I seem to go for the same thing. Anyway, my advice to you would be to think about it, and maybe make a list of what you like and dislike about your hometown and also about New York. Just remember that no one can take away the fact that you got offered the job. And remember, you don't have to decide until next week."

"Thanks, John. This has been very helpful. Have a nice weekend and I will let you know what decision I make."

"Good. Just one last little thing. Promise me you will come to our wedding."

"What? When? And yes, I'll be there."

"Don't know yet. Planning on proposing next week."

"Wow, that's great news. Keep me posted." There was a knock on the door. "Hey got to go. Good to speak to you."

"And to you too. Have a nice evening."

Julia had let herself in and was now standing in the kitchen.

"You look very happy. Any particular reason for that?" It was so good to see him smile like that.

"Yeah, just spoken to my friend John, the one that had to go back to Montana because his mother was unwell. He just asked me to come to his wedding."

"Oh wow, and when is this wedding?"

"He doesn't know as they haven't set a date yet. I've never been to Montana. Have you?" Jason was now standing in front of her, and he put his arms around her. "By the way thanks for coming over."

"Yes, I've been to Montana, back when I was a child. My dad's sister lives out there and I have a cousin called Emma. She used to come and stay here with us during the vacations until horses took over her world. Think you might even have meant her."

"Don't remember. Anyway, I was thinking earlier that you might like to help me sort out the last photos that mom didn't do. I have found a couple of empty albums; it looks like she brought them but didn't finish the job." He stopped for a moment and wondered if it was one of the last things she did before she died.

"I would love to do that." Julia could see the sadness in his eyes. "Come here." She put her arms around him and gave him a hug and then a quick kiss. "But first we need some food. I've hardly eaten all day."

"What do you fancy?" Jason didn't really care what she suggested as long as he was together with her.

"Why don't we get a burger from Benny's as a takeaway?"

"Does he do that?" The takeaway suited Jason just fine.

They spent the evening looking at photos and arranging them in the albums Jason had found. Julia had another look at the album, which was full of pictures of Jason with his friends. She picked out a few she liked, and Jason went searching through the negatives for them. Now it was a question of where to get copies done.

"Pretty sure there isn't a place around here that does that sort of thing."

"I had a feeling that might be the case. Tell you what. I will get my PA to find a photo shop in New York and I will get them done there. I got to go up next week for a couple of days, anyway." Jason noticed Julia's face change when he mentioned he was heading back to the city and put his arm around her.

"I will only be gone for two days, I promise you."

"I know, but I can't help it." Julia was leaning against him with her head on his shoulder.

"Let's not think of it now." Time to change the subject quickly he thought. "Hey Andrew and his dad are coming to help me fix up the place on Saturday. Would you like to help?"

"Okay, I'm not working, so why not?" She looked at him, still with a touch of sadness in her eyes. "But I feel we have to be careful about this. I don't want people to think we are back together."

"Okay," he was trying to work out what she meant by that. If they weren't back together, what was this then?

"Sorry, that came out all wrong. I don't think I am ready for all the questions yet. Hope you understand."

"Yeah, I can understand that." He nearly let on that he knew her full story but didn't. It also reminded him he had to be careful, as the last thing he wanted to do was hurt her again. He had to find a way where they both could be happy, and preferably together.

Julia looked at her watch, it was nearly midnight.

"Gosh, have you seen the time? I better head home as I got to do the early shift tomorrow."

Jason looked at her and couldn't resist it.

"Do you have to go?" He immediately regretted it. "Sorry I shouldn't have said that."

"I would love to stay, but I think it's best if we go slowly here, okay?" She gave him a kiss and a hug. "I will see you tomorrow"

Jason reluctantly let go of her hand as she walked out of the door.

*

The house phone rang, and Jason's first thought was that something had happened to his dad. He did a quick check on the time. Or it could be Grace calling to tell him she was leaving her friend's house now. He was expecting a call from her.

"Jason Wild speaking." He was trying to sound calm.

"Morning Jason, it's Grace here. I hope to be with you in about an hour."

"Morning Grace. Looking forward to seeing you. I will have coffee ready for you."

Right, only an hour to go now. He did another quick check of the house. Jason had no idea how the day would go. His dad seemed happy for Grace to come, but how would he react when she stood in front of him? They would either hit it off and chat a lot or there wouldn't be much conversation going on.

Just as he had sent a message to Mrs. Anderson, a car pulled up. Jason opened the door and walked toward the car.

"Welcome. Hope the drive was okay for you?"

"Yeah, not too bad and I could remember the way too, which was helpful." Grace got out of the car and did a quick glance around. When Jason had called in last Sunday, he had mentioned the place needing a bit of attention and she could only agree.

"I can see what you mean by the place could do with a little attention. It was your mother's passion more than your father's, I think."

"I know. I have a couple of old friends coming around tomorrow to help me as I haven't got a lot of experience in gardening. Haven't told dad yet but I hope he will like it."

"I am pretty sure he will."

"Now let's get you indoors. There's fresh coffee ready. I have told dad we will be in later this morning."

"That would be nice," and they headed in, with Duke following behind.

As Jason poured the coffee, Grace had a quick look around the house.

"This is just like I remember it, and I can see what you mean about nothing being sorted." Jason was right when he told her about the state of affairs in the house. Poor Frank, if only he had read my letters and replied to me, she thought. She returned to the kitchen.

"Yeah, according to the neighbors, dad would like to do it with me and as I haven't been home a lot, it never got done."

"Okay, that makes sense. Have you two started to talk about it?"

"Yes, and no. I have apologized for what I said at the funeral and for the lack of visits. Dad says he could have done more, but he says it's in the past and we should draw a line under it. We haven't talked a lot about mom. He gets very emotional when I mention her. I think he misses her a lot."

"I know how he feels. Trust me, it isn't easy. At least I knew it would happen as my husband was very poorly, and although it was very sad, it was also a relief, as he wasn't suffering any longer. That wasn't the case with your mother, as I understand it. Neither of you had time to prepare yourself for it."

"I know. Still, I hope we can work it out and I will have to try and visit him more often."

Grace detected a change in Jason's voice. "What do you mean by that, Jason?"

"Well, the thing is," he told her all about the job offer and how it would be even more difficult for him to have time off. He even told her about Julia and how they had connected again.

"I have no idea what to do now. On the one hand, the job is all I have ever wanted, but on the other hand, I haven't felt as happy as I am right now in a long time. It's at times like this that I really miss mom. I could talk to her about everything. She was a good listener"

"I see. I remember your mom telling me about Julia. She was very fond of her, you know, and it hurt her when you two broke up. She always maintained that you two were meant for each other. And she said that one day you would see it, she just hoped you wouldn't be too late. Have you told either of them about the offer?"

"Nope, and I know that isn't good either."

Grace put her hand on Jason's and looked him straight in the eye.

"Listen, things have a way of working themselves out. All you can do is be honest with them. Tell them what is going on. And if you need to talk, you can always come to me. I hope you know that." She felt sorry for Jason and wished she could wave a magic wand that would sort it all out.

"Thank you, Grace. You are the first one outside work I have spoken to about it all." It felt good to get it all off his chest, and he knew she was right. He had to tell them both.

"Right. Shall we head to the hospital and see the old man?" Jason got up and grabbed his car keys.

"Yes, but would you mind if we visit the cemetery first?"

It didn't take long to get there. Jason had said nothing on the way. He was so busy worrying about how he would react once he saw the grave again. Somehow, he had to try to keep it together this time, but he had a gut feeling that it wouldn't be easy.

As they walked in through the gate, Grace put her arm into Jason's, and they walked together in silence. There it was: the flowers he had put down the other day were still there. They stood in silence for a little while. Jason didn't know what to do or say. He was also afraid that if he spoke, the tears would start again.

"I found you, at last, my dear friend." It was Grace that spoke first. Jason was now fighting to hold back the tears. Why was this so hard for him?

"I will keep an eye on your boys." Grace bent down and put the flowers down that she had brought with her. That was it. Jason couldn't hold the tears back any longer.

As Grace got up, she turned and looked at him.

"I take it you haven't been here many times." She put her arms around him.

"I really miss her, never really realized how much until now."

"I don't think you have ever allowed yourself to grieve, Jason. Of course, you miss her. We all do and it's quite normal and nothing to be ashamed of."

"Thank you." He hugged her.

They stood for a while before eventually heading back to the car.

{ 15 }

The hospital parking lot was busier than normal, so Jason had to park further away from the entrance.

"Right. Are you ready to see the old man?" Jason looked at Grace.

"Yeah, I'm ready. Are you ready?" She looked at Jason. His reaction at the cemetery had surprised her a bit but also made her realize Jason hadn't really come to terms with the loss of his mother. This wasn't just a question of healing things between him and his father. In order for that to happen, he had to allow himself to grieve. She couldn't help thinking about what state Jason's dad would be in.

They walked across the parking lot and through the entrance. Grace stopped for a second.

"Does your father still like chocolate?" She hadn't brought anything but suddenly had a thought that it might help if she came bearing gifts.

"I think so. How can you not like chocolate?" Jason laughed. "I will wait over by that door while you go and get it." He pointed across the room to a set of doors, which was the way to the ward. The doors kept opening and closing as people kept coming and going. Jason didn't take any notice of them as he was busy checking up on emails and messages before turning his phone off.

He jumped when someone tapped him on the shoulder and quickly turned around to see who it was. To his surprise, Julia was standing there right behind him. She had spotted him as she was coming through the door and thought it would be fun to surprise him.

"Hi! What are you doing here?" Jason thought of giving her a hug but controlled himself. This was a public place, and he wasn't sure if she would appreciate it.

"I just popped in to say hello to your father and to see how he was getting on." Before she could say any more, someone spoke behind Jason.

Neither of them noticed Grace coming out of the shop. She stood for a little while and watched them. It was pretty clear to her that they belonged together. Finally, she made her way across the hall.

"Right, got him some chocolate. Now, who is this nice young lady you are talking to, Jason?"

Jason stood between them looking from one to the other.

"Julia, this is Mrs. Smith: my mother's friend; Grace, this is Julia. She has been looking after dad up to now and is also a best friend of mine."

"Oh yes, hello, and please call me Grace. No need to be so formal. Nice to finally meet you, Julia. I have heard a lot about you." Julia looked puzzled at Jason and Grace carried on, "Oh, Alice spoke a lot about you."

Jason was keen for this conversation not to end up all about his and Julia's past.

"We shouldn't hold you up and I suspect dad is getting impatient."

"Yeah, he is really looking forward to seeing you, Grace. I will speak to you later Jason," she gave him one of her lovely smiles and left.

"I can see your dilemma, Jason. Julia is really a lovely lady. Just like your mother described her to me whenever she spoke about her."

"Yeah, she is." Jason was still following her with his eye and gave her a wave when she went into the elevator. "Right, we better head in and see dad before any more hold-ups."

*

"There you are. I have been waiting for you." Frank was sitting in his chair next to the bed looking at the door, wondering when they would get there. He was feeling nervous about seeing Grace, mainly because he knew it would bring back memories of his late wife.

"Yeah, we had a few things to do first. How are you, my dear? Been such a long time." Grace went over and kissed him on the cheek. "And what have you been up to?" Meanwhile, Jason had found a chair and put it next to his dad's so Grace could sit next to his dad. He then went in search of one for himself.

The next couple of hours went by really quickly. They covered a lot, even Jason's job offer, which he made his dad promise that he wouldn't tell Julia about.

"Jason, I am very proud of what you have achieved and

whatever you decide to do, you have my full support, even if it means I won't see you much."

"Thank you, dad, that means a lot. But just to make it clear, if I say yes, it won't start until September, so I will still be here all summer. You never know, you might have had enough of me by then."

"I will never get enough of you, Jason, but I also know that you have to live your life."

"Your father is right, Jason. You have to live your life and be happy in it. No one can decide for you or tell you what to do. And sometimes you have to be brave and trust your decision. But remember that your father is here and happy to listen if you feel the need to talk about it. And you are always welcome to contact me as well." Grace reached out to take Jason's hand. "It will all sort itself out. It always does as long as you face it and do not try to run away from it."

"Thank you, and I will bear that in mind. By the way, I'm going to do some work on the place this weekend, dad. Hope you don't mind." Jason was keen to change the subject and couldn't help but laugh when he saw the concerned look on his dad's face.

"Don't worry, I'm not doing it on my own. Andrew and Alan will help me. And I get to meet Andrew's wife and son, too."

"I'm glad to hear that. I wouldn't like to see the result if you did it on your own." Frank could relax again now that he knew Jason wasn't going to do it all by himself.

The nurse came in to see if Frank wanted his lunch or if she should keep it back for him.

"You better have it now, dad. I'm going to take Grace to Benny's Cafe for lunch and I also need to get home and let Duke out." Jason got up and took his chair back to where he had found it.

"It was really nice to see you, Grace, and thank you for coming all that way." Frank had hold of Grace's hand and found it difficult to let go.

"My pleasure and I will be back soon, don't you worry." Hearing about the Saturday plans, she had an idea she wanted to run by Jason. She gave Frank a kiss on the cheek.

"See you soon my dear."

*

Benny's Cafe wasn't too busy and as the sky was clear and it was warm, they opted to sit outside.

"So, who have you brought along today, Jason?" Benny had come out to take their order.

"Hi, Benny. This is Grace Smith, an old friend of moms. Grace, this is Benny: an old friend of mine and the owner of this place. We have just been to see dad."

"Oh, how's he doing?"

"Fine thanks. Looks like he might come home soon, which will be nice."

"Will you be heading back to New York, then?"

"No, not yet. I'm working from here for the summer. Dad and I have a few things we need to sort out."

"Glad to hear that. I think we would all like to see a bit more of you. Now, what can I get you?"

Didn't take too long for their order to appear and they spent the next hour talking about the past, and the vacations they used to have together as families.

It was late afternoon by the time Grace was getting ready to head back to her friend, but just before she got into her car, she looked at Jason. Hearing Jason telling his dad about the plans for Saturday had given her an idea, but she hadn't managed to run it by Jason until now.

"I have an idea. Why don't I come back tomorrow and visit your father? That way you will have more time here to get things done, which, by the way, I think is a lovely idea."

"But are you sure you want to do that? It is a lot of driving for you." Jason was both glad and concerned about what Grace had just suggested. It was nice to hear she wanted to come back but he was concerned about the driving.

"Jason, I might be getting older, but I am still fit. Of course, I will. Your father and I have a lot of catching up to do. And I think it will be good for both of us if we have some time to talk, just the two of us. After all, we have been through the same thing."

"Okay, if you think you are up for the drive and happy to do it then yes, it would be very helpful, and I am sure the old man will be pleased to see you again." He couldn't help but smile. Grace looked happy and the day had gone a lot better than Jason had hoped.

After giving her a wave, he headed back indoors to get Duke's leash.

"You and I better go for a walk now."

Once back home, Jason got to work. Despite having said

he would take the day off he wanted to clear the long list of emails before the weekend. It was a rule he had set himself when he started at the company. There was nothing worse than starting on a Monday with a backlog of emails. Suddenly there was a knock on the door, and he looked at the time: nearly seven o'clock. He had been so busy reading and typing that he had completely forgotten about the time. Who could that be?

"Sorry, I didn't know if you were busy or not. Just thought it would be good if we could discuss how and what we do tomorrow?" It was Mr. Henderson.

"Oh yes, sure, no problem. I was just finishing some work. As you know, Mrs. Smith has been to visit dad, so I haven't been able to do any work."

"How did that go?"

"Very good indeed. In fact, she will come back tomorrow and visit dad, so I don't have to. It was her idea, and it will mean that I or we can get more done here."

"That's very kind of her. Hope your dad is okay with our project."

"Oh yes. He is okay with it as long as I am guided by you," Jason laughed. "He hasn't got great confidence in my practical skills, and I don't really blame him. And judging by the way he and Mrs. Smith were talking today, I think he will be happy with a visit from her without me."

"Well, I know what he is like, and don't you worry, we are only happy to help. Andrew says he will be here about nine o'clock. Would that be okay with you?"

"Yeah, I will make sure I'm up and ready."

"Okay. See you tomorrow then."

Back indoors, his phone was ringing. This time, it was Julia. She said she would come over if he wasn't too busy.

"I'm never too busy for you. See you shortly." He quickly packed his mini office away and put on a clean shirt. I got to get some washing done soon, he thought.

*

He was standing in the middle surrounded by people who all had their opinion on what he should do. Jason could see his dad, Julia, his boss, and there were some others, but he couldn't work out who they were. The circle kept spinning around, which made him dizzy, and he was trying to listen to what they had to say. The only thing they all agreed on was that they wanted an answer now. All he wanted was to get away from them all, so he covered his ears with his hands and ran until he was out of breath.

Jason woke up with his t-shirt sticking to him. In fact, the sheets were wet too. He sat up, confused, and realized it had been a nightmare. A quick look at the time told him it was five o'clock. It was too early to get up, but he couldn't get back to sleep. Instead, he stripped the bed and had a shower followed by some coffee while trying to work out what the nightmare meant. Yes, many people were waiting to hear what decision he would make, but none of them had put pressure on him and none of them had told him what they preferred his answer to be. The only one that was different was Julia, who didn't know about the new job offer but who had made it clear that it wouldn't work with him in the city and her staying here.

Last night, Julia had asked him about when he had to go back to New York. She had also asked if he had considered changing jobs. Instead of being honest and telling her what was going on, he had said he hadn't really thought about it, as everything had happened so quickly. Maybe a change of job was the answer - but what jobs were there for him here? Perhaps he should look into it - but how? He immediately thought of John and his new life in Montana. He had done it and sounded very happy about his decision from what Jason could work out. Would their boss be willing to do the same for him? It would mean that he would have to turn down the promotion.

Time for some fresh air, but first he had to put a load of washing on.

"Come on Duke. Let's go for an early morning walk." It was a beautiful morning. The sun was already up and the birds exercising their vocal cords. There was no one else out and about this early on a Saturday morning. This is really the best time of the day, he thought, and I won't ever have this in the city.

*

There was a knock on the door and in came Andrew with his wife Amy and son Colin.

"Morning! I brought help with me. Well, Colin is going

back to mom; not sure he would be good for anything apart from distraction here."

"Nice to meet you, Amy." Jason looked at Colin, "I'm pretty sure you're not as bad as your dad says." He gave Colin a smile.

"Nice to finally meet you, Jason. I have heard a lot about you." Amy reached over and gave Jason a hug with her free arm. She had Colin on the other.

"Oh, should I be concerned?" He looked from Amy to Andrew and back to Amy.

"Don't worry, only good things. Anyway, Colin and I are going to head back to Grandma. Hopefully, I will come across and help a bit later. It depends a little on how this young chap settles. He's teething at the moment, so can be a bit grumpy."

"Okay. Sounds good. The more the merrier. We will see you later."

Julia and Mr. Henderson came in as Amy was leaving.

"Look who I found outside," Alan nodded toward Julia.

"Hi, Julia. Long-time no see." Andrew went and gave her a big hug. He then looked at Jason. "Have you forced her to come and help?" He laughed.

"No, I just told her what we were doing, and she offered. Isn't that right, Julia?" He wanted to give her a big hug but kept it to a smile. Andrew looked at them both and although he was no relationship expert, he was pretty sure that something was happening between them. All he could think was that the last thing Julia needed was for Jason to hurt her again. He made a note that he would have to have a word with Jason later.

Jason had made coffee for everyone, and Alan explained what the plan was for the day.

It turned out to be a rather successful day with a lot of fun and a lot of talking. Grace stopped in to see how things were going before heading to the hospital and she came back later after lunch to let them all know the good news. The nurses had been so impressed with Frank's progress that they thought it highly likely that he could go home perhaps as early as Tuesday.

"Right, we better carry on so we can have it all done before supper." Mr. Henderson did a quick walk around to see how far they had got and what was left to do. Not a lot, just a little bit of cleaning up and cutting the grass. Grace took Jason to one side.

"Now I know you mentioned you had a meeting in New York. Just so you know, I'm happy to come and stay so you can go."

"Yeah, that's right, but I can't ask you to do that. I will postpone the meeting." Jason didn't know whether to be happy or worried about the news of his dad coming home.

"Don't be silly. I will come on Tuesday and be here when he comes home. What day was it you were going?"

"I was going to go Tuesday late afternoon. My meeting is on Wednesday, but I can move it to the following day and leave on Wednesday instead. Are you really sure you want to do this?" He had to admit that it would be good to get the trip done, as it would hopefully give him some answers.

"Yes, I will, and I think it is important that you go so you can get your thing sorted out. I will be here Tuesday afternoon unless there is a change of plan from the hospital. See you then." Grace hugged Jason and waved goodbye to the others.

They finished the jobs that Alan had planned and Jason even had time to cut the grass. Alan and Julia headed back to the Hendersons' house while Jason made sure the house and shed were locked. Andrew had stayed behind with Jason. He had been waiting for a moment when it was just the two of them.

"So what's going on, Jason? I see Julia and you must be getting closer, but at the same time, you look like you have the world on your shoulders."

Jason took a quick look around to make sure no one was close by to hear what he said. Whispering, he quickly told Andrew about his dilemma.

"Man, you got to speak to her. She, of all people, has been through so much. I know it won't be easy, but you got to be honest with her. I'm not sure she could cope with another heartache."

"Trust me, I know. Just haven't had the right moment yet."

"Okay, but the longer you wait, the more difficult it gets and the more it will hurt. Right, come on let's go and see what mom has made for us." Andrew had made his point and he could only hope that Jason took his advice.

They spent the evening sitting on the Hendersens' patio, enjoying the lovely BBQ that Mrs. Henderson had put together. Amy had to listen to all the stories about what

Andrew and Jason used to get up to when they were young. By the time Jason and Julia were heading back to the house, it had gone past midnight. Jason unlocked the door and then took Julia's hand.

"There is something I need to tell you, Julia. Can we go in?"

"Yeah, what's up Jason? You look rather serious." She had noticed as the evening went on Jason had become quieter. He hadn't said a word on the way home either.

He sat down on the couch and asked her to sit as well. Julia did as she was told. She didn't like the look in his eyes and was trying to work out what could have happened that had made him so sad.

"There has been a development in my job situation." He couldn't look at her so instead he was looking at her hands which he was holding.

"What kind of development?" Julia had a feeling that it wasn't going to be good news.

"They have offered me a promotion and I have to give them an answer on Wednesday."

"Okay. What kind of promotion and what does this mean?"

"Head of Investment. It would mean extra work and more traveling. It is a job I had my eyes on for a long time, but now after what happened to dad, I am not so sure." He looked at her. Her face had changed, and she looked like she was in pain.

"What are you not so sure about?" She had let go of his hands and moved away from him a bit.

"I mean, coming back here and seeing you, being with

you. I love you, but I also know that I can't ask you to move to New York." He tried to take her hands again, but she wouldn't let him. "Please say something." He couldn't bear the silence.

The news had hit her hard, but strangely enough, she knew it was coming. Deep down, she knew this was going to happen, so why had she let herself get so involved? Why did she think he would change? He loved his job, and it wouldn't be fair to ask him to leave it just because of her. She took a deep breath and looked at him.

"Jason, I can't tell you what to do. That wouldn't be right. It is something you have to sort out on your own. Yes, I love you too, but is that going to be enough? You have a career in New York, a job offer you have aspired to. What would you do if you come back here? It wouldn't be the same, and would that make you happy?" The tears ran down her face now. Jason wasn't much better, and he had no answer to her questions. In the end, Julia got up.

"Jason, I think it is best that I go now. I have something I need to do tomorrow, but I also think that it would be best if we didn't see each other until you have worked out what you want. I wish you all the best." She gave him a kiss on the cheek and quickly left.

Jason sat on the couch for a while, too numb to move. What had he done? Well, he had done the right thing by telling her, but where had that got him?

He woke up the next morning feeling exhausted. He couldn't remember what time it was when he eventually made it into bed. His muscles were aching from climbing up and down a ladder cleaning all the gutters around the house yesterday. It was Sunday and apart from visiting his dad and taking Duke for a walk, there wasn't really a lot to do. He grabbed some coffee before heading out with Duke.

They walked down the road and passed the house that was for sale. Every time he walked past it, he wondered who would buy it. At the end of the road, he decided to take a different route and after a while, without really realizing it, he ended up at the gate to the cemetery. Really! How could that be? He wasn't sure what it was, but something must have brought him here. He looked to see if there were any signs up that said dogs weren't allowed in but couldn't see any.

"Well, Duke, shall we go and have a look?" He did a quick scan round. There was no one else to be seen, so he opened the gate and headed in.

Soon they were standing next to the grave, and he bent down to feel the grass. No dew, so he sat down. He thought of all the things that had happened the last couple of weeks, all the questions he would have asked his mom if she had been here. He was pretty sure she would have given him good advice. She had always been good at that in the past.

Suddenly, he heard a car door slam and quickly got up. He quickly wiped his face as he didn't want anyone to see he had been crying, then looked at Duke.

"Come on old boy, let's head home."

{ **16** }

As Jason walked in, he was still going over everything that had happened the night before and didn't see that his dad wasn't there. It wasn't until he said good morning and didn't get a reply that he noticed the bed was empty. Slightly panicking, Jason looked around to see if he had moved, but there were no signs of him. As he headed back to the receptionist to ask if she knew where his dad was, Frank came walking back from the bathroom together with a nurse.

"I thought for a minute you had legged it." Clearly relieved to see his dad, Jason gave him a big smile. So nice to see his dad up and walking with no aids.

"I had you worried," and Frank laughed. "Just been for a shower, the first proper one in weeks. At least that's what it feels like."

Jason gave him a hug before he sat down.

"Dad, you have no idea how pleased I am to see you walking like this." That was true. One of Jason's worst fears was that his dad would have to rely on others for even the basic things. So, seeing him walking like this was amazing.

"At this rate, Mr. Wild, I think you will go home soon. We just need to make sure you drink enough fluid and are eating." The nurse made a few notes in a folder at the end of the bed and left.

"I shall be glad to get home to Duke. Speaking of home, how did you get on yesterday?" Frank was eager to hear how it had gone but something puzzled him. Jason looked different today, but he couldn't work out what it was.

"Great, and no need to look so concerned. Here, take a look at these." Jason got his phone out and brought up the pictures he had taken during the day.

He had made sure that he had before and after photos of most of the things they did. There were some of Julia, Andrew, and Mr. Henderson, plus some from the evening.

"Looks like you had fun. Thank you so much for doing it." Frank looked through them all a couple of times. It amazed him how much they had managed to do and how good it looked afterward. It brought back memories of how the place used to look when Alice was alive.

"Yeah, we had fun." The tone in Jason's voice had Frank baffled. Something must have happened, but what? All the pictures were full of cheerful faces.

"What's up, son? I'm not good at mind reading, that was your mother's specialty, but my guess is that something is bothering you. Does it have something to do with Julia by any chance?" It had to be, there couldn't be any other reason.

Jason was sitting with his head bent down, staring at the floor, and he whispered a yes.

"Did you tell her about your promotion?" Again, all he got was a yes.

"Son, I don't know what happened and what was said,

but I know that it always pays to be honest. I take it Julia didn't take it well?"

Jason took a deep breath and looked at his dad and then told him about the conversation he and Julia had had the night before.

"I don't know what to do, dad. I love her, but I also love my job. She is right. What would I do if I came back here?"

"I'm not sure, but maybe it would be worth finding out what opportunities there are before you decide?"

"I don't know. Can I ask you something?"

"Yeah, go ahead." Frank had taken Jason's hand.

"How did you know mom was the right one?"

"Well, I think I just did. I remember taking her out a few times and it just felt like we had known each other for a long time. She made me feel so happy and relaxed."

"Do you ever go to the cemetery?" As soon as he had said it, he regretted it. "Sorry, dad I shouldn't have asked that question."

The question rather surprised Frank and, for a second, he wasn't sure how to answer it.

"Yes, I do. Why are you asking me about that?" He looked at Jason and wondered what was going on in his head.

"Well, I somehow ended up there this morning on my walk with Duke." Jason was looking at his hands. He didn't want his dad to see that he was struggling to keep it together.

"That was rather a long walk. Did you go in?"

"Yes," and suddenly with the tears running Jason told him all about the three visits he had done in the last few days and how he had reacted.

"Dad, I wish mom was here. She would tell me what to do."

"No Jason. She would say that you will have to work this out for yourself, but as long as you follow instinct and what you really want deep down, you will be fine. She always said that things have a way of working themselves out."

"I'm not so sure this will." Jason took a deep breath and looked at his dad. "I really hate the way we ended things last night, and I had hoped we could meet up today, but she says she is busy all day."

"Give her some space, don't push it. Remember, she has had her fair share of traumas already."

Jason just nodded and wiped the last few tears away. His dad was right and all he could hope was that things would work out okay in the end. One thing was sure, he couldn't go on like this.

"By the way, it was really nice to see Grace again yesterday." Time to change the subject, Frank thought. "We had a good chat about everything. We talked a lot about mom which was hard but good. I haven't really had a chance to or wanted to talk it through with anybody until now. And we arranged that she would come and visit us, or me when I'm back home. Maybe you could take me to her place one day."

"I'm so pleased, dad." Jason couldn't help thinking that if his dad had only opened the letters, he wouldn't have spent two years on his own. He nearly mentioned it but thought he better not to. The important thing was that they were back in contact with each other.

"I shall be more than happy to take you." Before he could say any more, a doctor came in.

"Morning Mr. Wild. I hear from the nurses that you are doing very well. If you keep it up, I think we should be able to send you home in the next couple of days." He turned to Jason, "I'm assuming that there will be someone there to support him?"

"Yes, I will be there. In fact, I plan to stay with dad for the summer. We have a few things we need to do together."

"Good. Let's aim for Monday or Tuesday at the latest. We will do some blood tests tomorrow and as long as the results are okay, you can go home."

"Thank you, doctor. I shall look forward to that." The prospect of going home had Frank smiling from ear to ear. He turned and looked at Jason.

"Did you hear that, son? I'm going home."

Jason waited until the doctor had gone before saying anything.

"Yes, I did dad, but I have a minor problem."

"Yeah, I know you have to go to New York. I'm sure I can manage one night on my own. Just let me get home."

Jason laughed. He didn't mention that he had arranged things with Grace. No, this was a slightly different kind of problem he was thinking of.

"That wasn't what I was thinking of dad. I can move that. No, my problem is that I can't cook, so what do we do about eating?"

"Well, son, you must have a very short memory. Have you forgotten that I have been on my own for two years and I'm still alive? I might not be brilliant, but I can cook simple things, and so can you if you put your mind to it."

Jason could see the funny side of that.

"Okay. I'm sure we can work something out." Although his problems hadn't gone away, Jason was feeling a bit better with the prospect of his dad coming home.

*

The first thing Jason did when he got home was phone Grace to give her the news.

"That is lovely Jason. I will be there Tuesday afternoon." Grace didn't tell him she had already started to pack a few things for her stay. After their chat the day before she had come up with an idea that might help Frank talk about his loss.

"Are you really sure you want to do this? Don't feel you have to as I can move my meetings." Jason didn't want Grace to feel she had to come. His meetings could be moved.

"Don't be silly, Jason. Of course, I will do it. When do you have to leave?"

"Well, my meeting was Wednesday morning, and I had planned to go Tuesday late afternoon, but I will move it to Thursday and probably leave midmorning Wednesday if that is okay with you?"

"Don't worry about me, I will be there and yes, we will be fine."

"Thank you, Grace, that is very kind of you. I will be back on Thursday evening."

This would, in fact, work out better for Jason. On the way back from the hospital, he had come up with a plan. There were a couple of things he wanted to check out in town before heading to New York. He could do that Wednesday morning as he was leaving. That would also give him plenty of time to talk to Mr. Patterson late Wednesday afternoon and leave him with just the meeting on Thursday.

There was still nothing from Julia. Should he let her know about his plan? He didn't want to do it via messenger so it would mean that he would have to go and see her at her parents' house. That would involve the risk of meeting her parents. He sat for a while with the keys in his hands, but in the end, he decided that the best thing would be to get everything in place and then speak to Julia. Instead, he tried to focus on work and the things that were happening in the coming week. He sent a note to Mrs. Anderson about the change of plan. She must have been checking her emails because it didn't take long before Jason's phone rang.

"What are you doing working on a Sunday?" He knew well enough to know that she would be keeping an eye on the emails.

"I was just preparing myself for the coming week. And yes, I will get the meeting moved."

"Thank you"

"So, what's happening?" Mrs. Anderson was more inter-ested in hearing how Jason's dad was doing.

Jason told her all about his dad's progress and that he would bring him home tomorrow or Tuesday.

"And before you say anything, Grace, my mother's old friend, is coming to be here with him while I'm in New York."

"Okay, but are you really sure you don't want to postpone it for a week?"

"No, I need to come into the office as I have to give Mr. Patterson an answer. He needs it before Friday."

"Answer to what?" Mrs. Anderson pretended she had no clue what he was talking about.

"You know what, but it is a bit more complicated. I will explain it when I see you on Wednesday." Jason was keen to get off the phone so he could read the message that had come through. Could it be Julia?

"Okay. Looking forward to seeing you Wednesday. I will send you an email with confirmation about the meeting."

His heart was beating faster as he pressed the button to see who it was from. To his disappointment, it wasn't Julia but instead John Jackson.

"She said yes. Wedding in September and you are invited." That was all it said. Now, what do you reply to that when your own life seems to be a mess?

"Congratulations. When in September?"

He got a response almost immediately. "Will get back to you when I know a date. How's it going?"

Well, what was he going to say? Jason wasn't in the mood for talking right now, so he just said that he had a busy week ahead of him with his dad coming home and a meeting in New York. He finished up by saying that he would catch up with him later in the week.

"Okay. Will look forward to hearing from you. Good luck."

Well, it wasn't so much good luck he needed but more clarity on what would make him truly happy. And that was really down to him to work out. No one else could tell him. Was he prepared to take a risk and change the path he was on?

Whatever he decided, he had to have a meeting with Mr. Patterson, and Wednesday seemed to be the day. He looked at the time and decided that as it was Sunday, he would email rather than phone. What should he tell him? There wasn't any reason to tell him anything apart from that he was hoping to reach the office by mid to late afternoon on Wednesday and to ask whether it was possible to meet with him then. What he didn't tell him was that he had a couple of things to check out in town before leaving, and they could have an influence on his decision.

*

Jason called the hospital and asked if the receptionist could pass a message on to his dad, and tell him that due to work, he was going to be in late today. He then headed into town. There were a couple of places he wanted to visit. By the time he got to the hospital, it was late morning.

"You are a bit late today, son?" his dad looked at him with concerned eyes. "Everything okay?"

"Better late than never, dad. Sorry I had some work calls come up that I had to deal with first." He hoped that would be enough explanation.

"Is this about your job? Have you given them an answer?" Frank was still looking concerned.

"No, I have told them I will do that when I get there on

Wednesday afternoon. And before you say anything, Grace is coming to stay with you while I am gone. I take it you are still coming home tomorrow?"

"As far as I know I am, but Grace doesn't need to be there. I can look after myself."

"Well, I will have to leave Wednesday morning and won't be back until late Thursday, which is almost two days. I don't think it's a good idea for you to be on your own for that length of time. Besides that, who is going to walk Duke?"

"Okay, but I'm still sure I would be fine on my own. It's a long way for Grace to drive."

"I don't think you have an option, dad. She is very determined about coming."

"Well, it was nice to see and speak to her again the other day. Oh, have you heard from Julia?"

"Nope, not a word. Has she been to see you?" He looked down at the floor, as he didn't want his dad to see how painful it was for him to talk about her. To his relief, the nurse was heading toward them.

"Right, Mr. Wild, your blood results are all good. The physio will do one last assessment of you after lunch and if that goes well, you should be able to go home today. How does that sound?"

"Very good, I would say. Not that I can complain about this place, but I would prefer my own house."

"I know. I think we all do. Any questions?"

Jason suddenly had a bit of a panic. "Is there anything I need to do or take care of before dad comes home?"

Somehow, it hadn't crossed his mind to think about that before now.

"I don't think so. Do you sleep upstairs?"

"No"

"Well, in that case, I don't think so. The only thing that I would advise would be to remove any loose carpets and rugs as they are a trip hazard."

"Okay, don't think there are many of those. What time do you think we can go?" Frank was keen to get home.

"I would think you would be free to go by four o'clock. Would that be okay with you?" The nurse was looking at Jason now.

"Yeah, that will be fine. I will pop home and sort out a few things and then come back later to get you. Is that okay?" Jason could see how happy the news had made his dad.

"Of course, it is as long as you come today. Can't wait to see Duke."

"I will get your papers ready and sort out your medication. And don't forget, if you have any problems, just give us a call."

Jason got up. "I will be back in a couple of hours, dad. Don't go anywhere." He gave him a hug and quickly left. On the way home, he stopped at the store to do a bit of shopping. Next on the list was to take Duke out for a bit and then a quick look around the house to check for trip hazards. After checking his emails, he returned to the hospital to collect his dad.

"Here, let me help you out to the car. Now, remember to take it steady when you walk about, no rushing around." The nurse gave Jason some papers and a bag with his medicine. She had also packed all Frank's belongings and put them in a bag on the bed.

"I will." Frank took hold of her arm while Jason picked up the bag and they headed for the exit.

*

Jason parked the car and got out. He could hear Duke barking in the house.

"I think someone knows you're home now." He opened the passenger door and helped his dad out of the car.

Frank stood for a little while to get his balance. All this moving around was quite tiring. The physio lady had been right when she had warned him, he would get tired easily to start with. She had told him to just do a few steps, then stop for a bit before caring on. As he was standing there, he looked at the front of the house. They had done an excellent job on it.

"Thank you, son." Frank had tears in his eyes.

"Thank you for what?" Jason looked puzzled and then it hit him. "Oh yeah. Hope you like it. I will take you on a tour later, but first I think we need to get you in. You look like you could do with a rest, and I think Duke is keen to say hello."

They hadn't been home long before there was a knock on the door. For a second Jason hoped it would be Julia as he had sent her a message to say that he had brought his dad home. He hadn't had a reply yet. It wasn't Julia, but instead Mr. and Mrs. Henderson.

"Hope we aren't interrupting, Jason, but I saw your father get out of the car earlier. Is he really home?" Jason had mentioned to them that his dad was likely to come home today. He guessed that Mrs. H had probably been keeping an eye on things.

"Yeah, he's here. Come on in. Would you like coffee?"

"Only if you're having. We won't stay for long. Just thought we would welcome him home and see if there is anything we can do."

They stayed for about an hour chatting about this and that. As they left, Mrs. Henderson took Jason to one side.

"Now, please let me know if you need any help. I'm happy to cook a meal for the pair of you."

"Thank you and don't worry, I will." He didn't mention the fact that he was away for a couple of days and Grace was going to be there while he was gone. It would only lead to more questions and right now he just wanted to be alone with his dad. Jason headed straight back to his dad once the door had closed.

"Son, I think I need to have a little rest now. Hope you don't mind." It had all been overwhelming for Frank.

"Not at all, dad. I have some work I need to look at anyway." Jason was walking right behind his dad into his bedroom.

"I think I will just lie on top with that blanket over." Frank pointed to a blanket that was on a chair in the corner. "Please come and get me if I am not up in an hour, otherwise I might not sleep tonight." Frank had got himself comfortable and Jason unfolded the blanket for him.

"No problem, dad. I will leave the door ajar. Give me a shout if you need me."

He returned to the kitchen and cracked on with work. He was so busy with it he didn't notice his dad coming into the kitchen. Jason immediately looked at the time.

"That was a quick rest, dad."

"Yeah, I just needed to relax a bit. Fancy a little walk outside, or are you busy?"

"No, this can wait. Just let me close it all down." He still had a few things he needed to do, but they could wait. He had emailed Mrs. Anderson and given her an update and said he wouldn't be available for the rest of the day. She was fully understanding and had replied saying that she would take care of anything that needed dealing with.

The sun was still brimming from a blue sky even though it was now late afternoon. Well, some might call it an early evening as it was nearly six o'clock. After a little walk around in the place, they sat down on the patio.

"What shall we do about dinner, dad? I can get something from Benny's if you like?"

Frank looked at him. "I think we can do better than that. I have an old BBQ in the shed. Would you mind going to get it for me?"

Jason quickly went and opened the door to the shed. He hadn't actually been in to have a proper look yet. He found the BBQ at the back and dragged it out. It looked like it hadn't seen daylight for a while.

"Bit dusty, think it could do with a good clean," Jason carried it over to the patio.

"Yeah, hasn't been used for a few years, but I think it will clean up. Shouldn't be anything wrong with it." Frank was about to get up, but Jason told him to stay sat down.

"Dad don't overdo it. Tell me where I can find what we need to clean it and I will do it."

Soon Jason got it looking good again.

"I fancy a small steak with some bread and salad, you know, like mom used to do. That can't be too complicated to do. What do you think?"

"Sounds good to me. Let me make a list of what we need, and I will do a quick run to the store. Now please don't do anything while I'm gone, dad." Jason gave his dad a firm glance.

Somehow, they managed to cook dinner and Jason was surprised by how good it tasted.

"Cheers to the chef." Frank raised his glass of water.

"Cheers dad."

"I haven't sat out here like this for... well, ever since your mom passed." Frank was staring out at the backyard and Jason didn't really know what to say. All he knew was that in order to move on, they had to talk about her and their memories of her. It wouldn't be easy. He took a deep breath.

"Yeah, I remember we used to sit out here most of the summer when I was younger."

"It was your mother's favorite thing. I miss her, Jason." Frank was beginning to feel overwhelmed by emotion.

"Me too, dad." Jason could feel the tears coming, mainly because he could see his dad's eyes welling up. He got up and pushed his chair closer so he was sitting next to him. They sat for a while without saying anything, just holding hands.

"So, have you decided what to do?"

"Nope, not really. It's so difficult. What do you think I should do?" he looked at his dad and hoped he had some kind of miracle answer to his question.

"Son, it doesn't matter what I think. Do what you think is best. Follow your instinct and whatever that is, give it a go. But remember this: No matter what you do, I will always be proud of you and support you." Frank had put his hand on Jason's shoulder.

{ 17 }

The first night went with no problems. Jason had suggested that they kept their bedroom doors open a little so his dad could call him if he needed to get up or had issues. It hadn't been the best night's sleep for Jason, mainly because he was worried about his dad. He had woken up at one point in the night and decided to go and check that his dad was okay. By six o'clock he gave up on sleeping and got dressed. He made himself some coffee and looked through his emails. The house was silent, not that it had bothered him before when it was only him and Duke. He looked at the time, it was closer to eight than seven now. Should he have a look? Just as he got up, he heard voices.

"Morning old chap. That was a better night's sleep." A few minutes later Duke came into the kitchen followed by Frank.

"Morning son."

"Morning dad. Did you sleep okay?"

"Yeah, best night's sleep in years, I think. How about you?"

"Yeah, not too bad. Would you like some coffee and a bite to eat?" Jason didn't let on how worried he had been during the night.

"That would be nice. Are you already working?" Frank pulled out a chair at the table and sat down.

"Yeah, thought I would get a few things done for my meeting on Thursday. Then it's done and we can do things together." He brought the coffee to Frank. "Is toast okay for breakfast?"

"Yes, that is fine, I don't need a lot. What time did Grace say she would be here?"

"Late afternoon I think she said." Jason made a note that he had better check that out. "I better take Duke out for a quick walk in a minute."

While walking, Jason called Grace to let her know how the night had gone. She told him she would aim to be with them between six and seven and then asked if there was anything she should bring.

"Don't think so. We will sort out some dinner but can't promise you it will be good." He couldn't help but laugh.

"I'm sure it will be fine. Would it be easier if I bring my own bedding?"

Bedding. Jason hadn't thought of that. Where was Grace going to sleep? Well, he could always sleep on the couch tonight and she could have his room.

"No need for that. I'm sure we have plenty of spares." Right, better get home and sort that out he thought.

"I will see you later. Bye Jason."

Once inside Jason went straight to find his dad.

"We haven't talked about this but where is Grace going to sleep?" He didn't let on that he had actually spoken to her. "I can sleep here on the couch."

"Don't be silly son. There is a bed in the little room at the end." Jason had only opened the door once and looked in. It was full of all his mother's sewing things.

"Well, we had better take a look at it." Jason took a deep breath and opened the door. He knew it wasn't going to be easy for either of them but there was no way around it. The room hadn't been touched since Jason's mom died and it was full of all sorts of things. Looked like she had used it not only for her sewing and repairs but also for storing things. Neither Jason nor his dad knew anything about sewing and Jason wished Julia had been there. She would have known what to do. Jason still hadn't heard from her despite having sent her a message to say that he was heading back to New York for a couple of days and that Grace would stay while he was gone. He had asked if he could speak to her on his return as he had something he wanted to tell her in person. Jason looked around the room, then turned to his dad.

"What shall we do?"

His father looked at it, there wasn't that much on the bed, so he suggested they moved that and put it all on the table by the sewing machine for now. That would make room for Grace to sleep.

"Maybe we can get her to help us with it?" Frank looked at Jason, "but only if you are happy with that?"

"Yeah maybe," Jason started to clear the bed. The next thing was to find some sheets and make the bed. It felt strange handling his mother's things and Jason couldn't stop thinking that his mother had been the last one to touch all this. His dad was right, maybe Grace could help them with that room. At least it would be a start.

Once done, Frank said he needed a rest and went to sit in his favorite chair. Jason could do with some fresh air to clear his thoughts.

"I might just take Duke for a quick walk then if you don't mind?"

"You carry on son."

He headed in the direction of the house that was for sale. Once past the sign, he looked back to see if anyone was around. Looked like it was only him and Duke.

"Right let's do this!" He took his phone out of his pocket and dialed the number.

"Mark Wright here. How can I help?"

"Jason Wild here, just wondering if it was possible to come in tomorrow morning, say nine o'clock?"

"Yeah, no problem. I will see you then."

*

Frank needed a rest after lunch and Jason decided he could really do with one as well but didn't mention it. Once he had made sure his dad was in bed, Jason headed to the living room and sat down on the couch. Before he knew it, he had swung his leg up and made himself comfortable. Didn't take many seconds before he was fast asleep.

The phone rang and suddenly Jason was wide awake. He ran to the kitchen to answer it. It was Grace and she thought she would just let them know she was leaving now.

"Thank you, Grace. Drive carefully and we will look forward to seeing you when you get here." Jason looked at the time, it had gone past three. He reckoned with a bit of luck she would be there just before six.

"Who was that?" Frank appeared in the kitchen.

"Oh, it was Grace. She just wanted to let us know she was leaving now. She aims to be here by six, which reminds me, what are we going to cook for her?" Jason was making coffee. "Would you like one?"

"Yes please, and I don't know about dinner. How about sticking to what we know we're good at? What do you think? At least we know it tastes okay." Frank couldn't help but laugh.

"Good plan dad. I will go and get what we need." Jason couldn't stop smiling. It was so nice to hear his dad laughing and looking happy. He had expected him to be angrier and more negative – but there had been none of that. Maybe it had all been something Jason had imagined. Last night they had touched on the fact that when Jason returned later in the week, they would start going through some of his mother's things. It wouldn't be easy but they both knew it had to be done.

After coffee, Jason made a list and went shopping. He returned with a couple of bags and had just unpacked them when Grace arrived.

Jason showed her to her room. He apologized for the state it was in and then said that his dad had suggested that she might be able to help them sort through it.

"I know it might seem silly but at least it is a start." Jason looked nervously at Grace and hoped she wouldn't say no.

"Jason I will be more than happy to help out. And you are right, it will make a start."

Jason left Grace to sort out what she needed to do while he and Frank cooked dinner. Grace had offered but Frank had insisted that they would be okay.

"This is delicious. Well done to both of you." Grace had put down her knife and fork.

"Thank you, well it is the only thing we can cook so far but I'm sure that we'll learn many more over the summer." Frank raised his glass of water and looked at Jason, "What do you think son?"

"Oh yes. I'm up for a challenge."

They spent the evening talking a lot about Alice. To start with Jason found it a little uncomfortable but as the evening went on it felt good to hear all the stories. Yes, there were times when he got a bit tearful; it was almost as if the tears were a way of letting go of the pain, he had been ignoring over the last two years.

In the end, Grace turned to Jason.

"So what time are you off tomorrow and when do you plan to return?"

"Plan to leave no later than nine o'clock and should be back early Thursday evening I hope." He mentioned nothing about the meeting he had arranged in town before heading to New York.

"I hope the old man behaves himself while I'm gone," Jason gave his dad a big smile.

"I am sure he will be fine. We got plenty to talk about." Grace looked at Frank and Jason couldn't help but smile. He was so pleased he had opened the letters and made the call. Something told him he might end up seeing more of her in the future, which wouldn't be a bad thing.

*

Jason was making good progress, with less than two hours to go. His meeting with Mark had gone well: it was just a short one. Mark had promised him an answer by Friday.

He had phoned Mrs. Anderson and asked her to check out a couple of things for him. At no point had she questioned why he needed it which had pleased Jason. He wasn't really in a position to say too much at the moment, there were still a few things that needed to go his way for it to work.

Jason looked at the fuel gauge: less than a quarter of a tank wasn't enough to take him all the way. He decided to do a pit stop and also get some coffee. As he walked back to the car, a message came through. It was from Julia. He could feel his heart rate go up and quickly made it back to the car before opening it.

"Hope your meeting goes well, drive safely, and hopefully I'll see you when you return". A million things went through Jason's head, things he wanted to ask and say but, in the end, he decided they could wait until he saw her in person, so he simply replied "Thank you. I will look forward to that. X." He couldn't stop reading the message over and over. In the end, a man in the car behind him rolled down his window and shouted:

"Hey man, are you finished or what?"

Jason quickly started the car and headed back out on the road. Suddenly the next couple of days couldn't go quickly enough and he could only hope that everything would go as he had planned it.

He reached the office mid-afternoon and Mrs. Anderson was so pleased to see him. Jason gave her the flowers he had bought as a thank-you for all her help over the last couple of weeks.

"Thank you, Jason - these are lovely. Mr. Patterson says you can come up when you're ready"

"Okay let's get this over with then." Jason left everything in his office including his phone and went to see his boss.

Jason spent over an hour with Mr. Patterson, and they had a good discussion about Jason's decision.

"Thank you so much for your understanding, Mr. Patterson," Jason reached out to give a handshake.

"That's not a problem. And I'm pretty sure we can find a solution that will suit everybody. I will get back to you beginning of next week. Oh, and Jason let's just keep it between you and me for now, okay? Have a safe trip back tomorrow."

"Thank you and yes I won't say anything, well apart from when I speak to John as you recommended." Jason closed the door behind him as he left and headed back to his office feeling rather relieved and happy.

Once back in his office, he sat down. What had he just

done? Was it the right thing to do? Who knew? But he had to trust his instinct as his dad had told him. Mrs. Anderson knocked on the door, she had all the information he needed for the next day.

"If you don't mind, I will head home now Jason."

He looked at his watch. It had just gone half-five. He looked up at Mrs. Anderson:

"Yes, please do. It wasn't my intention to keep you here, sorry about that. I will see you tomorrow."

"Yes, see you in the morning, and thank you for the flowers - that was very kind of you. Now just because you are back here doesn't mean that you should work late." She had that firm look on her face.

Jason stayed for another hour checking he had everything he needed for the meeting. Hopefully, with a bit of luck, they wouldn't hit any problems and he could wrap it up fairly quickly tomorrow.

Once out on the street, he thought of dinner. Where should he go? Much to his surprise, he didn't really fancy eating out but instead went and bought a few things he could heat up once he was back in his apartment. Not quite the home-cooked meal but definitely better than sitting in a restaurant on his own. As he was eating, he flicked through the channels but couldn't find anything that inspired him so instead he phoned his dad to check how it was going.

"We are doing very well here. What about you?"

"What have you been doing today?" Jason was trying to avoid the question as he couldn't and shouldn't really tell anyone yet.

"Well, Grace took me for a little walk across to the Hendersons' where we had coffee. I have to say it was rather nice to get out and about a bit. How about you son? Have you spoken to your boss yet?"

"Believe it or not I have actually bought some food and am sitting eating it in my apartment. Think that's the first time I've ever done that -" he paused for a moment. Should he or shouldn't he tell his dad? No, he had promised not to say anything so probably best to stick to that. "I saw him briefly when I got here, and we are meeting again tomorrow." Not quite true but it bought him some time.

"I have to say it feels a bit lonely sitting here on my own. Looking forward to coming back," Jason had no idea where that came from, but it was the truth. He was lonely.

"We miss you too and are looking forward to seeing you tomorrow evening. Grace says she will stay until Friday as she doesn't really want to drive home in the dark and doesn't want to leave me before you get back. I have told her I will be fine, and she doesn't have to worry but she won't have it."

"Okay, I will let you know when I leave. See you to-morrow dad, love you."

"Love you too son."

Jason quickly tidied up after dinner which wasn't that difficult, and then went and packed a few things that he wanted to take with him. He wasn't sure when he was going to be back in the apartment again. Once all that was done, he grabbed a beer and sat down to look at his phone. He pulled up Julia's message and read it again. It was very tempting to send her a message explaining everything, but no, he had to stick to the plan. Things could so easily be misunderstood when relying on messages going backwards and forwards. No, he wanted to tell her face-to-face in the right place as he had planned. That would be the only way to do it. Right, time for bed, and Jason turned his phone off.

Jason had found it difficult to sleep with so many things going around in his head and when the alarm went off it felt like he had only just dropped off. Not what he needed on a day like this. Not only did he have a very important meeting that required his full attention, but he also had a good four-hour drive later on. A quick shower and coffee were needed to get going. And more coffee as he reached the office. By the time he headed into the meeting he was well awake. It took a little longer than he would have liked but he managed to strike the deal which was the important bit. And it wasn't until he was back at his desk, feeling pretty good about his achievement, that he realized how hungry he was. Jason looked at his watch, it had just gone twelve. He had hoped to be leaving his apartment no later than one which was not going to happen. He was debating whether to grab a quick lunch here or to get some once he was on his way. Mrs. Anderson had read his mind and looked firmly at him:

"Jason, have you had anything to eat today?"

For a moment he considered telling her that he had but then realized that she knew him too well. There was no point trying to trick her.

"Yeah, a muesli bar first thing this morning, why?"

"I think you and I need to go and have lunch together so I can be sure you have had some before you start driving back to your father. Can't have you having an accident because you didn't have anything to eat!"

He was going to object but knew by the look on her face that he wouldn't get out of it, so instead, he said with a smile:

"Mrs. Anderson, would you like to join me for lunch?"

"I would love to." She quickly shut down her PC, and put the sign on the door saying, 'Out of Office.'

They spent the next thirty minutes talking about Jason's plan to sort his mother's things together with his father over the next couple of weeks. Jason mentioned they would start with his mom's sewing room as Grace had offered her help.

"Do you know how long you are going to be gone?"

"As you know Mr. Patterson has said that I can work from dad's place all summer if I want to. It depends a bit on how we get on. However, I will be back for the odd meeting. So don't worry you will see me from time to time. Maybe you could make a trip out and visit me there?"

"I don't know. I have never really been outside the city," she laughed. "I am glad Mr. Patterson is so understanding towards you but then again you have worked hard and been very good to the company. No wonder they want to promote you."

"Yeah. Well now that I have had something to eat, I better be on my way." Jason wanted to stop the conversation before it got any further. He didn't like it when he couldn't be honest with Mrs. Anderson. Lying was not his strong suit and she was very good at reading between the lines.

"Okay. Drive safe Jason and I will speak to you tomorrow.

Could you please let me know when you have reached your destination?"

"Yes, I will send you a message and we will speak tomorrow."

A quick trip back to the office to get his things and he was ready to head for the exit. The subway wasn't too busy, and he managed to get a seat. He loved the subway when it wasn't too full of people, but he was looking forward to not having an hour-long commute to work every day. Finally, he unlocked the door to his apartment. One last quick look around to check he hadn't forgotten anything. Nope pretty sure it was all packed and ready. He grabbed the bags and headed to the car.

It felt really good to be on the way and he couldn't wait to be back home again. Jason had phoned his dad and told him he hoped to be back around seven o'clock. He had also sent Julia a message saying he was leaving now and asked if she would meet him the following day at two outside Benny's. It couldn't be any earlier as he was still waiting for Mark to get back to him. However, he was pretty confident that he knew the answer, but still. He had to follow the plan.

Traffic was easy and he had found a good station that played some nice music. Jason looked at the time, he had made good progress and it looked like he would get there before seven.

Finally, on the home stretch, he had just passed the sign that said ten miles to go. Jason was going over all the things he wanted to tell Julia, and in which order he would do so. He was debating whether to bring some flowers to give to her. It had never occurred to him that she could be working or even worse that she didn't want to see him.

Suddenly, out of nowhere, a huge deer jumped out in front of the car. Jason tried to avoid a direct hit but before he knew what was happening, he was rolling down the bank. Everything slowed down. The car eventually came to halt.

$$\{\ 18\ \}$$

Jason looked around. There was a ring of people surrounding him. They were all dressed in white. He panicked a bit. Where was he? He didn't recognize any of them apart from one: she looked just like his mother. Jason tried to say something to her, but she just put her finger up to her mouth in silent motion. He tried to turn around, but something was holding him back, he couldn't see what and tried again. Suddenly he could hear his name; someone was talking to him, but who?

Frank and Grace stood at the end of Jason's bed. Dr. Peterson and a nurse were standing on one side; on the other was another doctor and nurse.

"What is happening Doctor? Why is he so restless?" Frank was looking very concerned, and Grace had taken his hand to support him.

"This is normal when people are waking up after an accident like that, a bit like having a nightmare. Let's try and see if we can get him to open his eyes." Dr. Peterson turned to Jason and put his hand on his arm.

"Jason, can you hear me? Come on Jason open your eyes. You are in the hospital."

Finally, Jason opened his eyes. He looked around and tried to move but couldn't. Then he looked down towards his dad and realized the reason he couldn't move. His left leg was in plaster.

"What happened? Where am I?" His head was hurting, and he was trying hard to remember the day's event.

"Mr. Wild, why don't you come here and talk to your son? It might help him relax a bit." Dr. Peterson pointed to the other side of the bed. The doctor and nurse that were standing there stepped aside so Frank could come closer.

"Jason, you had an accident. A deer jumped out in front of your car. Luckily for you, there was another driver who saw it all and called for help." Frank took hold of Jason's hand and with the other, he stroked his hair. "You hit your head and have a broken leg."

"When did this happen?" Jason was still trying to work it all out.

"Two days ago. Can you remember what happened?"

"No, not really. Where did it happen and what was I doing?" He was trying hard to remember where he had been and why he was in the car.

"Don't worry, you're going to be okay son. You went to New York on Wednesday morning for a meeting and were on the way home Thursday afternoon. Do you remember that?"

"So, I was coming home?" Jason felt so confused. "What happened to the car? Is it badly damaged?"

"Yeah, I am afraid so. Andrew has picked it up and taken it to his place for now, but don't worry about that. The important thing is that you are going to be okay."

Jason turned to Dr. Peterson, "So what is wrong with me doctor?"

"As you can see you have a broken leg and concussion. Apart from that, you have some serious bruising from the seatbelt. It's fair to say that the seat belt saved your life."

"I remember nothing." His whole body was aching, but the headache was the worst and he felt so confused by it all.

"Don't worry about that for now, give it some time. I am pretty sure some of it, if not all, will come back. It might just take a little while. Now I would recommend you get some rest – that will be the best medicine for you. Do you have any pain anywhere?"

"Well, I feel like I've done a fair few rounds in the ring and my head feels like it's going to explode."

I will get the nurses to give you a top-up." Dr. Peterson turned to Frank and Grace, "I'm happy for you to stay for a bit but might be better to come back later. Any questions?"

Frank thanked him and then turned his attention to Jason.

"Well son, it looks like it will be me looking after you instead of the other way round." Frank bent over and gave Jason a kiss on his forehead.

"Are you going to be okay dad?" Jason saw Grace and then remembered something about his dad being ill.

"Yeah, I will be fine. Grace is more than happy to stay and help me." Frank turned to give her a smile.

Jason tried to reach out for her hand.

"Thank you, Grace, and sorry I have landed you in all this."

"Don't you worry about that; I have nothing else to do.

You get some rest Jason, and we will come back later. Okay?" She stoked Jason's head and thought of Alice.

The nurse came in to give Jason some more painkillers. He looked at her, now there was something about nurses, someone he knew but this one wasn't the person he was thinking of.

"Okay Mr. Wild, here are some more painkillers, which should make you feel better."

Jason looked at her, he didn't recognize the name, but he felt he should.

"Sorry, but do I know you? Or is there someone else here that I know?"

"Well, I looked after your father, but I think you might be thinking of nurse Taylor."

"Taylor yeah that sounds familiar." He tried really hard to think. "Julia? Is that her name?"

"Yes, that is correct." The nurse wasn't sure what to say. She was fully aware of their relationship. It had been clear to everyone when Jason had come in. Julia had tried to stay strong but had ended up passing out. The duty doctor had signed her off sick and her dad had come to collect her.

"Is she here?" Jason suddenly remembered something about needing to tell her something. But what? He couldn't remember.

"No sorry, she is on leave at the moment." She didn't and couldn't tell him what had happened.

"Oh okay. Do you know if I have my phone here? I think I need to look at it."

"No, your father has all your things and I don't think you

should worry about it now. Try to relax, your head needs to rest, not try to solve anything right now." The nurse looked firmly at him.

"Okay, but could you pass a message on to nurse Taylor for me? Just tell her I am here, and I would like to speak to her"

"Will do."

The painkillers must have worked because he felt a bit more relaxed and before he knew it, he had drifted off to sleep again.

*

Frank and Grace were on their way home. Grace was driving and without thinking, she had turned towards the cemetery. Frank looked at her.

"Why are we going here?"

"Not sure. Just feel I need to come here. You can come with me or stay here. I won't be long." Grace got out of the car. Frank thought for a little and decided that whatever the reason was, Grace probably needed to be alone for a bit.

"I will stay here if that is okay with you. Happy to come with you but I think you need to do this on your own."

"Thank you, Frank. I won't be long." She walked in through the gate and headed straight to the grave where she stood for a minute.

"I promise you I will do all I can to make sure he is going to be okay Alice. Now he is awake things are looking better. And yes, I will stay as long as I'm needed." She bowed her head and said a little prayer before heading back to Frank and the car.

"You okay?" Frank looked at her as she got back in the car.

"Yes, just needed a bit of time alone with her if you know what I mean."

"I do." He looked at her, there was something about her that made him feel good or happy, but he wasn't sure what it was. "She was always a good listener. I'm pretty sure she is grateful that you are helping us. Not sure what we or I would have done without you."

"I think you're right." Grace took Frank's hand, gave it a little squeeze, and smiled, "I'm more than happy to help. Now let's get home to Duke and have some lunch.

Later in the afternoon, they returned to the hospital to see how Jason was.

"I feel better. Hey dad do you have my phone with you?"

"No Jason and I don't think you should be using it right now. If you're concerned about work, I called your office yesterday and told Mrs. Anderson what had happened. She sends you her best wishes and hopes you get well soon. She also promised to let your boss know. Unless things change for the worse, we've to speak again on Monday. She sounds like a very nice lady."

"Yeah, she is one of a kind." He paused for a bit. "Hey, dad have you seen Julia? The nurse this morning said she was on leave."

"No, I haven't." Frank didn't let on what had happened. He only knew because he and Grace arrived at the hospital at the same time as Julia's dad. They had exchanged a few words and Mr. Taylor had said it was probably best if they didn't mention anything to Jason about it.

"I think she needs to be on her own away from it all. I hope your son recovers," Mr. Taylor had given them a nod and left. Grace thought he was a bit sharp but then Frank filled her in on what Julia had been through.

"Oh, that makes sense then. Poor girl."

"Jason, I'm sure she will be back soon. You focus on getting better so we can get you home." Grace had come up on the other side of the bed.

"I will try but it keeps bugging me that I can't remember anything from that day, not even the meeting I had."

"Mrs. Anderson assured me that there was nothing you had to worry about. If you like I can give her a call and check?"

"Could you ask her what I was doing there and if I have told her anything about my plans?"

"Will do. Now Andrew phoned earlier and said he would pop in and see you tomorrow morning. I hope that is okay with you. We will be back tomorrow afternoon unless you need us here."

"Thanks, dad." Jason's first thought was that Andrew could help him get in contact with Julia.

Despite all the beeping and people coming and going, Jason managed a reasonably good night's sleep, and it was obvious that he needed it. He felt a lot better the following morning. In fact, he felt so good that the nurses decided he needed to get out of bed. Well, easier said than done. He wasn't really in pain, only when they touched one of the many bruises he had, and there were a fair few. The two nurses had brought in a wheelchair for him, and the plan was for them to take him to the bathroom so he could wash. Now he couldn't have a shower with a foot in plaster, so instead, they parked him in front of the sink.

"Right Mr. Wild, time to see your bruises." The nurse helped him get his hospital shirt off. Jason was lost for words. He had never seen anything like it, and it sent a shiver down his spine. Suddenly he realized he must have been extremely lucky to still be here. He turned to the nurse, "Well, that explains why I am hurting all over I think."

"Yeah, I think so Mr. Wild. It will take a day or two for them to disappear I think but they should get less painful with time.

Once back in she helped him over so he could sit in a normal chair, and this was where he was when the doctor came in.

"I see you are up and about Mr. Wild. How does it feel?"

"Okay, bit shocked to see all the bruises."

"Well, you got off lightly. How is the headache today?"

"A lot better but I still can't remember anything from the accident or what I had planned to do when I got back. Is that normal?"

"Yes, that is normal. It will come back bit by bit, you just have to be patient. Everything else seems okay so I think you should be able to go home later today. How does that sound?"

"Well, I wouldn't say no to that."

"It will be on one condition. You have to promise to take it easy, and I mean take it easy." Dr. Peterson was looking over his glasses like an old schoolmaster. "Otherwise, you will be straight back here. I will get one of the nurses to call your father and ask him to bring in some clothes for you. And they will also teach you how to use crutches as you will need those. But I don't want you to get around too much to start with so only use them to get to and from the car etc. You will get an appointment to have your leg checked, probably the week after next, but should you experience any discomfort please contact us. Now, look after yourself. I think we have seen enough of your family in here for now."

"Thank you, doctor."

Andrew came in just as Dr. Peterson was finishing up. As it happened, they knew each other. Dr. Peterson used to live in Preston and was good friends with Andrew's father-in-law.

"Morning Andrew, what are you doing here?" Dr. Peterson reached out to give Andrew a handshake.

"Well, that man you have there was my neighbor and best friend when I was a child. We did everything together back then," Andrew waved to Jason.

"Well, he is a lucky man; not that he was at fault for the accident according to the police report. Anyway, I better be going. Good to see you and keep an eye on Mr. Wild. He has to take it easy, but I feel he might find that difficult."

"Good to see you too. And yes, I will keep an eye on him." Andrew then turned his attention to Jason, "Hey, what did he have to say then?" Andrew bent over and gave Jason a gentle hug.

"That I am free to go home later this afternoon."

"That's brilliant. I have to say that you have given us all a bit of a scare."

"I still don't know what happened."

Andrew explained what he had been told by the police when he had picked up the car. Basically, Jason didn't really have a chance according to the driver that was right behind him. He had done nothing wrong and wasn't speeding either.

"So how bad is the car?"

"Well let's just say that you won't be driving it again. I have taken out all the things in it and it's ready to go but I am holding on to it just in case you feel you need to see it."

"Thanks, Andrew." Jason was looking at the floor feeling a little unsure about it all.

"Jason this is going to take some time but my advice to you will be not to bottle it up. Keep talking to us."

"Have you seen Julia?" Jason looked straight at Andrew, he wanted to make sure he was telling him the truth.

"No, I haven't, isn't she here?" Andrew had been informed by Jason's dad not to say anything for now.

"Apparently she is on leave, but the thing is I can remember that I had something to tell her, and I wanted to tell her in person, I just can't remember what it was."

"Hey, it will sort itself out. If you like I can go via her house and see if she's in." Andrew had no intention of doing that but if it could help Jason then why not.

"Thanks, if you don't mind."

"I will see what I can find out and come and see you tomorrow – at home. I hear Grace is staying and from what mom and dad say it seems like she and your father are getting on quite well."

"I know and I am really pleased for them."

"Right, I will see you tomorrow."

Once Andrew had gone, Jason pressed the button. He was feeling rather tired and could do with a rest.

*

Grace parked her car as close to the front door as she could. Frank wanted to take Jason's bag in, but she told him not to.

"Remember you still have to be careful. Now go and open the door so Jason can walk right in." Grace had gone round to the passenger door and was helping Jason out. Not easy but she had tried it before when she looked after her late husband.

"Now just take it slowly Jason and I'm right behind you."

Jason was concentrating hard. Walking with crutches was easier said than done but somehow, he managed it as far as the couch, where he decided he would rest for now. Grace went back to the car and got the bag.

"You two have a rest while I cook dinner."

"You don't have to do that. I'm happy to pay for a takeaway." Jason felt bad about Grace doing all the work.

"Don't be silly. I love the fact that I have people to cook for." She disappeared into the kitchen. Jason had to admit he was looking forward to some nice food, not that it hadn't been good at the hospital, but it was hospital food.

"Dad, has Julia been in contact with you?"

"No haven't heard from her." Frank tried to look like he didn't know anything.

"I can remember I had some news to tell her, I feel it was something important but can't remember what it was. That is why I also need to look at my phone."

"You can have your phone tomorrow, that's the doctor's order. I spoke to Mrs. Anderson last night and she is happy for you to call her if you think that might help. Do you remember you got a promotion, and you were debating with yourself what to do? One of the things you were going to do while in New York was to speak to your boss. Do you remember that?"

Jason was trying to think. It all sounded familiar. He had a long chat with someone.

"Yeah, I remember talking to him and something about we would catch up at the beginning of next week."

"That's good. Maybe you can speak to him tomorrow and find out more."

"Yeah, but that still doesn't tell me anything about Julia. I have this strange feeling that I might have hurt her, but I can't remember why or what I have done."

Frank wasn't sure what to say. Andrew had called him earlier. He had been to Julia's house and spoken to her dad. Mr. Taylor had informed him that Julia had gone away for a few days. Jason's accident had stirred up memories and she needed to be alone for now.

"Dinner is ready!" Grace came in to give Jason some help getting up.

"It smells good." Jason sat down on the chair that Grace had pulled out for him. He hadn't noticed how hungry he was. This was by far the best home-cooked meal Jason had had for a long while. After the first few bites, he picked up his glass of water.

"A toast to the fabulous cook. How long can you stay?"

"I totally agree with Jason. This is delicious Grace. Thank you so much for doing this. Well thank you for offering to look after us; it appears we are not capable of doing it ourselves."

"You will be fine but I'm happy to stay as long as you want me." She looked at them both. The truth was that she really enjoyed the company. She and Frank had so many things in common and despite the drama around Jason's accident, they had laughed a lot together. She was pretty sure Frank felt the same way.

Jason looked at them both. It was the way they looked at each other; his dad really deserved to be happy. He could also feel his leg was beginning to feel a bit sore. The nurse had told him to make sure he sat with it up otherwise his foot would start to swell, which would make it uncomfortable because of the plaster. It was time to go to bed.

"Thank you so much for a delicious meal, Grace." Jason reached out and took her hand.

"Thank you, Jason."

"Well, if you won't mind, I think I will head off to bed. I'm feeling rather tired now."

Grace immediately got up and got his crutches.

"Here let me help you." She followed him to his bedroom

and made sure he was comfortable in bed. She asked Frank to find an extra pillow so she could elevate the leg in plaster. Jason was slightly embarrassed, but Grace pointed out that she was a nurse in her younger days and had seen worse.

"Looks like Duke is taking up residence in here," Frank looked at the dog.

"Well, that's okay. If you don't mind, could you leave the door ajar so I can call you if I need you?"

"Not a problem son. Hope you have a good sleep"

It didn't take long before he was out.

{ 19 }

Jason turned his head and opened his eyes. For a second he wasn't sure where he was. He tried to reach the table next to the bed which had a small lamp on it. Duke who had slept by his bed during the night had sensed he was awake and put his head on Jason's chest as to say, "Don't worry I'm here."

"Morning to you too old boy." Jason could smell fresh coffee and wondered what time it was. There was a knock on the door and his dad popped his head in.

"Morning. How are you feeling son? Did you sleep okay?"

"Yeah, I'm okay, what time is it?"

"Just gone eight o'clock. We checked in on you before we went to bed last night, but you were fast asleep. Grace is asking if you would like breakfast in here?"

Jason couldn't remember ever having breakfast in bed and it was rather tempting but on the other hand, he wanted to get out of bed.

"If you can cope with me not looking my best I would like to get up."

"Okay. Shall I get Grace to come and help you?"

"No, dad. I think I can do it with your help." It didn't matter that Grace had been a nurse once or was more than happy to help him. Jason didn't feel that comfortable with her seeing him in this state. Frank got the crutches ready and lent Jason a hand to pull himself up. He sat on the side of the bed for a bit just to get his balance.

"Could you get my robe and help me put it on?"

Soon Jason was standing up and looking a bit more respectable.

"I will just pop to the bathroom then I will be there okay."

"Okay, son. Give me a call if you need help." Frank headed back to the kitchen.

Soon the three of them sat around the table eating break-fast. It gave Jason a flashback to his youth. His mother had always insisted that they had breakfast together.

"Did you sleep okay, and do you have any pain?" Grace couldn't help it. The old nurse in her was concerned about him.

"I'm fine. Must have slept like a log. Can't remember waking up. My head feels a lot better, but the body is still aching a bit."

"You better take a couple of tablets, just to keep on top of it." She went to get the bag the nurse had given them.

"Thank you, Grace, and can I just say this is looking good." He pointed to the breakfast. He then turned to his dad, "Could I have my phone now?"

Frank handed it over and looked at him, "Now don't do it all in one go. Remember to take breaks."

"I will dad, don't you worry." He opened it and was surprised to see how many messages there were. To Jason's surprise, he turned the phone off and asked if there was more coffee. There was no rush, the messages could wait. He had all day to look at them.

"Think I will try and have a wash and a shave first." One thing he had never felt comfortable with was growing facial hair. It had never been his thing.

"Good plan son. Now if it is okay with you, Grace and I would like to sort out the room she is sleeping in. Grace has had a look at all the sewing stuff. Would you mind if we do that? Nothing is going to be thrown out without you knowing about it."

"That is fine by me dad. Once I'm dressed, I would like to go through all this here," Jason pointed to his phone, and I think Andrew said something about coming over as well."

"Yeah, Alan mentioned that this morning; we met when I was walking Duke. By the way, it looks like the empty house, you know the one you told me about, is under offer. Will be good if someone moved in there."

Empty house? Under offer? Jason tried to work out why that rang a bell with him; there was something about it, but he hadn't a clue why.

"Right, I think I will go and make an attempt to clean up and get dressed. That's if I have anything that would fit over this," he pointed to his plastered foot.

"Let me know if I can help, maybe we can modify a pair of trousers, that shouldn't be too difficult to do."

"Can you do that Grace?"

"Yeah, no problem. Let's go and have a look at what the options are."

Luckily Jason had brought some old clothes with him for

when they did the gardening last weekend and while he was in the bathroom trying to wash and have a shave, Grace quickly opened up the trouser leg that had to go over the plaster.

"There you are. Here, try this, I think this should work for now." She handed him the trouser. Do you want me to help you get into them?"

"Thank you, Grace. Yes please, I don't think I can bend down that far yet. I will have to buy some more, I think. Stuck with this for six weeks." It suddenly dawned on Jason how long he was going to be out of action, and not be able to drive. What would his boss say?

Once he was dressed, Jason slowly made his way to the couch. Frank brought his computer and phone in. First Jason wanted to look through all the messages on his phone. The first one was from Julia, he quickly opened it.

"Looking forward to seeing you tomorrow," it said. Totally confused he looked at the date and time it was sent and then realized it must have come through just before the accident. But the nurse at the hospital had said that she was on leave. This didn't add up, why was she hiding from him?

Jason carried on looking through the rest of the messages. There were a lot from all his co-workers, his boss, and Mrs. Anderson. Even some of his customers had sent him a message. He decided that rather than replying to each of them he would speak to Mrs. Anderson and get her to send a message out for now.

Then he came across a message from a Mark Wright. Jason couldn't remember knowing anyone with that name.

Looking at the date it had come through the day after the accident.

"Sorry to hear about your accident, hope you get well soon. Just to let you know they have accepted your offer." Who was Mark Wright and what offer was he on about? Jason was trying to think back, he could remember last weekend when they all had been together sorting out the gardening and he remembered bringing his dad home too, but after that, it all went a bit fuzzy.

The message from Mr. Patterson indicated he had made some changes, but what?

"Jason, hope you are okay. Just to let you know, I think I have worked something out that could work for both of us. Let me know when you are well enough to talk." What could that be? Somehow Jason had a feeling it was linked to both the message from Julia and the one from Mark, whoever he was.

"How is it going in here, son?" Frank had come in to see whether Jason would like some coffee as Grace was making one for them.

"It's going okay, dad. I am slowly getting there." For a second, Jason thought of sharing all the things he had come across so far with his dad but decided to wait a bit. Before Frank could say anything, the doorbell went.

"Who can that be?" Frank headed out to see and returned with Andrew.

"How are you doing?" Andrew declined Frank's offer to get a chair for him.

"I'm okay, but I could do with some fresh air."

"Good because I was going to suggest that if you are allowed out, I would take you out for a little drive?" Andrew looked at Frank, who already knew what it was about. Alan had asked him earlier.

"I see no reason why you can't do that, just as long as you promise not to overdo it."

"Will you and Grace be okay here?" What a stupid question that was. Of course, they would be fine.

"Yeah, we've got plenty to do." Grace had come in with a small bag.

"You better take these with you," she handed him his painkillers. "Have a nice time."

"Thank you. Dad, could you get my coat please?" While Frank went to get the coat, Grace and Andrew helped Jason to stand up. Slowly he made his way to Andrew's car. He was slowly getting the hang of using the crutches and working out which bruises were most painful.

"Those two seem to get on very well." Andrew gave Frank and Grace a wave as they left.

"Yeah, it's funny, I feel really happy about it. I know she's not mom, but in some ways, it feels as though she is. I remember years ago mom and Grace always talked about how everyone thought they were twins when they were young because they were so alike."

They passed the empty house and the sign had changed to "under offer."

"Hey, there is something I can't work out. Did I tell you anything about this house last weekend?"

"Yes, you asked if I could remember the name of the boy who used to live there. Why?"

Jason began to explain the various messages including Julia's and how none of it made sense to him, but at the same time, he had a feeling they were all connected.

"You told me last weekend you got a promotion and you had to give them an answer when you went back to New York last Wednesday."

"Promotion! I remember something about having had an interview but what has that got to do with Mark Wright?"

"Good question. Do you remember I told you, you had to speak to Julia and tell her what was going on?"

"Yeah, sort of. I've read the messages that I sent her. She didn't reply for a few days; she can't have taken it that well."

"Do you remember what I told you about her past?"

"Think so. Something about her losing someone." It annoyed him that he couldn't remember the details.

They were heading into Preston now.

"I want to show you something, Jason." Andrew had parked up at his shop. "But only if you think you are ready for it."

"Well, what is it?" Jason was puzzled. What was Andrew up to?

"I want to show you, your car before they scrap it. I think it might help you realize how lucky you were, and it might help you a bit to remember things."

"Okay," Jason hadn't seen that coming and he had to just think for a moment whether he was up to it. Did he really want to see it? He took a deep breath.

"Let's do it."

Andrew helped him out and they slowly made their way through the shop and out to the backyard.

All Jason could see was a rather flattened car with no roof. Andrew explained that they had to cut the roof off to get him out of it. Jason felt sick looking at it; how did he ever come out of that alive with just bruises and a broken foot?

"You okay?" Andrew was looking rather concerned at him. Jason's face was almost white.

"Sorry I'm going to be sick," and he turned around. Andrew was holding him, and once Jason had finished, he helped him back up. He found a chair for Jason to sit on and went to get him a glass of water.

"Sorry to put you through this but I think you will thank me for it later, and it might also help you to understand people's reactions." Andrew was thinking of one particular person but didn't mention that.

"I know you are right; it was just a bit of a shock to see it. I am really lucky to have come out of that alive."

"Yeah, but you are here now and that is what counts. Okay! Right, I think Amy has made some cake; her parents have taken Colin off for the day so why don't we go and see her."

"Okay." Jason couldn't really object to it as Andrew was the driver. Amy was rather pleased to see him and had indeed made cake.

"Coffee?" She pulled out a chair for him to sit on.

"Wouldn't say no." Jason looked around. "This place looks rather nice," he looked at both of them.

"Yeah, we like it. Amy still has a few ideas of things she wants to change but we are getting there," Andrew explained what they had done so far to the house and the plans for the future.

Jason couldn't help but feel there was a reason for the three of them being on their own.

"I take it Andrew showed you your car or what is left of it?" Amy was looking rather serious now.

"Yes, he did. Pretty grim site. The thing is I don't remember seeing a deer. The last thing I remember was passing the ten-mile sign, thinking that I was nearly home and how I was looking forward to it."

"They come out pretty fast and you were just unlucky."

"Hey, has Julia been in contact with you Amy?" Before she could answer Jason went on to explain about the various messages and the nurse telling him she was on leave.

"Well yes. I have spoken to her. She is pretty shaken up about what happened to you. You have to remember what she has been through, the fact that she lost her fiancé to an accident. She couldn't face that again which is why she has gone away for a few days."

Suddenly Jason remembered what Andrew had told him about her history. It kind of made sense now.

"Do you know where she is? I need to talk to her."

"She doesn't want to see any of us right now. The best thing you can do is get yourself sorted out. Have you decided on your job?" Amy had put her hand on his as a kind of support.

"I don't know. I've been told I had a meeting with my

boss last Wednesday and he has left me a message saying he thinks he has sorted things out to fit us both. What that means I have no idea. And I have another message from a Mark Wright who says that they have accepted my offer. I don't know who he is and what the offer is about."

"Wait did you say his name was Mark Wright?" Andrew looked like he had an idea.

"Yeah, that is his name. Do you know him?" Jason was praying that Andrew would come up with something that would answer his questions.

"No, but I think I know who he is. You know that house near your father that is empty, you asked me if I remembered the kid that used to live there?"

"Yeah." Jason was trying to work out where this was going, "I'm pretty sure he wasn't called Mark Wright

"I know, but the sign has changed over the weekend, and I think the agent that is selling it is called Mark Wright. Would you be buying a house?"

"I have no idea." Jason paused for a little, "I think I better get in contact with him. Maybe he knows what I've been up to."

"I think that is a good idea, Jason. Try and work out what it was you were planning and then we can try and get hold of Julia."

"Yeah, I know you are right. Just one problem. Not sure I want to let dad know that I might be buying a house if it isn't true or doesn't work out. How am I going to get to see Mark without dad knowing?"

"I'm free tomorrow, why don't I come over? We can just

say that I am taking you shopping, after all, you did say something about needing more trousers." Amy looked at them both.

"Yeah, that would be a great idea. I'm sure mom will be happy to have Colin for a few hours."

Jason looked at them both.

"Are you sure, would you do that for me?"

"Of course, we are here to help you. Should we say late morning? You could treat me to lunch." Amy smiled, "and if you could have a word with your boss before so you know what deal you have made with him. I am pretty sure it will all make sense then. And Jason, Julia will come round you just have to give her time. You two are perfect for each other, that was pretty clear to me last weekend."

"You think so?"

*

By the time Andrew returned him home, Jason was ready for a rest, and he spent the rest of the afternoon snoozing in bed. He was slowly beginning to remember things but there were still some gaps. As Andrew had driven past the empty house, he had taken a good look at it. He could see pictures of the insides of it but couldn't remember ever being in it. The sign did indeed say Mark Wright on it, and it could only mean one thing.

Jason had decided not to tell his dad or Grace about it as he wanted to know exactly what it was, he had planned.

There was no need to get either of them excited if it didn't turn out right.

While Jason had been out, Grace had been through his mother's sewing room and made a couple of piles of things. She suggested that while she was cooking Frank and Jason could go through it. There was a pile of things for repairs, one with a couple of unfinished projects; a pile of clothes that belonged to his mother. Then there were some books and materials. Grace said she would do the repairs and she would like to finish the projects that Jason's mother had started. The clothes were the difficult ones. Looking at it, Jason and his dad concluded that it was clothes she hadn't worn for some years and probably had planned to take to a charity but had just not gotten around to it. They decided that the best thing would be to give them to charity so someone else could make use of them.

It was strange going through it, and it brought back many memories. At one stage Jason could see his dad was getting a bit tearful. He put his arm around him.

"It isn't easy for either of us dad, but we got to do it. Mom would want us to."

"I know son, I'm just glad that you are here to help me go through it."

"So am I."

"I have to say it isn't easy for me either, we were so close back then when we were younger. But I also know from ex-perience that it is a process you have to do and once done you will feel better. That said, you have to do it at your speed. I am happy to help but please say if you prefer to do it yourself," Neither of them had noticed Grace standing at the door. She had come to see if they were ready for dinner.

"Grace, you have no idea how grateful I am. Well, I think we both are for what you are doing for us. Am I right Jason?" Frank turned to look at Jason, "And Jason, I hope you will be happy to help with the rest. I know your mother would want you to." There was a moment of silence. Jason was trying to get control of his emotions before he replied:

"Yes dad, I will be here." Jason thought of telling them what he had discovered but decided to stick to the plan.

"I know how close you two were and because of some silly argument I kept you two apart and for that, I'm truly sorry. And I or we would be grateful if you would help us sort out Alice's things," Frank had now turned to Grace.

"Don't be silly Frank it wasn't just you. I know my husband wasn't easy, trust me he wasn't easy to live with but that is in the past. I am just so glad that Jason called me." She walked across to Frank and gave him a big hug. "Getting back in touch with you and Jason has changed my life. The other day when Jason and I went to see the grave I felt something, it was like Alice telling me to keep an eye on you two to make sure you were happy."

"You went to see the grave?" Frank looked at Jason.

"Yeah, we did dad. I did tell you that when you were in the hospital. Don't you remember?" Jason was a bit surprised that his dad hadn't remembered that.

"Oh yeah, maybe you did." Frank was feeling a bit emotional now. Jason could see the tears and managed to get across to him.

"Come here, dad." Jason let go of the crutches and gave his dad a big hug.

"And yes, I agree with dad by the way. I'm more than happy for you to help us sort this out, Grace."

They spent the rest of the evening talking about Alice and the fact that it would have been her birthday the following Saturday.

"How about we all go out for dinner and celebrate mom on Saturday?" Jason looked at them both now sitting opposite him. "Well, if you are still here Grace?"

"That's a good idea, Jason. Will you come?" Frank now looked at Grace and Jason couldn't help but think how lovely they both looked, and it brought a smile to his face.

"Of course, I will still be here. Neither of you two can drive yet and yes, I would love to it." Grace leaned into Frank and gave him a smile.

"Well, that is sorted, and it will be my treat. If you will excuse me, I am off to bed now." Jason got up and hobbled towards his room. Once in bed, he thought of what had happened. Seeing the car had really shocked him but he was glad that Andrew had taken him. And his memory was beginning to come back. One thing he hadn't managed to do yet was to speak to his boss, but he could do that in the morning. He hadn't spoken to Mrs. Anderson either but had sent her a message asking her to thank everyone for all their kind messages and to say that he was okay but needed time off to recover. Something told him that he wasn't going to see a lot of the New York office. His phone rang and Jason wondered who that could be this time of the day.

"Hey, how are you? I have only just heard what has happened to you."

"Oh, hey John. I'm okay."

"Glad to hear that. What happened?"

Jason spent the next thirty minutes telling John all he knew and what he was confused about.

"I know that you and Mr. Patterson had agreed to you working from your dad's house on a similar deal as what I'm doing here. Now would you like me to come and visit you and help you set it all up?"

"It's all making sense now and I have a feeling that once I have been to see Mark Wright things will be very clear. The only thing then is Julia. I really hope she will let me explain things."

"I'm sure she will come back. Just give her some time."

"Thanks, John. Yes, I might take you up on your offer."

"Just let me know. Well, glad you're okay. I will speak to you soon."

So, he had turned the promotion down and it looked like he was moving back home. Now he just needed to speak to Julia. What was the point in doing all of this if she didn't want to speak to him again?

{ **20** }

Jason made the most of Grace and his dad taking Duke out for a walk. He phoned his boss and had a long conversation with him about his future with the company. It was all beginning to make sense now. Jason had mentioned his chat with John the night before and his offer to help him.

"I would make use of that offer; he has made the transition really well." Mr. Patterson then said that once Jason felt up to it, he should come to New York so he could sign the new deal.

"I'm really looking forward to this little project and I feel very confident that you will do well and make the company proud. Keep me posted on how you are getting on."

"I will and thank you for these kind words. I will keep you posted."

Next on the list was Mrs. Anderson. He had promised his boss not to tell anyone until the company had put out a press release the following day, but he wanted to thank her and let her know he was okay.

"Will you come back?" Jason could hear how concerned she was about the future and felt bad that he couldn't be honest with her, but it was too risky.

"Not for three weeks as I am signed off sick for now, but yes, I will be back to see you. I can't tell you more right now but don't worry it will all be fine. Who knows I might bring a friend." The minute he had said it he regretted it. The fact was he would love to take Julia to New York and show her the city, but he didn't know if that was ever going to be possible. First, he had to convince Julia to listen to what he had to say.

Amy turned up just as he had finished speaking to Mrs. Anderson and the dog walkers returned. Grace insisted on them having coffee before they went shopping. It gave her an opportunity to ask if Amy knew which charities there were in the area. Amy quickly wrote a couple down and then turned to Jason:

"We better be going. Are you ready to spend some serious money?" She gave him a big smile.

"How much are you planning on buying?" Frank was looking concerned, and Jason assured him it was only a couple of pairs of trousers.

"And he is buying me lunch for my trouble," Amy laughed.

"Good luck and enjoy it."

Once they had passed the empty house, Jason looked at Amy.

"If only they knew what I'm about to do."

"Yeah, don't think you are only buying a few pairs of trousers today," she laughed. "By the way, they really seem to be getting on well. How do you feel about that?"

"Yes, they are, and you know what, I am very happy about it. They are both still relatively young so why not let them enjoy life a bit? At least one of us is happy." He couldn't help but think of Julia.

"I know, but I am pretty sure you will be as well. Have you spoken to your boss?"

"Yeah," Jason thought for a second and then decided that telling Amy about it wouldn't hurt. The likelihood of her telling any of his co-workers would be very slim.

"Can you promise that what I'm about to tell you stays between you and me?" Jason looked very serious, and Amy agreed. Jason explained what was happening.

"I feel things are beginning to fall into place for you Jason." Amy was parking the car near Mark Wright's office. She got out and went to help Jason out of the car.

*

A couple of hours later they sat down at a table in Benny's and ordered lunch.

"I think this has been rather a successful day Jason. How do you feel?"

"I would agree. I am glad I have worked out what it was I was up to before the accident. However, I just hope this is the right thing to do." He couldn't help but think about what he would do if Julia didn't want to see him again.

"Don't worry, it will sort itself out."

What Jason hadn't realized was that while he was looking and buying trousers, Amy had sent Julia a message to find out how and where she was. Amy hadn't mentioned that she was with Jason as she thought she might not get a reply.

Benny brought out their lunch and looked surprised at Jason.

"Hey young man. Another lady? Did you have to fight that hard for her?"

"Hi, Benny. This is Amy, Andrew's wife, and she has very kindly taken me shopping. I had a bit of a run-in with a deer the other day."

"Oh, so it was you. I heard about it. From what I have heard you were lucky to get out of it alive."

"I know. I must have had a guardian angel with me that day."

"You let me know if there is anything I can help you with. Better get on, we are a bit busy. Enjoy your lunch."

"Thanks, Benny." Once he had gone Jason apologized to Amy.

"I have known him since I was a child. He hasn't changed."

"I know. Andrew has told me a lot about him and when we were dating, we used to come here regularly.

While eating their lunch, Amy told Jason all about how she and Andrew had met, and where he had proposed to her. Jason couldn't help but smile; it was pretty clear to him that his friend had definitely found the right one.

After another quick chat with Benny, they headed back to the car.

"Just want to do one more thing before I take you home, is that okay?" Amy looked at Jason. She had a plan and all she could do was hope that it would work.

"It sounds like I don't have a choice." Jason laughed; he had no idea what was about to happen.

Amy pulled up outside Julia's parents' house.

"Hey what are we doing here?" Jason suddenly felt a bit sick. "Is she here?"

"Come let's go and find out, shall we?" And again, Amy helped him out of the car, and they headed up the path. Once outside the door, Jason looked at her. She nodded towards the doorbell. Jason felt very nervous, his hand was shaking when he pressed the doorbell. After a little while, Mr. Taylor opened the door.

"Afternoon Jason. What do you want?" He didn't look or sound too happy to see who it was, and Jason couldn't really blame him.

Jason looked at Amy who just nodded, then he turned to Mr. Taylor.

"Afternoon sir, is Julia at home?"

"Maybe, why?"

"Could I speak to her please?"

"Not sure she wants to speak to you." But before Jason could answer Julia had popped her head around the inside door.

"Who is it, dad?" She almost froze when she saw Jason.

"Julia, please can I have a word with you? I have something important to tell you, please."

Mr. Taylor was about to say something, but Julia got there first.

"Dad, I got this, please give us a moment."

Mr. Taylor gave Jason a very serious look as if to say, "if you touch my daughter, I will get you," he then went back in, and Julia closed the door after him.

"Jason, what are you doing here?"

"For a start, this wasn't my idea. As you can probably tell I can't drive at the moment," he pointed to Amy. "But I'm glad she has taken me here as I have some good news to tell you."

"Jason, I don't know if I can do this, do us. Your accident freaked me out so much that I had to call in sick. I don't want to go through another heartache."

"I am really sorry about that." Jason was trying to work out how to tell her the news. He hadn't had a chance to think about it, but it didn't really feel right doing it here.

"There is something I want to show you, would you mind coming with us?"

She looked at him and then at Amy and back to Jason.

"Julia, I think Jason deserves to explain if you don't mind me saying so." Amy thought it might help to give them both a small push. "And I can either come with you or if you prefer you two can go without me. But only on the condition that you bring him home. I don't want to be in trouble with his dad or Mrs. Smith."

All Jason could think was please, please, please say yes. He didn't care if Amy was going to be there, just as long as Julia would hear what he had to say.

After what seemed like an eternity, Julia finally spoke.

"Okay I will come, and I can take him Amy if you want to get home." She grabbed her keys, opened the door, and told her parents she was going out for a little while.

Before Amy left, she made sure that Jason had his

shopping bags. Jason thanked her for all the help and gave her a big hug.

"See you soon and say hello to Andrew for me."

"I will. Now you two need to talk." Amy helped Jason get into Julia's car and then gave Julia a hug. "Trust me this is for the best. If you need to talk, call me."

"Thanks, Amy. I hope you are right." Julia got into the car and started it.

"So where is it you want me to take you?" She was still a bit skeptical about the whole thing but was willing to give him a chance to say what he had to say.

"If you drive back towards dad's house, I will tell you when to stop." Jason didn't know what to say. Julia didn't exactly look happy to see him and he was beginning to wonder if this was the right thing to do. It was a big change but was it worth it if he couldn't have the full package?

Julia didn't say anything either. She was trying to work out what it was he wanted to show her. Why were they heading back to his dad's house? Why wasn't he saying anything? She turned onto the road where his dad lived.

"So did you just want me to take you home?" Julia couldn't help but be a bit disappointed.

"Stop here by that sign." Jason pointed to the sign saying, "under offer" and Julia did as she was told.

"And?" She looked at the house. It made absolutely no sense to her. Why were they parked outside an empty house?

"Could you help me out please?" Jason opened the door and Julia quickly got out to help him.

"Come with me." He would have taken her hand, but he

needed both for the crutches. She slowly walked behind him up the path, still very confused.

"Jason, what are we doing here?"

Jason stopped and took a key out of his pocket. He then unlocked the door.

"After you." Jason signaled to Julia that she should walk in. He followed her and shut the door.

"Jason, what are you up to? What is this? What are we doing here?" She had a quick look into the next room.

Jason put his back against the wall and parked one crutch. With his free hand, he reached out to take Julia's hand.

"Julia, I know that I haven't treated you well in the past. I also know about your fiancé and his accident and fully understand why my accident must have hit you hard. But I would like to have the chance to explain what I was working on before the accident. You are standing in my new house; this is where I will live once it has been renovated. And I hope that I won't live here on my own. Before you say anything, no I didn't take the promotion, but instead, I will be working from here. This is my new home." The tears were running down his face now. "Julia, I love you and I really hope and believe that you love me too." Before he could say any more Julia hugged him and kissed him. They stood like that for a little while and Jason didn't want it to end but he could feel he needed to sit down.

"Sorry, Julia but I need to sit down, my legs are shaking." Julia had a quick look around and by magic, there was an old chair left in the room next door. She parked it right next to Jason.

"Please sit down carefully, not sure how strong it is. I don't want you to land on the floor." She held onto the chair as Jason slowly sat down.

"That's better." He kissed her hand. "Thank you."

Julia got down on her knees and rested her head on his chest. She could hear his heartbeat. What a lovely sound. Jason put his arms around her. They sat like that for a little while. In the end, Julia looked up.

"Can I take a quick look around?"

"Of course, you can. Just remember I haven't looked around it yet, only seen photos. Mark let me have the keys for a day or two so I could show the house to dad and Grace. Got to take them back as the paperwork isn't finished yet. Hopefully, it will be done by Friday."

After a quick look in all the rooms, Julia returned with another chair.

"Jason this is amazing. It will need some work done before you can live in it. I can't believe you have done it." She gave him a big smile.

"Julia, I want you to know that I had already made my decision before I went back to New York last Wednesday morning. A lot of things have happened over the last couple of weeks that have made me realize I couldn't go on living as I did. Seeing dad in that hospital bed was the wake-up call I needed. And as soon as I saw you, I realized I had never really stopped loving you." Jason reached for her hands, "I don't want to spend another day without you in my life, but I also realize that I couldn't ask you to move, so I had to make some changes."

"Sorry I didn't tell you the truth. I find it very hard to talk about and didn't want you to feel sorry for me. It has taken me a long time to get over it but then when I saw you on the stretcher covered in blood it all came back. You didn't exactly look very good, and I was shocked and collapsed. One of the doctors signed me off sick and phoned my parents. Think dad met your father on the way in." It was Julia's time to let the tears run but Jason wasn't much better.

"Come here," he put his arm around her. "I'm not going anywhere." They sat like that for a little while. In the end, Jason put his hand under her chin to lift it so he could see her eyes.

"So, what do you think of this then? I know it needs a lot of work doing but I think we can handle it." He was looking into the most beautiful eyes he had ever seen.

"I love it." Julia reached up and kissed him.

"Maybe we could ask your father to have a look at it – he is still in the building industry, right?"

"Yes, he is, and he will be more than happy to help us I think."

"Good. Hopefully, he will feel happier about me seeing his daughter. I got the feeling earlier that he isn't overly keen on the idea."

"He's just trying to protect me, that's all."

"Let's hope so. I also think it would be good for dad and Mr. Henderson to help a bit, especially with the ground. It is all a bit overgrown. Speaking of dad, I'd better get back before they start sending out a search party."

"Come on I will help you up," Julia gave him a hand so he could pull himself up.

A few minutes later they pulled up in front of the house. No one came out which Jason found a little strange, after all, he had been gone for quite a while. He opened the door to the house.

"Anybody home?" Julia followed him in.

"Yeah, we are in here son."

Jason looked at Julia, "Come let's go and surprise them."

"Look who I found." Jason went to sit down on the couch and indicated to Julia that she could sit next to him.

"We knew, Amy called in to let us know she had dropped you off with Julia and we shouldn't be worried. Good to see you, Julia. Would you two like coffee? We have just had ours."

"Actually, I think there is a bottle of fizz in the fridge. Would you mind getting that Grace? We have some news we would like to share with you both."

"Oh, that sounds very nice; what kind of news?" Frank had got up in search of some glasses.

Grace had returned with the bottle and Jason asked his dad to do the honors and open it.

"Well Mark Wright turns out to be the man who is selling the empty house and I'm the new owner of it. I'm moving back and will be working from here for now. And once the house is renovated, I will move across to that and I hope that Julia will join me."

"That is wonderful news son, I am really happy for you." Frank got quite emotional, and Grace went to support him.

"That is the best news I have heard in a while. Congratulations to both of you."

"Now as you can imagine, there is quite a lot to do both inside and outside of the house. Don't think it has had a lot of work done on it since it was built. I have the key and I was thinking we could look at it tomorrow morning. Might ask Julia's dad to come along as well. I have to give the keys back by the end of tomorrow as it's technically not mine yet; still waiting for some paperwork to go through."

Frank sat down again. The news had rather overwhelmed him a bit. Was his son really coming home? He took a deep breath and looked at Grace who was sitting next to him.

"I am really happy for you son. Now talking of news, Grace and I have been talking and as you know we have both been on our own for two years now. We aren't getting any younger but we both still have things we would like to do so we have decided, and I hope you won't mind Jason, to spend more time together."

"I think that is wonderful dad, couldn't be happier for you."

It was late by the time Julia left. They had arranged that she would come along with her father the following morning so they could all have a look around Jason's new house.

*

"What do you think?" Jason was sitting on the old chair in the kitchen. Frank and Grace had had a quick look around the house. They were waiting for Julia and her parents to come along. Jason had received a message from Julia saying they were running a bit late but were on their way now. He was a little nervous about meeting Mr. Taylor after seeing him yesterday, but Julia had reassured him that everything would be fine.

"I think this will make a lovely home for you son. I still can't believe that you are actually moving back here. Your mom would have liked it."

"Yeah, I know." There was a knock on the door, "That must be them." Frank went to open the door while Grace helped Jason stand up.

"Sorry we are a bit late, but dad had a customer calling him just as we were on our way out of the door," Julia went straight over and stood next to Jason.

"Morning Mr. Taylor," Jason reached out to shake Julia's dad's hand.

"Son, I think it is time you start calling me James." He shook Jason's hand. "Now what have we got here? May I?"

"Yes, please. Take a look around and let me know what you think." Jason then turned his attention to Mrs. Taylor who was behind her husband.

"Morning Mrs. Taylor," and again he reached to shake hands with her.

"Morning Jason. This is so exciting." Instead of shaking his hand she hugged him and then followed her husband.

"This is good Jason. Now have you got any thoughts on what you want to do?" Mr. Taylor had returned to the kitchen where Jason was sitting on the chair.

"To be honest I haven't really had any thoughts. I want to go through it with Julia first if that is okay with you."

"Yes, of course. But just so you know, I'm happy to help out here."

Grace and Mrs. Taylor walked into the kitchen.

"Why don't we all head back to Frank's house for coffee?" Grace looked at Jason.

"Fine by me. Where is dad?" Jason was looking to see if he could see him.

"Did I hear something about coffee?" Frank appeared with Julia.

"Yes Frank, I have offered to make it if that's okay with you?"

"Of course, it is. Then we can all sit down and talk about this exciting place."

Jason was the last one out and had the key for the door. Mr. Taylor offered to help him lock up and Jason saw his chance.

"Could I have a quiet word with you, Mr. Taylor?" Jason couldn't bring himself to call him by his first name.

"Yes, of course, why don't I drive you back?" Mr. Taylor turned around and told the others to head on. He would drive Jason home.

After a long chat over coffee, it was decided that once the house was Jason's, Julia's dad would come over and they could have a proper look at it.

*

The days that followed were quite busy, not only in terms of working out how to go about sorting out the house but also going through Jason's mom's stuff. The three of them had picked one of the charities that Amy had suggested and had packed most of the clothes. They then all went along to hand it over. It had been hard but at the same time, it felt good. Before they knew it Saturday had come along. Jason had booked the restaurant in Preston that he and Julia had been to.

As they had finished breakfast Frank had taken Jason to one side. He handed Jason a small box.

"Son, I want you to have this. It was your mother's." Jason opened the box and was lost for words. This was very beautiful.

"Thank you, dad. Are you sure you want me to have this?" He gave Frank a big hug.

"Yes, that is what your mom would want."

"Speaking of mom. Would you mind if we went to the cemetery first this evening?"

"No, I think that is a very good idea son."

Jason's phone rang. It was Mark Wright.

"The house is yours now Mr. Wild. Would you like me to come over with the keys?"

"That would be great." This was perfect timing for Jason. He quickly sent Julia a message to tell her the news and asked if she could come over. Next, he wanted to make a quick call. His dad and Grace had taken Duke out, so Jason didn't have to worry about anyone overhearing the conversation, but just to be on the safe side he went into his bedroom.

"John Jackson speaking."

"Jason Wild here. Have some news for you. House is mine now."

"Congratulation. When are you moving in?"

"No idea. Got a lot of work to do on it first but that's not why I'm calling." Jason opened the door just to check that no one was in and then told John about his plan.

"Well done. Let me know how it goes."

Jason could hear the front door close.

"Right, I got to go. Will let you know later.

"Anyone home?" Julia went into the kitchen. "Jason are you here?" She checked her phone to see if she had misunderstood where he wanted to meet her.

"Sorry just had to change my shirt." Jason slowly walked towards the kitchen.

"You had me worried for a moment," Julia met him and gave him a kiss.

"Sorry about that. We better head down and meet Mark."

Mark arrived just before them and handed Julia a folder with everything in it, including all the keys.

"Congratulations Mr. Wild. I wish you all the best with it." He shook Jason and Julia's hands and left. Jason was glad that he didn't hang around as he wanted to be alone with Julia.

"Come let's have another look," Jason headed for the door. Once inside he headed into the main room and turned to see if Julia had followed. He parked the crutches and took both her hands.

"Julia, you have no idea how happy I am right now,

standing here in my house with you in front of me. They say things happen for a reason and in these last few weeks, a lot of things have happened. It was scary for a while, but we have got through it and now it is time to plan the next step. So, I have spoken to your father and asked for his blessing." Jason put his hand in his pocket and took out a little box, opened it, and took out the ring. "Julia Taylor, will you marry me? Sorry I can't get down on one knee......"

"It doesn't matter. Yes, I will marry you," She put her arms around him, and they kissed.

"I hope it fits." Jason slowly put it on Julia's finger.

"Perfect. It is so beautiful." She gave him another kiss.

"It was my mother's engagement ring. Dad gave it to me and said mom would want me to have it. I hope you don't mind."

"That is so lovely Jason and I feel very honored to wear it. I will never forget her."

"Would you mind if we head back and tell dad?"

"Not at all Jason."

Frank and Grace had returned when they got back, and Jason told them that the house was now his.

"And we have some news too," Jason took Julia's hand and held it up so they could see it.

"Congratulation you two." Grace quickly gave them both a hug; Frank gave Jason a big hug.

"Son your mom would be very proud of you."

"Thanks, dad. I know it would have been mom's birthday today and that is what we are celebrating tonight, but would you mind if I ask Julia's parents along? It just seems the right thing to do."

"Of course, it is."

They left in good time as Jason had asked if they could stop at the cemetery on their way. Julia's parents came along. Jason and Julia had picked some flowers to put on the grave. And as they stood there altogether the sun broke through the clouds. Jason first looked up at the sky, and then he looked at Julia.

"I think mom is happy with my decision."

They all agreed.

The End